# Cool Communication

# Cool
# Communication

· · · · · · · · · · · · · · · · · · · · · · · · · · · ·

*A Mother and Daughter Reveal*
*the Keys to Mutual Understanding*
*Between Parents and Kids*

**Andrea Frank Henkart, M.A.,**
**and Journey Henkart**

*Foreword by John Gray, Ph.D.*

A Perigee Book

A Perigee Book
Published by The Berkley Publishing Group
A member of Penguin Putnam Inc.
200 Madison Avenue
New York, NY 10016

First edition: May 1998

Published simultaneously in Canada.

The Penguin Putnam Inc. World Wide Web site address is
http://www.penguinputnam.com

Library of Congress Cataloging-in-Publication Data

Henkart, Andrea Frank.
Cool communication : a mother and daughter reveal the keys to
mutual understanding between parents and kids / Andrea Frank
Henkart and Journey Henkart ; foreword by John Gray.—1st Peri-
gee ed.
        p.    cm.
"A Perigee book."
Includes bibliographical references.
ISBN 0-399-52400-2
1. Mothers and daughters—United States.   2. Parent and child—
United States.   3. Communication in the family—United States.
I. Henkart, Journey.   II. Title
HQ755.85.H453   1998
306.874'3—dc21                                          97-49229
                                                           CIP

Printed in the United States of America

10  9  8  7  6  5  4  3  2  1

We dedicate this book to the thousands of kids and their parents who contributed directly and indirectly to the stories in this book. We thank you for your honesty and trust in us.

. . . and to all the teenagers who have lost their way.

# Contents

# Foreword

*Cool Communication* reveals what parents need to know about their children and what children want their parents to know about them. Written by a mother-daughter team, this book demonstrates how kids and parents can coexist while maintaining mutual respect, strong communication skills, and high self-esteem. Andrea and her daughter, Journey, provide their readers with powerful tools that will make a difference in family communication immediately.

When parents have a deeper understanding of why their children behave the way they do, it facilitates the effectiveness of their parenting by making their job easier and less frustrating. The primary motive deep inside each child is to cooperate and achieve his parent's approval. When a parent can clearly hear and acknowledge a child's unique point of view, a child is able to surrender her resistance and express her cooperative nature. When a child's sense of self is supported, he is more than willing to receive a parent's direction and guidance.

At times, children are unable to clearly articulate their true needs. When a child is upset, angry, afraid, or sad and she is unable to successfully handle those feelings, it is a sign that her needs are not being met. By reading this book, parents will be better equipped to tune into the needs of their children and attend to their needs. It will also help children to understand that parents have needs, too, and there is much that a child can do to help his parents.

While all parents were once children, it is easy for them to forget anxiety and problems that can accompany childhood and adolescence. Journey's words will help parents gain insight into what their children are thinking and experiencing. By considering the child's point of view, parents increase their ability to communicate in a way that will be heard.

Often parents feel the frustration of not being heard and instead of changing their approach, they turn up the volume. While this tendency is automatic and very common, it is one of the biggest mistakes a parent can make. A parent sabotages the possibility of communication when he yells. The more intimidating a parent becomes, the less she will be heard. And, while intimidation may force a child into obedience, the only lesson he is learning is to mindlessly obey. Because there is a lack of understanding, the next time the parent will have to yell louder and the child will resent it even more. If a child is always told what to do, she will never develop the ability to be in control of, and responsible for, her own behavior.

Cool communication allows a parent to remain calm and yet deliver a clear and firm message about what is expected from the child. It also explains how to allow children to grow in their ability to make decisions for themselves and cooperate with their families. It provides new options that will work so parents, and their kids, don't become frustrated.

By making an effort to understand one another, par-

ents and their children can create an atmosphere of mutual trust. Whether the issue is messy rooms, curfews, or
dating, Andrea and Journey provide a much needed perspective from both the parents' and kids' sides in understanding the issue and, most importantly, how it can be
resolved.

More than just a book dealing with problems, *Cool Communication* reminds parents to say "I love you" and
"Thank you," which can go very far in fostering not only
cooperation from kids, but will help them develop positive
self-esteem. This book will also give kids the confidence
to cope with everyday problems on their own.

*Cool Communication* helps to bridge the gap between
parent and child through greater understanding, articu-
lation of both points of view, and validation of both the
parents' and children's perspectives. Andrea and Journey
have written a book that is not only greatly needed, but
can be easily applied right away. Although it takes time
and effort to learn a new approach to parenting, your
children will greatly benefit from this book.

Thank you for taking the time to be great parents.

—John Gray, Ph.D., author of
*Men Are from Mars, Women Are from Venus*

# Acknowledgments

It takes a labor of love to give birth to a book and that labor is never achieved alone, as any writer knows. So many people have been instrumental in the writing of this one. As the mother of this writing duo, there are many people I would like to acknowledge.

I give my loving thanks to my maternal grandparents, Della and Harry Richman, for showering me with unconditional love from the moment I took my first breath to the moment they breathed their last.

I offer my deepest gratitude to my parents for providing a path that encouraged me to look deeply into the art of communication skills, the soul of self-discovery, and the heart of love.

I want to thank my brother, Mark Frank, for showing me how siblings can overcome all obstacles, and still find their way back to love.

To my husband and best friend, Reggie, thank you for being the most patient, loving, and supportive human being I have ever known. Your unconditional love to our family and your dedication as a father are awe inspiring. I can't believe after all these years it just keeps getting better! I love you with all my heart.

To Journey Delena, my writing partner, my friend, my daughter. I admire your beauty and your sageness. You have graced my life and helped me to be the best mother I can be. This book would not exist without your precious guidance and your brilliant insight. *Namaste.*

To my gorgeous, talented, and very "cool" son, Quest, for continuously challenging me to look deeply into the truth of what this book is all about, and for reminding me how to be the best parent I can be. Your love and your tenderness make my heart sing. I love you deeper than you will ever know. Thank you for your patience, sweetie; now you may use the computer!

I want to give special thanks to John and Bonnie Gray. Thank you, John, for writing the foreword to this book. Thank you both for the loving, caring, inspirational support you have given to my children over the years. Your wisdom, your generosity, and your healing gifts to the world are ingrained in my heart. You are both divine lights that shine the way for millions. Thank you for always shining on me and my family. I am forever grateful.

To my dear friends—fellow writer Donna Germano, M.F.C.C., and Jeanne-Marie Grumet—thank you both for standing in as midwives to the birth of this book. Your invaluable support at labor's end was heartwarming.

Thanks to Joan Flax and Phil Clark for all of our late-night talks when the kids were young. Your words of wisdom, dedication to parenting, and never-ending friendship are a blessing. Thank you for your input and support.

To my artistic and talented long-distance friend, Ashley Collins (aka Carol Ann Birtwell), whose parenting skills are a true gift. Thank you for so generously sharing your expertise with me.

Journey and I both want to bestow appreciation and thankfulness upon our aunt, Barbara Richman Levine, for always providing us with an unbounded sense of family. Thanks, Bobbie, for always being there when we need you.

We both thank our beloved friend and guardian angel Reverend Ari Smith-Cordtz for continually chasing away the negative mind chatter, and for bringing clarity and light into the depths of our souls. We don't know how anyone can write a book without you lighting the way.

We also offer thanks to Reverend Karyl Teixeira for your contribution to our book, for your words of spiritual wisdom, and for so lovingly sharing the goodness in your heart with everyone.

To Shannon and Juliet Grumer, Journey and I want to thank you for your great advice, common sense, and guidance. You are both radiant examples of how teenagers can turn out.

We also thank Jordan Riak, Michael Pritchard, and Julie Sobaszkiewicz for your fabulous input in our book, and your endless faith in kids.

To our extraordinary agent, Carla Glasser, we give our loving thanks for your precious guidance, your creative gentleness, and your brilliant suggestions. A huge part of this book belongs to you!

We thank Patti Breitman for believing in the message we wanted to express, and who connected us to Carla. Your friendship and enthusiasm have meant so much to us both.

Very special thanks are due to our multitalented editor, Sheila Curry: part editor, part therapist, and part hand-holder. Thank you for believing in us from the beginning.

# Cool Communication

And correct
me.

And criticize
me.

And praise
me.

And hug
me.

And yell at
me.

My parents
smile at me.

All because
they love me.

Harry Pulver Jr.'s illustration from *Bringing Up Parents: The Teenager's Handbook* used with permission from Free Spirit Publishing Inc., Minneapolis, MN. ALL RIGHTS RESERVED.

# CHAPTER 1

# What Parents and Kids Want

The differences between parents and their children are vast. The adult brain has more than one hundred trillion connections, while the brain of a newborn is just waiting to form its connections. Adults have more life experience, more physical strength, more control, more power, and more know-how than an average child. Whether you have a baby, an adolescent or a teenager, your needs and desires are different from your child's. Parents have consistently told me that they want more from their kids. Parents want their kids to tell them what is going on in their lives and talk about their feelings. They want them to be respectful and kind. They want them to cooperate instead of acting belligerent, and to clean their rooms instead of being lazy. Parents and teachers say that many kids "just aren't living up to their potential." On the other hand, most children and teenagers say that their parents and teachers are too strict and "They just don't understand."

Parents have conflicts with their kids because we see the world one way, and our children see it from another perspective. We want our kids to talk to us about what is going on in their lives. We want them to be considerate and respectful of us and others, and we want complete cooperation whenever we ask for it. In our quest for this kind of behavior, our children challenge us to be fair or they rebel. They want freedom to make choices and to have more control in their lives, and they want everything to be fun and easy.

**Parents want the three C's from their kids:**
Communication
Consideration
Cooperation

**Kids want the three F's from adults:**
Freedom
Fairness
Fun

Parents and kids both want control and respect. Just as parents *want* to be heard, respected, understood, listened to, acknowledged, appreciated, and loved for who we are, our children *require* all of these things to be able to grow into their full potential.

Children come through us, not to us. They can be powerful and magical when we acknowledge them and honor them for who they truly are. Watch a little baby as she takes her very first step. You can observe her excitement and feel her passion for the newness of life. However, by the time many children are in elementary school, you can look into their eyes or observe their behavior and behold how their self-esteem, their individuation, and their excitement about being a child have been diminished. Most of their ecstasy for life is already gone. This is a crime.

It is our hope that *Cool Communication* will restore that joy in parents and their children.

We must teach our children to *honor* life, to *love* the Earth, and to *respect* themselves. Nurture your child in his wholeness and fullness by acknowledging who he is, not who you hope he will be. Lavish your children with love and understanding as you gently encourage them to be the best they can be. That may mean that sometimes you have to love them enough to say "no" when necessary.

By honoring our many differences, we can work toward eliminating conflict in our families. Growing together as a family does not have to be difficult, it can be magnificent. With empathy, compassion, respect, and understanding, we can create win/win situations within our families. It takes a continual, conscious process to build loving, lasting relationships with your children. Make every moment matter.

## *PARENTS:*

### *Andrea's Story*

Tradition has it that parents know best, yet most of us are thrust into this role of parenting without any previous training. It is not surprising that many well-intentioned parents repeat the same mistakes their own parents made. Sometimes it is difficult to know the best parenting approach to use with our children; after all, they do not come with an instruction manual. To confuse matters, teenagers seem to change the manual daily. Most parents want good relationships with their children; many do not know how to proceed. Many of us simply operate from an assumption of what parents should do and how things should be. We forget that each child is a unique individual, with a distinctive personality and approach to life. We look outside ourselves for advice, listening to the words of others and watching their examples. Sometimes parents simply forget to listen and respond from their hearts.

In today's complex world, children have to deal with a greater range of difficult and, more often, dangerous choices than their parents once did. Many of us were raised to be seen and not heard. Many of our parents believed that if you spare the rod, you spoil the child. As we approach the new millennium, simply teaching children to obey their parents no longer works; it merely creates a generation of people who learn to please and appease others. Children must learn intelligent and creative survival skills such as how to resist peer pressure, how to respond to choices and conflict, how to stand up for what they believe to be the truth, and how to develop a system of healthy values. Children require an emotional environment that allows them to become self-appreciating, self-assured and remain stress-free.

To enforce these ideals, many parents believe they have to nag their children so they do not forget, or constantly yell at them so they will listen; they tug them here, and push them there. I have seen parents manipulating their children in public—using gestures of disapproval, threatening, bribing, scolding, demanding, using ill-chosen words. I do not often see parents act as role models, encouraging their seedlings to grow in an environment of unconditional love and mutual respect. What I continue to see is an array of frustrated parents and their unhappy kids who grow up to be rebellious teenagers.

I once heard someone say, "Feelings from childhood do not go away, they just get pushed into the closet of your soul." Studies have shown that ninety percent of adult anger stems from childhood. Children seem to carry a collection of every neurosis society has: they can be whiny, abusive, manipulative, and violent. We must demonstrate more consciousness, awareness, and communication in our relationships with our kids, because this is what heals all our relationships and ultimately, our planet.

Recently, I witnessed a mother yelling at her young son. "Let's go!" she screamed. She spanked him on the bottom with such force that the little boy was knocked into the wall. As he began to wail, his mother screamed at him to stop crying as she dragged him from the store. That incident made a strong impression on me. I imagined how I would feel if I were in that little boy's shoes. I was grateful that I could just walk away from her authoritarian tirade.

The authoritarian parent acts as the family ruler. He or she expects to be obeyed without question; the children are treated as lower-ranking citizens on the totem pole. The parents' primary focus is to make sure their kids are doing what they think kids are *supposed* to do. Initially, kids may exhibit "good" behavior out of fear of their parents, or their own inability to make decisions. Without the opportunity to share in decision making and the freedom to make mistakes, children of authoritarian parents do not always end up using good judgment and often end up rebelling when they are old enough to speak up.

On the other hand, many parents who have bitter memories of restrictive households filled with limits and punishments tend to become permissive parents. Wanting to "undo" what their parents did, permissive parents offer no clear limits, responsibilities, or dependable consequences. They allow children to do whatever they please, as long as it does not disturb the parents' routine. The parent may appease or ignore the child, depending upon which better suits the parent's mood. This leaves the child frustrated, feeling anxious and insecure.

When a child is raised without healthy boundaries and allowed to run wild, she may grow up believing that no one is there to help and support her. This can create a very deep level of fear within her soul.

Some permissive parents try to set reasonable boundaries for their kids, but give in after their children have nagged or tested them for too long. Many of these kids have withdrawn completely from all parental influence, or have their parents wrapped around their little fingers. These parents must find the inner strength and the verbal communication skills to be able to love their kids enough to just say "NO" when necessary.

There are as many books on the most effective parenting techniques as there are opinions on the best way to raise children. Whether or not you identify with the authoritative or permissive parent, or a more democratic parenting style, everyone seems to agree that no matter what you do, when your children become teenagers, they will be inherently rebellious, negative, and untrustworthy. Many parents believe they have no power to prevent this "stage" from taking place.

I have worked with over three thousand adolescents between the ages of ten and sixteen who spoke freely about life, school, family, and friends. They have shared intimate stories about what is really important to them, how they view the world, and what life is like at home. I discovered that kids begin to listen and trust their own inner voice when they have been given the respect they deserve and the chance to make educated choices. They learn to apply reason to situations to avoid imbalance which creates struggle and disharmony. It is time for parents to step down from their self-appointed pedestals and listen to the voices of their children.

When problems arise in my own family, we consciously and lovingly strive to move through the difficulties that transpire in interdependent relationships. My husband and I do our best to model fairness and honesty. We take extra time to listen to our kids without giving unsolicited advice, to acknowledge and praise without shaming or blaming, and we love our children unconditionally: no strings attached. The result is a preteen son and a teenage daughter who are loving, trustworthy, respectful, and considerate. I am grateful to my children for so many things; they truly are my greatest teachers.

I sincerely believe that parents who have respect for themselves and compassion for those around them can maintain positive relationships with their children through all the various phases and stages of development. *Cool Communication* has been written to help parents and adolescents move through all the stages of growth with mutual respect, mutual trust, a sense of equal human worth, compassion, and unconditional love.

Children are our future. We must model ways for them to respect others and value life. We owe it to our children. Hopefully, they will someday care for their own children with the same love and compassion we gave to them in their formative years. Therefore, I am committed to providing parents with positive communication skills which help us all to learn, grow, and feel good about ourselves in our ever-changing world. Step by step, Journey and I offer ways for you to maintain balance, peace, and harmony in your families to create an environment where both adults and children can grow in love.

# KIDS:

## Journey's Story

I have wanted to write this book for a long time. When I was younger, I noticed there was a difference in the relationship I had with my parents and the relationship my friends had with their parents. When I was at a friend's house, I would get very upset when they would fight with their parents over stupid things, or when their parents overreacted to something my friend did.

When I was seven years old, my best friend, Jamie, and I loved to play with dolls. One day I went to her house and suggested that we play with her doll collection. Jamie said her mom had decided that she shouldn't play with dolls or toys anymore, and threw them all out. Her mom replaced her entire toy and doll collection with a bunch of books. Jamie was devastated. This is an example of parental control. Because Jamie never had any power at home, she found other ways to gain power by lying. Jamie lied to her teachers, her family, and her friends. At least she had control over the stories she told.

A few years later, I remember having lunch at Stephanie's house. When we finished eating, my friend asked her mom if we could have some candy for dessert. At that time I didn't eat candy. Her mom said to me, "Here, Journey, you can have some candy too, if you promise not to tell your mom." I was very surprised and confused. When I got home, I told my mom what happened because I had been taught not to tell lies, and I knew my parents trusted me. My friend's mom set a bad example by suggesting that I lie to my family.

I remember going to my friend Sara's house when I was about twelve. We were watching television and eating popcorn. Her mom walked in and said, "Sara, stop eating that! You're fat enough as it is!" Her mom grabbed the bowl of popcorn and walked out. When parents talk to their kids like that, it lowers their self-esteem. Sara's mom always put her down and compared her to other girls. She grounded her for everything. Sara's mom always acted strict and stuck-up. When Sara was fourteen, her mom put her on diet pills. Sara didn't want to take drugs; she was a nice person who just wanted to be loved by her mom. The truth is, Sara was never fat! When she turned fifteen, she desperately wanted to make her own decisions, so she decided it was cool to smoke and do drugs. Now she does everything she can behind her mother's back.

My life at home is very different from what most of my friends have experienced. My parents never call me names, because they know how much that will affect my self-esteem. My mom never decides if I'm too old for my things. It is my decision to choose what I want to get rid of and what I want to keep. I don't have any reason to lie to my family, because I don't really get punished, and I also don't want to lose my parents' trust. I know my parents are on my side and will always be there for me. When problems arise, we talk about it and everyone gets to share their feelings. We always try to come up with some kind of compromise or solution that works for us all.

One day my mom and I were flipping channels on TV when we saw the Montel Williams talk show about "disrespectful" teens and their parents. We were glued to the screen. The parents each spoke first and talked about how disrespectful and horrible their kids were. One mother said her child had hit her. *Everyone* in the audience went nuts! They were screaming at the teenager, calling her names and putting her down when she came onstage. She looked like she was ready to cry. These kids really did sound like horrible people. The parents said, "All we want is respect from our kids!"

Then the girls came out; there were four of them. They each told their stories. The girl who had slapped her mother said she had been physically abused by her mom many, many times before. The girl said she was only trying to protect herself because her mom (who was quite large) would sit on top of her! When the other girls told their stories, it was obvious that their parents had been treating them badly for a very long time. The teenage girls all said, "All we want is some respect and freedom from our parents!" The parents wanted respect, and so did their kids.

Hearing these lies and seeing all the hatred made me feel so angry. My mom and I kept looking at each other. We both knew we had some of the answers to make their lives easier. We had some solutions for solving their problems, but they couldn't hear us through the TV. That was very frustrating. It is also what moved me the most to write this book. I have so many ideas that might help, I just need a way for people to hear me.

When kids and their parents don't have good relationships, they lose that special connection of love. Many relationships between kids and parents need help. What my mom and I are doing in this book is giving kids and their parents techniques they can use to improve their relationships. My mom gives techniques for parents to use, and I give techniques for kids and teenagers to use. We hope the information we give to you throughout this book will help so you can create peace within your family.

# CHAPTER 2

# Understanding Our Differences

## *PARENTS:*

### *Resolving the Differences Between Parents and Kids*

In order to create lasting, caring relationships with their children, parents must realize that their viewpoints, ideas, thoughts, reactions, responses, needs, and desires differ from those of their kids. As our children grow, the gap between "us" and "them" grows too. While there are practical ways to bridge this gap, the differences seem so vast at times that it appears as if children come from a different planet altogether, where language, style, and attitude have values and characteristics of their own. To illustrate this idea, Journey and I came up with a playful idea that explains our theory.

Once upon a time, somewhere over the rainbow in a land far, far away is a place where children come from. This kids' world is quite different from planet Earth where mom and dad now reside. Where children come from, life is a constant party. There are balloons and toys throughout the land, and simple beauty is everywhere. A kid just has to wish on any one of the million stars overhead, and everything is at his or her disposal. No one ever says "no," and there are very few rules. The rules that do exist in this imaginary world are quite simple. The Kids' Rules are:

- Behave like a star and let life revolve around you.
- Be open to receive anything new.
- When you do receive something, it is yours and does not have to be shared.
- Resist authority when it does not suit you.
- Everything can go your way if you insist long enough.
- When you get your way, you can choose to be happy or sad. Your mood swings are completely up to you.
- You do not have to pick up anything. Magic angels are at your service to put everything away for you.
- Take risks because you are invincible.
- Be unique, or join the crowd and be like everyone else. The choice is yours.
- Be open to receive love.
- Believe in yourself and your ability to do anything.

Kids expect to be the star no matter what and are quite surprised when they discover life on Earth does not revolve around them. Parents expect their kids to follow their time schedule, quickly learn their rules, and do things the way an adult would expect it to be done.

When a baby is born, the parents take one look at this tiny, helpless human being and assume the loving little bundle now belongs to them. They quickly develop parental amnesia. They completely forget about the rules in Kids' World. Until the fateful day their child says, "NO!" followed by, "GIMME" and "MINE!" Some parents are startled as they realize their children relate to life from a completely different perspective.

As adults begin to understand why children act the way they do, they can more readily accept the idea that it is quite normal for children to think, feel, communicate, and respond differently than their adult counterparts. After all, where kids came from, life was perfect. When the bubble bursts, the reality of everyday routines begin to run kids' lives, and parents continue to want their children to think as they do, feel what they feel, and respond to life with the mind of an adult.

We have all heard parents say, "Stop acting like a baby," "Why can't you do what you're told?" or "How could you be so irresponsible?" A two-year-old will say "no" for similar reasons that a seventeen-year-old stays out after curfew; they are seeking independence and control over their lives. As kids continue to think and respond differently than adults do, and demand reasonable control over their lives, adults become angry and frustrated. This anger and frustration can create friction which leads to a breakdown in the relationship.

By the time young children have been transformed into teenagers, their parents often say, "I'm living with an alien!" Teens have often told me, "My parents are from another planet!" Adolescents also complain that adults can be selfish, they say embarrassing things, they eat weird food, they listen to dumb music, and they want everything their own way. Sound familiar? That is what most parents say about their kids!

---

Children are messengers from a world we once knew, but we have long since forgotten.
—*Alice Miller*

---

Given all of our differences, everyone in the universe still responds to love. When adults respectfully and lovingly speak to the heart of the child, conflict can be avoided.

## Know Yourself

To speak heart to heart and to love your children unconditionally, it is important to know yourself. It helps if you know who you are and what you believe. What do you *really* think about life? What do you value in yourself and others? What makes you respond to situations as you do? You have to put all aspects of your life into perspective: how you felt growing up, how you relate to your family now, how you react in current relationships, feelings about your job, and your feelings about yourself.

Many parents have discovered that their parenting behavior has a lot to do with the way they were parented. Some parents have said:

- I automatically say "NO" to my daughter for just about everything. My parents used to do that, and I vowed never to do it to my kids. Now, here I am on automatic pilot. Sometimes I have to say "no," but when I do it every time, I make myself crazy! I'm working on just being aware of how often I say no, so I can start saying "Yes" more often, and being open to her needs.
- When my kids fight, my buttons get pushed big time. I had a big brother who used to beat me up all the time. Somewhere in the back of my brain, I want to protect my kids from the feelings that I had as a kid. So I always get really mad when they fight. It's ridiculous because we all end up in a

screaming match with both kids crying and angry. I'm working on helping my kids work through their anger instead of bringing up my old childhood feelings of anger and help-lessness.

• While going through marriage counseling, I realized I come from a long line of very strong, matriarchal women. In my family I nag my kids, I nag my husband, and I'm pretty much a control freak. That rubs off onto my kids of course. I had to look pretty deep into myself to realize how controlling I am of my kids' lives. It creates unbelievable rebellion which just creates more tension, friction, and anger. So, we're working to-gether in family counseling to be more un-derstanding, less controlling, and more forgiving. It's not so easy to change who I am, but it's worth it in the long run, because my kids won't push me away as much if I can be less controlling and more understand-ing.

• My parents spanked all of us kids, so that's always been my normal reaction when I didn't like what my kids were doing. My wife doesn't believe in spanking, so we argued about it all the time. It created a lot of prob-lems in our relationship. Now I pay more at-tention to my reactions and I deal with each situation on an individual basis. I don't spank the kids anymore, but the automatic urge still comes up. I have to watch my own issues with anger and power.

Kids have their own questions and concerns about life. A boy in one of my seminars said, "Not all kids want to admit it, but it's scary growing up." Kids want to know if their parents are strong enough to support them as they grow and change. You can count on your kids to test limits and find buttons you did not know could be pushed. Lively, intelligent, spirited kids are the ones who seem to push the hardest. These are the kids who need strong role models. It would be a shame to pulverize the strong-willed, spirited nature of a child. Love your children; care for them, be flexible and understanding, and be strong enough to say "no" (or "yes") when appropriate. Above all, do not be afraid of your children.

Growing yourself while raising your children can be a juggling act at best. Throughout this book you will notice that we suggest ways that families can find a middle ground where both parents and kids can relate together in peace and harmony. But raising kids is not always harmonious. There will be many times when your young child defies you, or your teenager sees you as the enemy. As they get older, many teens prefer to "hang out" with their friends rather than spend time with you. This stage is a normal part of growing up. At that time your kids are no longer malleable, controllable, or manageable.

As their hormones rage, some kids also rage against their parents. This can be painful for parents to experience, and can cause parental burn-out which may show up as neglect or anger. When you are angry you do not have to be the brutal authoritarian, and your kids are not necessarily the authority. When your children present you with various situations, watch how you act or react to their behavior. Check in with yourself to see what your own needs may be, and find ways to help yourself through the trying times.

One of the best ways to see yourself through the eyes of your child is to look at how you react when your buttons get pushed. When you are aware of your actions and reactions, you have more insight into why you do and say the things you do. For some, this means getting therapy or family counseling and getting to know your inner self on a deeper level. For others, this kind of soul searching may involve consciously healing old patterns of negative behavior by using meditation, reading self-help books, or attending local support groups. If you have a child with special needs or learning disabilities, hook up with support groups, or find the experts who can give you and your child the guidance you need. Taking care of yourself is one of the best examples you can set for your kids.

## How You Respond to Your Child

I watched a young mother play with her two-year-old son in the video arcade of a local mall. They finished a game and she immediately said, "Okay, we're leaving now. Let's go." The little boy looked as if he didn't understand. She gathered up her purse and packages and said very harshly, "I said let's go NOW." The little boy just looked at her. The mother then grabbed her son's arm and yanked him in her direction. "I'm getting really mad," she warned. Her two-year-old sat down on the ground and looked up at his mom with a sad look on his face. "Cut that out," she demanded, as she picked him up forcefully. The frustrated mommy began verbally abusing and threatening her son. "I'm never, ever, taking you to play another game again. You're a bad, bad boy. Do you hear me? You're BAD. That's the last time I take you anywhere with me." And she walked off. The little boy looked at his mommy and started to cry.

There is a more appropriate way to respond to this type of situation. The mother could have given her son a time frame for leaving, telling him that this was the last game they would play. That would have allowed him to prepare for their departure in his own mind. When it was time to go, the dialogue might have sounded like this:

*Mom:* "Let's go now," as she takes her child by the hand.

*Child:* "I don't wanna go," starting to cry.

*Mom:* Acknowledging his feelings she says, "I know you don't want to leave now, but I have to get home. We can come back to play another day."

*Mom:* As she continues to acknowledge him she says, "I'm sorry you're so sad. Let me carry you, Mommy's going to give you a ride!" She scoops him up in a loving embrace and carries him off.

She could hug him, give him kisses, tell him she loves him: anything that helps him feel good about himself, keeps his self-esteem intact, and lets him see her as the caring, concerned mother who really does need to get home. Even if the child is screaming and crying, continue to acknowledge his feelings, remain calm, and treat him with love and respect.

## How You Respond to Your Teenager

While the previous situation involved a mother and her young son, I have seen parents and teenagers in clothing stores have a similar experience when the parents want to leave and the teens want to try on just one more thing . . .

- Tired of waiting, the exasperated parent begins to lose patience.
- Insistent, the teen grabs more clothes and puts them on anyway.
- Anger builds, as the provoked parent becomes agitated and critical.

- The teen becomes hostile and smart-mouths back.
- The parent starts to walk out of the store, swearing and threatening never to go shopping with a teenager again!

Teens have a need to feel that they have some semblance of control. They can feel powerless when the balance of power tips in the parents' direction. If your teen is dawdling in a store and you want to leave, a respectful conversation with a few boundaries sprinkled in might work better than threats or angry words.

*Parent:* I really have to get home now.

*Teen:* Wait, Mom, I just want to try on these last few outfits.

*Parent:* I told you five minutes ago that I was reaching my limit. I'll give you another five and then we are out of here. Okay? Five more minutes.

*Teen:* Okay, okay. Do you like this outfit or this one, or the other one?

*Parent:* To be honest, I don't really like either one on you. I prefer the first one you tried on. That one looked nice. Come on, pick one and let's go. Your time is almost up.

*Teen:* Can I just try one more, please?

*Parent:* Look, I agreed to go shopping with you, and you agreed to honor my time limit. I want to be fair to both of us. You can come back another time, but I need to go now. Will you please help me get home on time?

Remember to:

- State your needs in a calm, gentle voice.
- Be generous by giving a few extra minutes if you can.
- Do not criticize your child's taste in clothes.
- Give her the opportunity to make up her own mind.
- Remind her of the time limit agreed upon so she can be clear about the boundaries.
- Give her responsibility she can handle: by asking your teenager to assist you in getting home, you have put reasonable power and control into her hands. *This gives her a sense of pride.*

---

Think about how you would want to be treated if you were in your child's place.

---

Imagine you were your teen at that moment when the parent got very angry. Put yourself in her shoes. Now imagine you were shopping with your ideal parent. Ask yourself, how would you want your ideal mother or father to handle this situation? How would you want her or him to treat you? How would *you* want to be treated? When you are with your own kids, watch how your buttons get pushed and look closely at how you respond to various situations so you can become more aware of your actions.

## You Are Not Your Child

The way we want our children to be is not necessarily *who* they are going to be. Parents must let go of the notion that they are creating their children in their image. Your job is to guide your kids into adulthood, not make them little versions of yourself. Parents often point out how their kids resemble them when they were children. They say, "I was like that as a kid," "I did that when I was his age," or "I looked just like that when I was little." Parents can celebrate the similarities they see in their children by simply acknowledging the likeness, without the expectation that their children must turn out like them. While you may see many similarities, this child is *not* you. This is a different human being with his or her own DNA, gene patterns, and thought processes.

What is important to remember, however, is how you felt as a child. Even if you had the most ideal family situation, there is most likely a place in your own childhood where there was some hurt. There may have been a time when you were not heard, listened to, or completely acknowledged. There may have been a teacher, a next-door neighbor, or another family member who said or did something hurtful or offensive that you still remember today. As an adult you know what that pain feels like. It is precisely this kind of pain that most parents want to protect their children from. From this desire to protect, parents tend to overpower. From this place of feeling overpowered and misunderstood, kids do everything they can to fight for their freedom.

By parenting in a new and different way than your family did, or other people who influenced you did, you can create a strong sense of self-esteem and balance in your children while also creating it for yourselves. Raising a human being takes integrity, honesty, compassion, unconditional love, and a lot of patience. It is not always an easy task, especially if you do not treat yourself that way.

---

A child's life is like a piece of paper on which every passerby leaves a mark.    *—Ancient Chinese Proverb*

## When Problems Arise

Parenting is not an easy job, and the job description is ambiguous at best. To make the relationship between parent and child flow, you must be on the lookout for problems that come up along the parenting path. They are not always easy to see or figure out.

As was the case for Michelle. She is a single mom on welfare. She is going to school to get a degree so she can work and support herself and her young daughter. She said:

> I don't have time for myself. I just go through the day and get things done. My daughter has to toe the line because there is no room for any nonsense around here. She's rebelling a lot lately and I just don't know what her problem is. I think she's doing okay in school, but at home, look out! She's stubborn, but then I guess I am too. She keeps telling me I don't understand her, and she says I'm mean. I'm dealing with her stuff and trying to do my homework at the same time. Things are tough around here.

Michelle is feeling the stresses of life and has to focus on her homework so she can finish school and make a better life for her daughter and herself. What Michelle does not realize is her daughter perceives that stress and feels a sense of abandonment as Michelle places her focus on the routine of getting through her day.

A child usually does not clearly verbalize the problem at hand. Most children are not in tune with their own feelings enough to say "Mom, I'm feeling left out and anxious. I miss our time together and wish you didn't have to go to school so we could just play together like we used to. The stress and all-work-and-no-play attitude is really getting to me. It's affecting my concentration in school and I'm starting to get very angry."

What the child does do, however, as Michelle's daughter has exhibited, is act out, become angry and rebellious, and have problems at school. The parent often does not make the connection, because the rebellion and problems at school do not appear to have any relationship to the issues going on at home. Michelle needs to uncover the reason behind her daughter's anger and find time to give her the attention she craves, while making time to nurture herself.

When problems arise, it is important to be aware of what is going on within yourself. One father in my parenting support group said, "I consider myself to be a gentle, caring dad. My wife and I always try to listen to and respect our two teenage sons. But every now and again I find myself screaming and threatening just like my dad did. I can't believe I do that!" When I asked him what he does after he realizes what he has said or done, he responded with "As soon as I realize what I have done, I immediately either apologize to my boys or somehow let them know my judgment was wrong. I make sure I listen to what they have to say about it and honor their space when they want to be alone. My dad always harped on us. He never apologized and he never really listened. My boys usually thank me for being fair. When they tell me I'm 'cool,' I feel like my extra efforts pay off." This type of honest, considerate interaction helps the developing child learn strong family values and self-respect.

---

It takes extra effort and energy
to parent in a positive way.

---

23

## When Kids Rebel

When children rebel, they are not saying "I'm bad, please keep ignoring me and punishing me." Rebellion is the children's way of asking for more attention, asking to be heard and acknowledged from *their* perspective according to *their* needs. Sometimes it may mean "I need space instead of smothering."

When your child or teen is acting up, is a change in *your* behavior warranted? When you are angered or frustrated by things in your life, your children may reflect your behavior. They get angry, frustrated, or crabby. If you yell or nag, they will yell back, ignore you, or sulk. Check in with yourself to see if your children are consciously or unconsciously responding to your changing moods. Before you lash out and blame them, you might just give yourself an "attitude adjustment." Deal with your own feelings and emotions in an appropriate way. If you are really angry, take time to cool off before you lash out at your kids, which just pushes them farther away. Set an example for the children who look to you for guidance.

Look at how *you* respond when your child does push you away, or acts rebellious or stubborn. Do you get angry, or do you try to understand from your child's point of view? Are you quick to ground your teen, or do you talk about how you both feel and then work out an agreement? Do you lose your cool, or do you remain calm and deal with the situation from a place of inner strength, respect, and love? How would you want your boss or your spouse to talk to you if the tables were turned?

Family members are affected to a certain degree by the moods, emotions, and feelings of those around them. This kind of interdependent behavior is essential in healthy families. This normal, highly desirable, interactive behavior is often confused with negative, "codependent" behavior which implies that someone else sets the mood for your behavior all the time.

Encourage your kids to speak up and respectfully say what they feel by listening to them, giving them opportunities to share their thoughts, and respectfully avoiding criticism and judgment. Teach them assertiveness by giving them the opportunity to challenge your decisions. Let them know they can verbally, and respectfully challenge what you say without any repercussions. Teach them to discuss. Be willing to say "You're right, I'm wrong." When they know they can be open and honest without being criticized, they will feel safe to express themselves. This is not the same as encouraging argumentative or disrespectful children. Learning calm debate and decision-making skills helps create strong minds.

## Take Time for Yourself

Sometimes parents just need a break. As a parent, it is vital to take time for yourself. Find ways to relax and gather your strength. Perhaps that means taking a five-minute walk, or taking a bath, or sneaking a magazine into the bathroom so you can be alone. When your baby is napping, lie down and relax. When your child is in school, do something for yourself. Go to a bookstore and browse, get a massage, treat yourself to lunch or a movie, listen to self-improvement tapes, or take a coffee break. Treat yourself well to avoid feeling overwhelmed or overburdened.

A single mother of a teenage son was in a parenting class I gave at a local health club. She said, "I work all day, and then I come home and spend time with my son. Most of the time I feel burned-out. So about three times a week, after my son is in bed, I go out to the local coffeehouse and have a great cup of coffee. I just love to sit by myself with nothing to do and no time constraints. It's my way of finding peace in my hectic life."

What a gift to willingly make time for yourself and to consciously value those moments that belong to you alone. Make those minutes or hours precious to you. Make them count. When you have nothing left to give, your child senses that something is missing and will act out in ways that may not even be related to the issue at hand. When you feel refreshed and fulfilled, you have more to give to your child.

---

Take good care of yourself because I'm counting on you to take good care of your children.

—*Dr. Louise Hart*

---

## Make Equal Time for Your Children

As an adult, when you want acknowledgment at work or attention from your mate, are you really asking to be ignored? When children demand attention, they are not asking to be ignored either. They will not "act out" or require "negative attention" when they always know the positive love and attention we all so desperately crave is readily available to them at all times. Help them to feel heard, and the negative behavior will fall away. Make equal time for your child on a daily basis.

Even the busiest parents owe it to their children to:

- hug them.
- read with them.
- go grocery shopping together and buy food they like.

- listen to how their day went.
- be patient and compassionate.
- tuck them in at night (even if they are big).
- listen to their dreams.
- ask them what they think.
- help them reason things out.
- keep laughter and joy alive in the family.

Your children are in your safekeeping for such a short period of time; they grow up and move away in the blink of an eye. Cultivate family togetherness while time is on your side. I am not denying that you have stress and worries; just leave them behind for a while as you make time to lovingly, respectfully, and joyfully interact with your child. Create a bond and a sense of family that will endure through peer pressure, teen turmoil, and the everyday bumps and bruises of life.

## You Have to Give Respect to Earn Respect

As children travel through the numerous stages and phases of growing up, many parents find their children to be disrespectful. Parents must demonstrate what respect is before their children can understand it. Just because you are the parent does not mean you deserve respect; **you have to give it to your kids to get it.** You can beat anything into children to make them succumb. They will obey out of fear, but they will not have respect. If they feel uncomfortable or unsafe telling the truth to their parents, children and teenagers will sneak around or lie to protect themselves or to avoid being grounded or punished.

A few years ago, Journey and I had a conversation that reflected this concept:

*Journey:* Mom, some of my friends are starting to go out really late at night.

*Mom:* Where are they going?

*Journey:* Well, they're going into the city to go dancing and stuff.

*Mom:* Their parents are letting them go to the city?

*Journey:* Not exactly. They're mostly sneaking out.

*Mom:* So, what are you asking here?

*Journey:* I'd like to go, but I don't want to sneak out.

*Mom:* You have never snuck out before, why would you consider doing that now?

*Journey:* Well, would you let me go if I asked?

*Mom:* I don't really want you going into the city. I don't think you can get into clubs anyway, because you're underage.

*Journey:* Mom, everyone gets in.

*Mom:* Listen, this is brand-new information for me to think about. I hear what you want, and I also know how this makes me feel. I have a lot of concerns and fears that come up for me. I want to think about this before I can give you any kind of an answer.

*Journey:* Mom, if I were a parent, I think I would want to know where my kid was. I don't want to have to sneak or lie like other girls I know. I want to be able to tell you the truth. But if you say no to everything I want to do, then how will I ever get to experience the stuff all my friends are doing?

*Mom:* I don't really want you to do what all your friends are doing.

*Journey:* Mom, I'm not going to do anything stupid or illegal.

*Mom:* I know you won't, I trust you. But I still

> want to give this some thought so we both
> feel comfortable with the outcome.

I needed time to think about all this. I have to keep remembering that my daughter is not three years old anymore, and I can no longer control all her activities. As she grows up, new situations continuously present themselves, and her values shift and change. My husband and I are constantly developing and reevaluating the scale of permissible behaviors and activities that harmonize with our family's beliefs and ethics.

Later that day, Journey and I discussed the inherent dangers of going to a club in the city. We discussed what I could do to be fair, and what Journey could do to ensure her safety. We talked about waiting to have some of these experiences until she could be the one to drive, because I would trust her behind the wheel of a car. She told me she would never jeopardize her life by getting in a car with a friend who was drinking. Taking a taxi or calling home were two of the options she explored during that conversation. We talked calmly for two hours, openly discussing our fears, our needs, and our hopes.

I have so much respect for my daughter and her ability to see things in a logical manner when she is given the opportunity. I am proud to have raised her so she feels safe enough to be open and honest with me. By the time our conversation was over, Journey realized it was inappropriate for her to go to the city, but she uncovered many of the other things I was willing to compromise on. I agreed to let her stay out a little later after the upcoming school dance. I agreed to let her go to a midnight showing of a film with a group of her friends when it came to our neighborhood. She promised to continue telling me the truth. We ended our conversation with a loving hug.

As parents, you must show your children how to behave by demonstrating healthy behavior, and remember to forgive yourself when you do not always succeed. Admit your shortcomings. Take time to think things through. Be respectful toward your kids and other people around you. Be flexible enough to change your usual parenting responses when necessary. Teens really respect their parents when they are flexible and respectful. By letting go of your own ego, you can step aside from yourself and allow yourself to see through the eyes of your children. Remember to put yourself in their shoes. Trust your children's inherent desire to trust you as a parent.

## Create Loving Memories with Your Children

We all have different needs at different times: babies want to eat when we want to sleep; kids want to play when we want to rest; teens want to go to the mall when we want to unwind. Take care of yourself and nurture your own inner child. Look into the innocent eyes of your children, and find love. See yourself as loving and capable in all that you do. Loosen up, relax, and have fun with your kids. You are creating the memories your children will remember for the rest of their lives. Think about how you would want to be treated if you were a kid, then practice compassion by listening and being gentle.

This book is not intended to eliminate all problems. Instead, it provides parents with basic underlying tools for deeper understanding and enhanced communication between parents and kids. By remembering our differences, and by looking deep into our own selves, we can transform the inevitable problems we encounter in raising children into opportunities for increased caring, trust, and mutual respect. I heard someone say that children do not exist to fulfill their parents' needs, but parents do exist to fulfill the needs of their children. Learn from your kids; they are your greatest teachers.

## *Personal Goals*

1. Remember what it felt like to be a child.

2. Bear in mind that kids think and react differently than adults do.

3. Put yourself in your child's place and imagine what any given situation might feel like from where he or she stands.

4. Do not expect your children to be just like you—they are unique individuals.

5. Treat your children with the same respect you want for yourself.

6. Trust and honor your ability to be a good parent.

7. Watch how you react to your child when you are angry.

8. Pay attention to the words you use when speaking to your kids.

9. Have compassion for what your kids may be going through, especially if they are teenagers.

10. Take time to reenergize yourself so you have more to give.

# *KIDS:*

## *Resolving the Differences Between Kids and Parents*

Have you ever noticed that adults can be really weird? Parents usually don't understand things the same way we do. That's because they are older than we are and they interpret things differently. It isn't their fault; it's just the way they are. My mom and I asked over 2,500 pre-teens and teenagers to describe how adults are different. The most common responses were:

- They always want to be in control.
- They have more power over us.
- My parents swear, but I get grounded if I swear.
- My parents get angry all the time, but I'm never allowed to express my anger.
- They treat us like babies.
- They think that just because they're older they know better.
- My parents always tell me what to wear.
- They talk differently to impress their friends.
- They think that if I do chores I'll be a better person.
- My dad yells at me to clean my room, but his room is a total mess.
- They call me names and always put me down.
- They think I'm lazy and stupid.

- My mom threatens me to get me to do homework.
- When there are problems at school, they always believe what the teachers say.
- My parents always call me a spoiled brat. I hate that!
- My dad smokes cigarettes and then tells me never to smoke.
- My parents drink wine with their friends and then tell *me* not to drink and drive.
- They never include me in major family decisions.
- They don't trust me.

---

Parents can't help being weird; it's just the way they are!

---

When parents treat their kids with disrespect, it lowers kids' self-esteem. Kids feel as if they have no control over their own lives because they aren't given the chance to make their own decisions. When kids aren't allowed to make their own decisions, they have a harder time making positive choices when they are older. Some of the things kids have told me are:

- My parents make me feel like I'm a nobody.
- I feel like I'm not important.
- I feel like I don't matter.
- They give our family dog more love and attention than they give me.
- Sometimes I wonder why my parents had kids in the first place.

Sometimes parents treat their kids unfairly because the kids don't meet their expectations, or because they are repeating what their own parents did, or they just think this is the right way to raise children. Parents usually want their kids to be just like them, but the truth is, we are completely different.

## Why We Are So Different

Here is a theory that my mom and I came up with. It may sound a little far-fetched, but if you use your imagination, it will help you understand the differences between kids and parents.

There are so many old wives' tales that explain where babies come from. Some say babies are bought from the store, or found in a cabbage patch, or dropped on your doorstep by the stork. Our theory is that there is a land far, far away where kids come from. In this land for kids only, life is fun. There are toys all around, kids run free, there are no rules and no one to tell them what to do. Kids get to be kids.

- Imagine being able to make a mess and not have to clean it up.
- You can eat candy for breakfast, cake for lunch, and ice cream for dinner without getting a stomachache.
- You can play in the rain and as soon as you're bored, you're dry.
- You don't have to worry about catching a cold because no one ever gets sick.
- There is no school; everyone already knows what they have to know.
- Every day is Christmas. You always get presents. When you are bored with your

toys, they are magically replaced with new toys.

- You can stay up all night and you won't be tired the next day.
- There are personal robots that cook and clean for you.
- If you don't like your food, you can eat something else.
- There is no such thing as pain. No one can break an ankle or sprain his or her wrist.
- You have no curfews or limits. No restrictions or laws. There are no kidnappers or murderers. No police officers or parents. No worries or problems or anything bad.

But, there are just a few rules that you do have to follow:

- You are the star and everything revolves around you.
- Everything can go your way just because you want it to.
- You can stand up for yourself no matter what.
- When you do receive something, it is yours and does not have to be shared unless you want to share it.
- You have the right to resist authority when it does not suit you.
- You don't have to say please or thank you unless you want to.
- Don't eat vegetables, because kids are allergic to them!

I sure could get used to these rules. The only problem is, once kids are born, they forget all about how life used to be. Being born creates some kind of amnesia. Even though kids don't remember where they have come from, they have all kept their old habits. We still expect to have everyone and everything revolve around us. We continue to believe that if we talk back or insist for long enough, things will go our way; and some of us still think that we're allergic to vegetables!

Parents have completely forgotten that kids come from a distant, faraway land where wishes do come true, and the basic rules of life are different than they are on Earth. Instead of talking to their kids in a way that they can understand better, parents treat their kids as if every one of them has a problem following rules, directions, and general instructions.

## Unreasonable Parents

Parents can be very unreasonable, like when they are listening to totally boring music. While driving in the car you ask your mom, "Can I listen to my favorite radio station?" She responds with "I'm the driver, so I get to pick what kind of music I listen to, and I don't want to listen to that!" Or she might just give you a flat-out "No!" It's really unfair when parents just say no and don't provide you with a reason.

Have you ever been punished for something that you thought was so unimportant? Sometimes your parents might give you their reason for saying no, but refuse to hear your side of the story. One girl said:

> I wanted to wear shorts to a party, but my mom said, "Wear a sweater or you might catch a cold." I told her I knew I'd be running around and dancing, which would keep me warm. She said I either had to wear the stupid sweater or

I was grounded. I couldn't talk to her. She gave
the final word and that was that. She's such a
control freak.

Adults have weird ways of doing things. In order to get
more respect from your parents, I have provided you with
helpful hints throughout this book to help you better understand and appreciate the differences between you and
them.

## Parents Are Not So Bad

Even though you might think adults are out to get you
and make your life miserable, the truth is most parents
love their kids very much. You may never hear the words
"I love you" from your parents, because some adults don't
feel comfortable showing their emotions. In that case, you
have to show them how to express their feelings.

One teenager told me:

No one in my family ever hugged. In fact, I
didn't even realize that was what families did.
Then I saw a lot of my friends hugging their
parents, and I decided to try it. I hugged everybody: my parents, my brother, my grandma,
even my aunts and uncles. The more I hugged,
the more I got hugged back. At first they all
thought I was weird, but after a while my family became a hugging family. I've always felt
like I taught my family to love each other more.

If you feel that your family doesn't say "I love you"
enough, here are a few things you can do. Before you walk
out the door to go meet your friends somewhere, say,
"Bye, I love you!" or before you go to bed, say, "I love
you guys. Good night." It's not so hard to do, and your
parents might be surprised. Give your parents hugs once

in a while: when you wake up in the morning, before they leave for a meeting, or anytime you feel like it. Sometimes the best way to teach something new to someone is to be an example.

---

Listen with your eyes and heart, more than your ears and brain. *—Anonymous*

---

## Make Your Life Easier

In this book, there are many examples of how to make your life easier. One way to make things easier for yourself is to keep remembering that parents think differently than we do. For example:

- Parents usually have high expectations for their kids. If their kids can't live up to those expectations, they think the kids aren't trying hard enough.
- Some parents think that in order for us to grow up strong, it's up to them to toughen us up so we will be able to take care of ourselves when we're older.
- Parents who ground their kids don't do it to be mean; they usually do it because they think it is the right way to teach their kids a lesson.

Sometimes there isn't much that we can do to change our parents because they have been on this planet for a longer amount of time than we have. There are special ways you can teach your parents, which I talk about in other chapters, but the most important thing is: You have to **want** to make your life easier. The relationship between you and your parents doesn't have to be full of anger, hate, and distrust. You have the power to make a difference. If you know the right techniques and when to use them, you can change the relationship you have with your parents to make it better.

Life is supposed to be filled with truth, happiness, understanding, and love. The way to find it is here for you. This advice is easy to follow if you are willing to do the work.

## Stop Those Fights

We relate to life one way; our parents relate to life another way. This is the cause of most misunderstandings and fights. But wouldn't it be nice if you didn't have as many fights with your parents as you do now? You can stop most fights before they happen by checking in with yourself to see if what they are saying is really important to you. If it isn't, then don't make a big deal about it.

For example, if you're leaving for school and your dad says, "Put your jacket on," don't argue. Instead of arguing and trying to explain that no one wears jackets at your school because it's not cool and they always get in the way, just say, "Okay." Take the jacket with you and leave it in your locker if you don't need it. Hopefully he'll respect you for listening to him, and he'll be happy he doesn't have to argue with you. Plus you won't have to listen to any of his long, boring lectures about getting sick when you go outside without a jacket!

## Don't Lie

The intention isn't to lie to your parents; it's just to avoid fights and keep peace in your family. If your dad says you can't go to someone's house, don't tell him you're going to the library when you are really planning to go to your friend's house anyway. That creates distrust. Once you've lost your parents' trust, it is really hard to gain it back. If you do lose the trust your parents had for you, here are some ways you might be able to regain it:

- Ask permission to go places instead of just telling your parents you are leaving.
- If you don't want to ask permission, at least discuss your plans so they feel that they have some power and control.
- Call home if you are going to be late.
- Promise to do something and then do it to show them you can follow through with your promises.
- Don't do anything that you know will make your parents angry when you are trying to win back their trust.

Telling the truth has nothing to do with being a kiss-up; it's just one of the many simple ways you can keep peace in your family. And it really works!

## Keep Cool

If you can't talk to your parents without yelling at them, accusing them, or putting them down, then you need to wait until you cool off; otherwise you may just get yourself in trouble. No matter how hard it may be, you have to remember to control your temper so you can show your parents you have self-control.

Some parents think kids are disrespectful, lazy, irresponsible, untrustworthy, and immature. When you can show your parents that you aren't all the terrible things they might think you are, it will be easier for them to give you the freedom, respect, and trust you deserve.

If something comes up that you really want to do and your parents won't let you do it, try to reason with them by discussing it. The trick is to *calmly* let them know why something may be so important to you. Usually the best time to explain things is not in the heat of the moment. It is definitely not a good idea to try to work things out during, or even right after, a fight. Whenever you decide to talk to your parents, make sure they are in good moods. They will listen better when they don't have so many other things on their minds. The way to find out if they are in a good mood, and if it is the right time to talk with them, is simply by asking. Remember to keep calm.

> *You:* Mom, is this a good time to talk to you?
> *Mom:* Sure. (Even though she said that, you can tell you don't have her full attention.)
> *You:* Mom, I really need to talk to you. When you stop what you're doing and pay attention to me, I feel like you're really listening. Is this a good time to talk, or should I wait till later?
> *Mom:* Give me a few minutes to finish what I'm doing, and then I can give you the attention you deserve.
> *You:* When should I come back?
> *Mom:* How about in ten minutes?
> *You:* Okay. I'll be back in ten minutes.

Even though this conversation probably sounds stupid to you, just know that it works. Adults want us to be reasonable (reasonable according to them anyway!). Don't forget that adults think differently than we do, and they react differently too. When you stay calm and handle things in a way that works for both of you, you get heard and things have a better chance of working out.

Whether you believe you can, or believe you can't, you're right!
*—Henry Ford*

We all lose our tempers at least once in a while. Because parents are human, too, sometimes they blow up for no apparent reason. I use a great technique called "Duck, Dodge, and Walk Away." I have used it many times with my parents. Just recently, my mom lost her temper big time. She was mad about something, and I knew it had nothing to do with me. I said something to her, and she started screaming in my face. I quickly remembered that this was her problem, and it was not about me. I just let my mom yell and scream. Her words flew past me instead of getting to me. As I ducked and dodged her words, I was reminded of the game little kids play at school called dodgeball.

In this game, you have to move around to avoid being hit by the ball. In the same way, when your parents scream at you, you have to pretend to duck and dodge so their words don't make you mad. When she finished yelling I looked at her, and sympathetically said, "I'm sorry you're so angry, Mom." Then, when I was sure she was finished "talking" to me, I walked away. Walking away isn't something you can do all the time, because your parents will think that you're being rude. But when you are able to do it, it makes it much easier to get out of the line of fire.

## If at First You Don't Succeed

It might be really hard to get these ideas down and follow through with them at first. You might think, "I'm not going to fight with my parents today. If they tick me off, I'll just go along with it." Then after they say or do something, you start screaming your head off. That's okay, because you made the first step which was to agree to try to make your life easier! You may not be able to stay calm each time your parents make you mad.

Just because you cooperate with them once does not mean they will let you do whatever you want after that. It's a gradual process. When you get these suggestions down and you are able to control your temper, your parents can get used to talking to you with respect.

The more often you use these techniques, the quicker your life will begin to change. It may be hard to change your ways at first, but if you really want more freedom, more respect, more choices, and more trust from your parents, you have to change some of your old habits. Hopefully, your parents will have more respect for you and they will treat you better. If it doesn't work at first, don't give up. Keep trying. They will get it eventually!

## Understanding Our Differences

Parents often expect us to think the way they do. We often expect parents to be more like us. Sometimes we have to remind ourselves that kids and parents are ***supposed*** to be different. If we forget about our differences and expect our parents to be like us, we end up disappointed and experience unnecessary conflicts.

For the next couple of weeks, become aware of the differences between you and your parents. Look at how their differences affect you and how you act toward them. Realize what you do when their differences bother you. Focus on what you can do to bring more peace into your family. Set an example for others to follow.

It is important to remember that adults can be really weird, and you might not always get along with them. Even if you don't always agree with what they say or do, your relationship doesn't have to be full of anger, hate, and distrust. If you use the ideas in this book, the relationship between you and your parents can only improve.

---

### *Personal Goals*

1. Remember that adults see the world differently than you do; it isn't their fault—it's just the way they are.
2. Find as many ways as you can to make your relationship with your family easier.
3. Stop yourself before you make a big deal out of things that really aren't very important.
4. Count how many times you can control your temper in one day. Save your energy for when you really need it.
5. Keep calm as often as you possibly can.
6. "Duck and dodge" your parents' angry words to avoid getting hurt or angry.
7. Try responding in a way adults think is "mature," and watch their reaction.
8. Give your parents an occasional hug and watch their response.
9. Keep peace in your family by always telling the truth.
10. Keep using the techniques for better communication until they work!

---

# CHAPTER 3

# Be an Example

## *PARENTS:*

*Model the Behavior You Expect*

We are our children's first teachers. Our influence, be it negative or positive, is all-encompassing. We are powerful role models. The way we parent has an effect on the way our children will relate to every experience for the rest of their lives.

Teach your children by becoming a living example in your daily life. The art of parenting takes a little bit of wisdom and a lot of common sense. Influenced by peers and cultural conditioning, children look to you to provide emotional stability for them.

Embody the values you want your children to possess. Do you swear? Drive fast? Gossip about your friends or family? While you may view these actions as harmless, your child watches you and learns similar behavior.

## Set Good Examples

- If you have two glasses of wine with dinner and then get into your car after a very full meal, what message does your child understand?

—Can your teen truly comprehend that a couple of beers may be potentially deadly for him?

• When someone cuts you off on the freeway, do you angrily speed up to cut him or her off, swearing as you go?

—Who teaches teenagers about driving courtesy?

• The frustrated mommy slaps her young child and says, "Don't hit your brother again."

—Does a young child learn to control her temper and work things out, or does she learn by example?

• The exhausted dad screams at the kids to stop yelling.

—When your preteen is upset, is he able to talk about his problems or does he scream and throw a temper tantrum?

*This confusion and hypocrisy destroys adult credibility in the mind of a child.*

Think about the kind of examples you set for your children. We know school-age children can be very cruel, and some teenagers are rude and disrespectful. Where did they learn that kind of behavior? Children are not born cruel, nasty, or competitive. Children pick up behavior from their circle of influence: family, friends, school, media, and television. What kinds of things do *you* say about your family, your neighbors, or the waiter in a restaurant? Become aware of the powerful influence you have on your children.

I became acutely aware of just how influential parents

can be one day when I was driving car pool. Someone cut me off on the freeway. I had to slam on my brakes with a car full of teenagers in the backseat. I took a deep breath and changed lanes to get away from the idiot playing car-tag. One of the thirteen-year-old girls sitting in the backseat of my car said, "I can't wait until I can drive. My dad lets me drive in parking lots and he's teaching me to go fast. He's so cool. You should see him drive. If someone cuts him off, he speeds up and cuts them off. He flips them off and screams and laughs. He's so cool. I love my dad. Hey, how come you didn't chase that guy and flip him off?"

I merely said, "I don't think playing games with cars is safe. I don't want to waste my energy and I don't want to risk anyone's life. I feel much better just changing lanes and getting out of the guy's way." I can only hope that this girl's circle of influence includes me.

---

Children are unpredictable. You never know what inconsistency they're going to catch you in next.
—*Franklin P. Jones*

---

It is your responsibility as a parent to model positive, healthy, safe behavior for your children. Parents enjoy being told they are "cool," or that they are loved, but it is not worth anything if it stems from irresponsible parenting.

## Children Live What They Learn

Children have very sensitive radar; they pick up values and behavior from all directions and then assimilate it. In fact, children pick up various behaviors from the moment you put them in your arms. It is a subtle process that continues as they grow.

A mother in my parenting class related this story:

> A group of parents car-pooled for a fifth-grade field trip. As the parents stood in a group waiting for the teacher to tell them which way to go, I stood on the sidelines and listened to them all talking. They were gossiping! They were talking about the way some of the other moms dress. They were talking about who drove what car. Some of the mothers were making blatant judgments about everyone, as their daughters stood around listening. I couldn't believe my ears! These were the mothers of the same girls who tease my daughter unmercifully. No wonder the girls are so nasty; they learn it at home!

Another parent chimed in and said:

> My daughter is in high school. She always complains that the girls are so snobby and won't let her into their cliques. I didn't really understand what the problem was until I went to an orientation meeting at her school. Every time I tried to introduce myself to another parent, I was appalled at how snobby they were! I'm a well-educated, well-dressed woman and can converse with the best of them, but they were in their own cliques and acted like I wasn't welcome. These were grown women! This is the example they show their own daughters, who continue the snob cycle.

Another mother said:

> I have taught my kids not to gossip. I have taught them to respect other people's property.

I have taught them to have compassion for others. But when my daughter tries to uphold her belief system by not making fun of other kids, and by not throwing around her classmates' notebooks, she is shunned by the other girls. They call her a bitch because they can't understand why she isn't like them. I thank God she isn't like them, but it's hard for her.

For children to grow into caring, compassionate human beings, they must first see that caring and compassion take place in their home. Your own behavior becomes ingrained in the persona of your child. In an article in Newsweek magazine (Feb. 19, 1996) entitled *Your Child's Brain,* Sharon Begley writes, "If emotions are repeatedly met with indifference . . . brain circuits become confused and fail to strengthen." The article goes on to say, "It's the pattern that counts. A baby whose mother never matched her level of excitement became extremely passive, unable to feel excitement or joy."

You are instrumental in the developing personality of your children. Give them tender loving care when they are tired, cranky, or having a rough time. Show compassion when they have made a mistake or they have let you down. Demonstrate true understanding when they need it the most, by listening and by being fair. When you are having a bad day, try to be as loving and fair as you possibly can. This does not mean you have to be in a good mood all the time. As life unfolds, deal with your issues in the best way you can without taking it out on your children. By taking responsibility for your own actions you can admit to your mistakes, face your fears, deal with your negative behavior, apologize, and get on with your life. Model the behavior you expect.

Teach your children to be kind by treating them and others with kindness. Encourage them to respect others and enjoy life. Balance the seriousness of peer pressure, homework, chores, and stress by encouraging your children to burn off excess energy by being silly. Be playful and laugh with your kids; you are never too old, or too mature to have fun.

Remember that kids are not adults in little bodies. They have characteristics that differ from ours. It is natural for children to be self-absorbed, or "selfish." As they grow and learn by example, they do begin to consider others around them. Show your children how to be kind to others and praise them for every little bit of generosity they display.

---

As the twig is bent the tree inclines.

—*Virgil (70–19* B.C.*)*

---

## Teach Respect

A primary responsibility of parents is to teach their children respect. You can do this by respecting them and other people in your life. If you are a single parent, demonstrate what positive relationships look like as you interact with friends, family, and the people around you. If you are divorced, do not bad-mouth your ex-spouse in front of your kids.

If you have problems relating to your "ex," it is rarely, if ever, the direct fault of your child. If you are in a committed relationship, let your children see that Mom and Dad love, honor, and appreciate each other. Show affection, hug your family. By using the ideas in this book, you can give concrete demonstrations of love, understanding, trust, and respect to your children.

If your relationship is less than ideal, find ways to enhance your communication skills and respectfully work out your differences. Show your children that even when problems arise, they can be dealt with in a civilized manner. Get counseling, take a seminar on relationships, listen to tapes, or read books on enhancing relationship skills. Be tactful and respectful to those around you.

- If you impart kindness, children will learn to be kind.
- If you show respect and play fair, children will learn to be respectful and fair.
- If you encourage feelings, children will learn to feel.
- If you demonstrate tolerance, children will learn to be tolerant.
- If you practice forgiveness, children will learn to love themselves again.

---

Mankind owes to the child the best it has to give.
—*U.N. Declaration*

---

## Teach Kids to Express Themselves

Allow your children to express their disappointment, anger, and frustration by listening to what they have to say. If you listen and understand from *their* perspective, your children will feel safe to come to you whenever they have a problem. Begin this when they are young, and you will eventually create a safe haven for your teenager. If you already have teens, it is never too late to start listening. Don't correct their grammar, mannerisms, or slang. Be helpful, listen, and continue to understand from their perspective; remember to put yourself in their shoes.

As you allow your children to express themselves fully, use patience and understanding. Whining and nagging can be obnoxious to the adult ear, but it is a normal form of communication for kids. It is just another way children respond when their needs are not being met. Unfortunately, many children are abused physically and verbally when they whine or nag, but you must remember it is a stage they will eventually outgrow. "Use your words," parents say to their whining child. "You two work it out," they say when two youngsters are fighting. Children only have the words if they have learned them. Parents must help their children learn how to express themselves.

To a whining child who wants something, you might say:

• "I want you to use your regular voice. That high-pitched whining hurts my ears!"

Keep repeating this in a *calm* manner. Then say,

• **"Tell** me what you want. **Show** me what it is you want so I can understand."

After the child has shown you or told you what it is she was whining about, you can remind her gently:

• "Thank you for using your regular voice. When you use your regular voice, I can hear you, and then I can understand what you want."

For example: After discovering what your child was whining about you can say, "I understand that you really want a candy bar, but I don't want to buy candy today because we had a lot of sweets yesterday. You can pick out your very own box of crackers or a bagel. Which one do you want?"

If you respond in this way, your child feels heard and understood. By providing him with an opportunity to choose between crackers and a bagel, you give your child choices. The choices are limited; they are within a structure you feel comfortable with. Yet, your child feels he has reasonable control over his life, which lessens the need to rebel.

To a nagging teenager who wants to go somewhere, you might respond with:

- "I need you to stop nagging me."
  The trick is to keep repeating this in a calm manner. Then say,
- "Look, this isn't a good time to talk to me about that. Ask me later when I'm done with my work, and we can work something out."
  After your teenager has stopped nagging you, you can tell her:
- "I really appreciate it when you don't nag me. When I'm being nagged, I don't want to help, I just feel like saying no. When I'm being respected, I feel like doing things for you."

For example: Tell your teenager, "I have some things I have to get done this morning. If you give me time to finish my work without nagging me, I won't feel resentful. I'll be willing to drive you later because I won't be pressured for time."

When you respond in this way, your teenager has an opportunity to hear what you feel and what you need, without feeling threatened or put off. In addition, you have provided her with reasonable options she can handle. She can choose to give you space and reap the benefit of going shopping later, or she can continue to nag and lose the privilege. You empower your child by giving her reasonable choices that allow her to make wise decisions for herself.

Give your kids feedback about unacceptable behavior and its inappropriateness so they can learn what acceptable behavior is. By clearly explaining yourself, you simultaneously express your needs while giving your kids the opportunity to take responsibility for their actions. As you continue to respond in this way, you begin to form the groundwork for continued open communication.

## Help Them Work It Out

We are not perfect, yet we often expect perfection from our kids. Adults don't always have the necessary communication skills to work out problems in their relationships, yet we expect great interpersonal skills from our children. We must give them the tools so they can begin to understand how to work things out.

A father in my son's karate class was yelling at his bickering son and daughter to stop fighting.

"You two work it out yourselves," he bellowed.

I watched his children tremble at the tone of his voice.

His daughter walked over to him and meekly said, "But, Daddy, we don't know how to work this one out."

"You'll just have to figure it out, you're big enough. Go do it now, and stop fighting," he ordered.

Of course, the children continued fighting, the father got very angry, and they all left the karate studio in anger and embarrassment.

If the father had used sensitivity, compassion, and good communication skills, the conversation might have gone like this:

> **Father (firmly):** "It makes me sad when you two fight. Please stop now."
> **Sister:** "Well, he started it."

*Brother:* "Uh-uh, she started it."
*Father (gently):* "Look, I want you two to figure out how you can stop fighting."
*Sister:* "But, Daddy, we don't know how to work this one out."
*Father:* "Try your conflict management skills. Remember what we do at home?"

• First you each take a turn to tell what happened without interrupting each other.
• Then, after each one of you has spoken without being interrupted, you tell the other person how you feel about the situation. Remember to describe all of your feelings about what happened without calling names or saying mean things.
• Then, even if you don't agree, you both try to come up with a solution that works for both of you. "Would you like me to be the referee? I'll be glad to help you reach a conclusion so everyone feels better about what's going on. Let's go do it outside so we have some privacy."

You can squelch fighting by giving your kids clear messages about what kind of behavior you expect before fights begin. Parents who have never spoken to their kids this way may find it difficult at first. As with any new idea you may try, practice makes it better. You will find, however, that this form of communication is more efficient and works better in the long run. Take your time to learn these new skills and be patient with yourself when you do not do it exactly the way you intended to.

No one ever said parenting was easy. It is a job that

can be challenging and exhausting, but stating what you really mean does not have to be hard. Watching your children express themselves and work out their problems can be very satisfying. Working it out, using good communication skills, and demonstrating to your children the best way to deal with a given situation does take extra effort, but the end result is worth it.

---

Kind words can be short and easy to speak, but their echoes are truly endless.

—*Mother Teresa*

---

Demonstrate "working things out" in your own relationships by modeling fair fighting. When couples, friends, or family members disagree, discussions often quickly turn into battles. We hurt each other deeply by blaming, accusing, resenting, doubting, and demanding. The secret to avoiding arguments is through honest, respectful, loving communication, and forgiveness. While it is perfectly normal to disagree, ideally an argument does not have to be hurtful and controlling. Use marital spats to teach problem-solving skills to your kids by showing them how you work through your disagreements. You must learn to be honest and direct without hurting or offending the other person. "Saying it like it is" can deeply hurt someone's feelings. While you may not reach a conclusion or come up with a solution, it is okay if you both agree to disagree. Let your kids see that you are willing to hear the other person's side of the story, and if the fight escalates, let your kids know that Mom and Dad can really disagree and still love each other.

Kids can only turn a negative situation into a positive one if they have good role models. Consciously choosing to debate, discuss, and argue constructively and respectfully can be immensely helpful to neutralize tension with your own children when conflicts arise. Remember that angry discussions usually just promote more angry discussions. When your child is misbehaving, "work it out" with her. Give her words and techniques for getting along. Teach her how to play fair. The tendency toward anger diminishes when a person can share his feelings and feel that he has been heard. Understanding and connection with others create healing. Practice using good communication skills in all your affairs.

## Teach Them to Negotiate

Kids who do not have a sense of power in their lives, or who do not feel respected by the adults who influence them, feel the need to manipulate, or "kiss up" as kids call it. People who are treated as individuals and given the respect they deserve do not need to manipulate; they learn to negotiate—to express their concerns and desires, to be straight and honest, and to work things out so that everyone's needs are heard and met. This is not the case for most kids.

Because they are not treated with high esteem and faith, and because so many parents believe they "own" their children, many kids do not feel they are taken seriously. In relationships, couples often manipulate each other to get unspoken needs met. On the television show *I Love Lucy*, the immortal Lucy Ricardo constantly manipulated her husband, Ricky, to get what she wanted. Adults "brown-nose" their bosses to get ahead. Kids go overboard or "kiss up" when they want their parents to be nice to them, or to get them in a good mood.

While the expression "kiss up" may sound offensive to the adult ear, it is merely a tool that many kids believe they must use to negotiate with their parents. When they have to be careful of their parents' reactions, or fear repercussions of any kind, they use the "art of the kiss up" to butter their parents up. Once "buttered," adults tend to be in better moods and are often more generous with their affection and rewards. Kids know this and use this technique to get their needs met. When they have been treated with respect and honesty, when they have been taught good communication skills, and the lines of communication are open and safe, kids can negotiate from the heart.

## Temper aggression

Teaching values is a very delicate endeavor. We must remember that children relate to the world differently than adults do, and they filter our words and actions through their own viewpoint.

In my baby-sitting seminar, one of my students was exploring ways to get more baby-sitting jobs. He said he played soccer and that there were always little kids running around at the games. I asked him if he could baby-sit for a sibling of one of his opponents. The conversation was shocking:

*Jason:* "NO WAY," he replied with horror.
*Me:* "Why?" I asked, rather astounded at the intensity in his voice.
*Jason:* "Because they're the enemy. When I play ball, my parents want me to kill the other team. There's no way they would let me baby-sit for someone from the other team's side. They're the enemy!"
*Me:* "They're just little kids watching their brothers play ball. They don't want to kill you," I reasoned.
*Jason:* "There's no way. I hate them, they're the enemy," he insisted.
*Me:* "So, you think your parents hate your oppo-

nents and don't want you to associate with
them in any way?"

***Jason:*** "Yeah. I know my parents, and there's NO
way!"

The competitiveness, anger, and aggression coming
from this otherwise sweet twelve-year-old boy was
astounding. What kinds of examples were his parents setting for him? Even if it was meant as a joke, this child
took the word of his parents very, very, seriously. If he
believes he must consider innocent siblings of his opponents "the enemy" in sports, how does the mind of a
teenager transform this thought and the energy behind
the thought into treating humankind with gentleness and
kindness?

My own son felt this confusion and inconsistency one
day when we were visiting the Monterey Bay Aquarium
in Northern California. After patiently standing in line,
it was finally his turn to view a hands-on exhibit. Suddenly, an adult pushed my son out of the way and boldly
said, "My son is next, he's been waiting." My son replied,
"I was next. I'm after that girl." The man yelled at my
son, saying "My son has been waiting over there for a
long time, now it's his turn." As his little boy walked up
to get in line, the man once again pushed my son out of
the way and pushed his son into line. My son said, "Please
don't push me." The man responded, "Don't tell me what
to do. Get out of my way."

I could not believe what I was witnessing: a grown man
pushing little kids around and shouting in front of crowds
of people. I quickly intervened and said, "Please don't
push my child." He began shouting, "Shut up, lady. My
kid has been waiting and your kid cut in line." Having
waited with my son, I knew that he had not cut in line.
I said, "You have no right to push children, and you are
setting a terrible example here." This aggressive, pushy
father did not care about setting an example as he con-

tinued to rant and rave. To avoid making a huge scene, I then told his child to take his turn, and instructed the man once again, "Don't push little children!" As we moved away, he called out loudly, "Bitch."

As the other children frantically began pushing and shoving to secure their place in line, one little girl began to cry. Her mother said, "Let's get out of here. These kids are all so rude." Unfortunately, it is the children who become the tragic victims of aggression and animosity.

For this world to survive, we must show our children how to be caring human beings. Because we are the most influential role models on the planet, our influence is all-powerful. We must teach kindness, respect for ourselves and others, and we must teach peace.

## Teach Kindness

What you say and how you say it gives a direct message to your kids about their own self-worth. Every interaction you have with your children has the tremendous potential to make a negative or positive difference in their lives. You hold the power. You can choose to hurt or to heal, to bruise or to inspire. The choice is yours.

Speak calmly and be firm when necessary. Shouting creates tension in your home and teaches your kids to raise their voices in order to get heard. Nagging teaches kids to whine and beg for things they want and cannot have. Remember that in Kids' World, children can do whatever they please, whenever they please. They often forget they have to tune you in, not tune you out.

When I start to lose my temper or begin to sound mean, I try to catch myself right away. I take a deep breath and apologize to my children; after all, I am contributing to the adults of the future by treating them with kindness and respect.

After losing my cool when my son did not clean up his

mess one day, I went to his room and knocked on his door. When he let me in, I told him I was sorry:

**Me:** I'm so sorry for yelling at you. You probably feel really bad right now.

**Son:** Yeah, you were so mean.

**Me:** I'm really sorry. Sometimes I get so angry and impatient, and it's not fair for me to yell at you. I didn't mean to hurt your feelings.

**Son:** You did hurt my feelings, Mom.

**Me:** I'm sorry for hurting your feelings. You don't deserve to be talked to like that. No one should get yelled at. You are a wonderful person and I love you. I love all the special little things you do. Messes are not such a big deal. I should have been more patient. Will you please forgive me? *(This is really what I say!)*

**Son:** Okay. But can we not yell at each other anymore?

**Me:** I'll work on not yelling and you could work on picking up your stuff when you're finished playing, okay? I'm counting on you to help keep our house in order.

**Son:** Okay.

**Me:** I want you to pick up your stuff. Will you please do it now?

**Son:** Sure.

This kind of discussion can move an angry situation and imbalance of power to a place of understanding, consideration, and mutual respect. It teaches children to be kind, flexible, and compassionate. It gives them the freedom and the safety to make mistakes, while showing them how to forgive. Forgiveness does not imply that you condone what the person has done; it affirms that the person who made the mistake still deserves to be loved. Later that evening, my son threw his arms around me and said he loved me because I'm "such a great mom." Now when he loses his temper, he often catches himself and apologizes immediately. The change is astounding.

You can also show kindness and compassion in a novel way: be kind to animals and nurture the innate connection between children and their pets. Teach your children compassion and empathy by creating a safe, nurturing, loving environment for their pets. As you lovingly and diligently care for a sick or aging pet, you are inadvertently demonstrating how your own child might care for you when you are old. People who abuse animals rarely stop there. According to the Humane Society, studies show that people who abuse their pets are also likely to abuse their kids. The parent who comes home and kicks the dog is probably just warming up. Teach your children respect for *all* living things through your own actions.

---

Kindness is the connection that links us all together and strengthens the bonds within our communities, neighborhoods, and families. —*Rosalynn Carter*

---

## Encourage Feelings

You do not have to carry the burden of always being right. Let your children see you complete with your flaws. It makes you seem more real. If your children see you upset, it will not harm them, as long as you do not make them feel responsible for causing you to be upset or making you feel better.

Let your children see you cry. Both Mom and Dad can allow their cleansing tears to flow. There is no shame in crying; it is a normal, natural part of feeling. It is also the way babies communicate when they cannot speak. Over seven hundred preteens and teenagers have told me, "My parents hate when I cry." They told me their parents say things like:

- "Stop crying. You have nothing to cry about."
- "Stop crying, or I'll *give* you something to cry about."
- "Don't cry. You don't look pretty when you cry."
- "Cut it out. You're okay."
- "Big boys don't cry."
- "Don't feel bad. You'll forget all about it tomorrow."

These comments negate the way your child is feeling. All the kids agreed that when they cry, it is for a reason that means something to them. Sometimes adults cry "for no apparent reason." Put yourself in your child's shoes and be compassionate. What may seem irrelevant or frivolous to you may be of great importance to your child. Be supportive of your child as he experiences pain or sorrow. Lend an ear and listen without judgment.

Many people tend to back away from normal human emotion and self-expression. Allison and Robert were in my parenting class. They told me their son's first-grade teacher called them to school for a meeting. The teacher told them their six-year-old son was a "crybaby" and needed to toughen up. "He's too sensitive. He always talks about his feelings," she complained. When they asked about his schoolwork and his grades, the teacher assured them that he was doing fine academically. "You just need to make a man out of him, that's all," she scolded. Unable to "deal with" a kind, considerate, sensitive boy, the teacher wanted to change the inherent nature of the child.

Robert told the teacher:

> Look, we're proud our son isn't an inconsiderate, insensitive, rude little guy. Sure he cries sometimes, he's a kid. But we're glad he talks about how things make him feel, because we're trying to cultivate a sensitive young man with a positive attitude. Can you imagine how your class would be if all the six-year-old kids could express their feelings without whining or blaming other kids? It would probably make things a lot less stressful, that's for sure.

We are living in a time when men and women are discovering the balance of the masculine and feminine within. Psychologists are encouraging men to cry and get in touch with their feelings. Medical doctors tell us to let out our emotions and stress in healthy ways through therapy, meditation, and laughter to avoid disease.

---

Tears that do not flow make other organs weep inside.
—*Michael Pritchard, child advocate and comedian*

---

Kids watch how you behave in addition to what you say. The best lecture is a good example of how you live your life. Let your children see how you respond to negative and positive issues in your life. Encourage your children to feel their full range of emotions. When kids feel safe enough to express their full range of emotions at home, parents must be prepared for everything from passivity to volatility to emerge. Help them find outlets for their ever-changing thoughts and feelings.

- Let your kids talk on the phone to share their innermost feelings with friends.
- Give your son or daughter a punching bag or pillow to let out aggressive behavior.
- Encourage your kids to do volunteer work so they can help others instead of constantly dwelling on themselves.
- Read with them to open their minds to the infinite possibilities of life.

Think how good you would feel if you had safe outlets for all of your feelings. Create a safe, nurturing home environment in which your children can count on being loved, guided, respected, and heard.

---

### *Personal Goals*

1. Teach your children to love by loving them and loving yourself.

2. Be true to yourself because your children can sense when you are not.

3. Be a caring human being.

4. Set reasonable boundaries.

5. Model honesty.

6. Apologize when appropriate.

7. Demonstrate your willingness to work things out.

8. Honor your commitments, and always try to keep your promises to your children.

9. Say what you mean and mean what you say.

10. Don't preach. Practice what you teach.

# *KIDS:*

## *Get Your Parents to Appreciate You*

Have you ever wanted to reverse the roles with your parents? Now is your chance! It's your turn to take responsibility and teach your parents a few things. Since you have been raised to believe your parents are in charge of raising you, it's probably very hard for you to understand this idea and believe that you can do it. It's up to you to set examples for your parents so you can create trust, communication, and respect in the relationship you have with them.

## Ways to Get Appreciated

Do you ever feel unappreciated by your parents? Sometimes parents don't realize that you do things to help them out. If you start to do things that aren't part of your regular routine, they might start to appreciate you more often. Some simple ways to get your parents to appreciate you are:

- Carry in the groceries from the car.
- Bring in the mail.
- Take breaks from teasing your brother or sister.
- Say please and thank you more often.
- Do the laundry.
- Set the table even if it's not your job.

- Do the dishes.
- Take the dog for a walk without having to be told.
- Make your own lunch for school .
- Offer to make dinner if you know how to cook.
- Clean your room the first time you're asked (and shock them!).
- If you are asked to do something, do it immediately before someone gets mad.
- If you drive, offer to go to the store or take your sibling to a friend's house.
- Take phone messages for your parents and remember to give the messages to them.

Your parents may think you're crazy if you start doing these things regularly, but they will notice that you're doing things you haven't done before. Adults like that. They think you are maturing, and hopefully they will start appreciating you.

## When Your Parents Don't Appreciate You

If you still don't get appreciated even after a few weeks of helping out, bring it to your parents' attention by telling them that you have been doing things for them that you don't usually do. You can say something like:

- "Hey Mom, did you notice that I brought the groceries in for you?"
- "Since I had nothing else to do, I folded the laundry."

- "Here, I remembered to give you the phone messages this time."

If they respond with something like "It's about time," or "Better late than never," just pretend you are ducking and dodging from what they are saying so the words don't make you feel bad. Then try to get out of the situation without talking back to avoid fights.

---

You have the power to keep peace in your family.

---

Sometimes you might feel that your parents make a bigger deal when you do something wrong than when you do something right. If this is the case, it may be a good time to make a deal with your parents:

*You:* Mom, I've been helping out a lot around the house, and I feel like I don't get appreciated.

*Mom:* I do plenty of things and nobody ever thanks me.

*You:* I'll try to appreciate you more often, if you appreciate me too.

*Mom:* Why can't you just do what you're supposed to do without making such a big fuss?

*You:* In order for me to do more things without a big fuss, I need you to appreciate the things that I do.

*Mom:* Why???

*You:* Because when I get appreciated for doing things, I don't mind doing more.

*Mom:* Okay. I'm willing to give it a try.

Another example might be: If it seems as though your dad is always mad at you, you might think, "Why would I want to make him happy, he's always so mean to me?" If that's the way you feel, just try the appreciation thing for a while. When you help, appreciate, and acknowledge your parents more often, it may make them want to be nicer to you, and they may help you out in return.

## Remember to Acknowledge Your Parents

Everyone likes to be acknowledged when they have done something good, and they like to know that the things they do are well liked. We all know the best way to train an animal is to give it a reward right after it has done something good. Even though your parents aren't animals, you can train them in a similar way. When your parents do something you like, let them know right away by praising them. This could be something like:

- "Thanks for driving me."
- "The dinner is really good."
- "Thanks for buying that for me."
- "Thanks for letting me go to the party."

If you praise or compliment them right after their "good deed," there is a better chance they'll do something nice for you again. The reason people repeat their actions is because they realize they are liked and appreciated.

If you feel that your parents don't appreciate anything you do, try to appreciate them for everything you possibly can. It makes them feel good about themselves (even if they don't show it), and they will be nicer to you. It's not your job to tell your parents what to do, but you can teach them by being an example. Acknowledge and appreciate your parents if you want them to do the same to you. In other words: Treat your parents the way you want them to treat you.

There is a pattern that develops by appreciating your parents. At first it might seem ridiculous, but in the end it works out in your favor:

- When you tell your parents how much you appreciate what they have done for you, it makes them feel better about themselves.
- When they feel better about themselves, they tend to be in better moods.
- When they are in good moods, it makes them easier to be around.
- They are more generous and fun when they are in a good mood.
- There are fewer fights and life is much easier for everyone.

Here is an example of how this technique works:

If my mom drives me to a friend's house and I get out of the car without thanking her, she would probably feel used and she might be upset with me. She might not want to go out of her way to drive me to a friend's house again, or anywhere else for that matter. All I have to do is show some appreciation and say thank you, and my mom will probably be willing to take me somewhere another time. Why make it hard on yourself when you can make it easy?

## *Please* and *Thank You*: the Magic Words

It usually doesn't take too much effort to make adults happy if you use the right techniques at the appropriate times. Experiment to see what works for them. *Please* and *thank you* are two words that make adults happy; in fact, they call them the "magic words." For example, when a little kid asks an adult for something, the adult says, "What's the magic word?" They keep asking until the child says "please" or "thank you." Since adults are really different and they think and do things differently than we do, each time we use the "magic words," it's a big deal for them. They think we sound polite and well mannered. When we don't say "please" or "thank you" it makes adults think we are really rude.

When you say "thank you," it acknowledges what your parents have done. Thank them for driving you to school, cooking dinner, taking you to a friend's house, or even taking you to the orthodontist! It's very simple; acknowledge your parents and watch the benefits come back to you.

---

Good thoughts are the power that makes my mind flower;
Good deeds are the seeds that I sow.

—Positively Mother Goose

---

Saying "please" and "thank you" is usually a very difficult thing for kids to remember because in the land where we came from, saying "please" and "thank you" were optional rules.

## Getting on Your Parents' Good Side

It's pretty obvious that parents won't appreciate anything you do if they're angry with you. Sometimes you may need to go out of your way so you can get on your parents' good side. When they feel better about themselves and they're in better moods, it's probably easier for them to share their happiness and appreciation with you.

You may feel that your parents are always mad at you no matter what you do for them. I interviewed some kids and asked them how they get on their parents' good side. Even though parents might think the word *kiss up* is rude or inappropriate, that's the word most kids use when describing how they work with adults to get what they want in their relationships:

- Erica is thirteen. She said, "I kiss up to them. I try to look at the problem from their point of view so I can see where they are coming from. Then I move in from that angle. It works for me almost every time."
- Hillary is fourteen. She said, "It's pretty simple. I kiss up to them. I do stuff I don't normally do, and it makes them happy. But it works!"
- Margot, age fourteen, told me: "You have to gain their respect by living up to their expectations. That way they trust you more and you get more freedom."
- Gina is fifteen. She said you have to "kiss up. Do everything you're told. Follow the rules. Me and my mom have this agreement where we trust each other and I can tell her everything without getting in trouble. You have to be honest, then they trust you."

• Max is fifteen. He said, "You kind of have to kiss up to them. You have to do what they ask you to do. You have to show a lot of respect for them."

• Dan, age sixteen, said, "I usually try to offer to do things that they usually have to ask me to do, like mowing the lawn, reading to my little brother, or dusting and vacuuming. When I do those things, they see me as being helpful, and they like me! Then when I ask to do something they normally wouldn't let me do, they think, 'He's been really helpful' and they let me go out."

• Ben, age eighteen, says: "I tell them I love them a lot and I act nice. It works for my family most of the time."

• Josh is twenty-one. He said when he was a teenager the way he got on his parents' good side was always "definitely school related. If I got a good grade I would definitely mention that. If something good happened in one of my classes, I'd let my parents know about it. I also told them what I was doing. When I included them in my social life by letting them know where I wanted to go, they were always more willing to say okay."

## No Kissing Up in This Relationship

Almost everyone I have talked to has said that you have to kiss up to get what you want. But I found one person who said that he doesn't have to kiss up just to get what he wants from his parents.

• Aidan just turned sixteen. He said, "I don't kiss up. I either get what I want or I

don't. Kissing up is a waste of time. My relationship with my parents is open, not false.
I can talk to them and they listen. Our relationship is better than most of my friends'
relationships with their parents. It's more
comfortable and relaxed. I consider myself
pretty lucky."

I can relate to Aidan's relationship with his parents
because it is very similar with my parents. I don't have
to worry about kissing up to get what I want. I ask and
we discuss. If I don't get something that is very important
to me, I discuss it more with my parents. No matter what,
they always listen to me. They don't always agree with
me, but at least they always listen to my point of view.
We usually end up working out an agreement or a compromise of some sort.

Helping out and appreciating your parents is a way to
create a good relationship with them. I used to remind
myself to do extra things around the house to get my
parents to say "yes" more often, but now it just comes
naturally. We all work together to help each other out.
We have trust and respect for each other. Ever since I
was a baby, my parents have acknowledged me for all the
good things I've accomplished. They've encouraged me,
praised me, and given me support in everything that I've
done. They're always on my side and ready to stand up
for me whenever I need them. My parents have always
treated me like a person, not like a lower-ranking kid.

## How to Use the Act of Being Nice to Work in Your Favor

For those of you who aren't able to communicate well,
keep practicing the skills in this book. Here is what you
can do to make your life easier until that happens.

When you want something, sometimes the only way to get it is if you act nice to adults so they realize you deserve it. *Suck-up, Kiss-up, Goody-Two-Shoes, Teacher's pet, Daddy's girl, Mommy's boy* are some of the names that we're called when we act really nice to adults. The names are stupid, but what matters is that being considerate makes a difference in your relationships.

For example: You want a new stereo and you don't have enough money to pay for it. If you're nice to your parents, help them out around the house, and don't cause fights with your siblings before you ask them to help you buy the stereo, you have a better chance of them helping you than if they were upset with you. What you do, how you act, and what you say affect adults. The more you appreciate them and the more you treat them with respect, the quicker you will see results. This technique works for everyone involved because you get what you want, and it makes the adults happy because they see you being cooperative. It's what they call a win-win situation: everyone is happy.

You have to be very careful not to abuse the power of the "kiss-up." Make sure that you are nice to your family and you help them out and do things for them not only when you want something. If you're nice to your parents only when you want something, they will catch on and then you won't ever get appreciated for anything, and you'll never get what you want. Even though this might sound "sneaky" to adults, please realize that sometimes this is the only way some kids can get what they need.

---

No act of kindness, no matter how small, is ever wasted.

—*Aesop*

---

There are two major benefits for not abusing the power of the kiss-up:

1) Whenever you want something and you act really nice to your family, they won't see any difference from the way you act at other times. That way they won't suspect anything before you even get a chance to ask for what you want.

2) If you help out and act nice to your family as much as you can, they'll be nicer to *you* more often, and chances are they'll be more generous.

This technique can work at school, too:

• For example: Your teacher says your entire class won't get any homework for the whole week if everyone is nice to the substitute teacher. So the whole class "kisses up" to the sub; you all do what she tells you, and you don't cause any problems. The substitute thinks you're a good class. She tells that to your teacher, and you don't get any homework for the whole week. The process is pretty simple.

In order to create a win-win situation, you need to be respectful and considerate of others. But most of all you need to create a special relationship with yourself. When your family or friends piss you off, if you believe in yourself, trust yourself, and know yourself on a deep level, you can handle any situation.

## Appreciate Yourself

To make a positive difference in your life, the most important thing you can do is respect yourself. I have met a few preteens and teenagers who seem to get in trouble all the time. They don't seem to have much self-respect. They hang out with the wrong crowd, get bad grades, or they are involved in some kind of illegal behavior.

I met one fifteen-year-old guy who had great self-respect, and who chose to wear strange, out-of-the-ordinary clothes. Aaron was a nice guy with a very high I.Q. He had a great relationship with his parents and worked part-time in his parents' art store after school. The way he dressed made some people judge him as a punk. Some of his friends from school weren't allowed to hang out with him, because their parents thought Aaron would be a bad influence on them. The adults judged him by the way they saw him on the outside, instead of getting to know him better.

People may judge you by the way you dress or by the people you hang out with. For example, you might not like to smoke pot, but if you hang out with a group of people who do, then you might be judged as a druggie. There is an old French saying that translates to: "If you show me your friends, I'll tell you who you are." There are some other old sayings in English like:

- Water seeks its own level.
- Birds of a feather flock together.
- If you lie down with dogs, you wake up with fleas.

When I first heard those expressions, I didn't understand the real meaning. But if you really think about them for a while, and you think about who you are, who you want to be, and who you want to hang out with, those old expressions start to make a lot of sense.

You have to look around you and see what's happening in your life. Some people aren't happy with who they are, yet they don't do anything to change. By living your life with self-respect and self-appreciation, you can have a different outlook on life. When you respect and appreciate yourself, you can work on getting your parents to appreciate you.

## Don't Give Up

Sometimes it's hard to break old habits, and it may be surprising for your parents if you suddenly start trying to communicate with them. Be ready for possible failure and extreme tension within your family. Whatever happens, don't give up. Stay with it and keep trying. After a while you will get used to these techniques and strategies. Trying new things can be tough.

If you're having a really hard time, find friends who you can talk to when you're angry or hurt, so you don't keep your feelings inside and end up exploding with anger. Sometimes talking things out can make you feel better. Use the skills in this book to find ways to talk to your parents. Treat them with respect so they'll treat you with respect. Do things to get appreciated by your parents and don't forget to appreciate them, too. Try this for a while and see if it makes a difference in your life. You might be surprised by what happens. The worst that can happen is that you'll end up with more trust and respect from your parents. Now how bad could that be?

If you think to yourself, "I don't need my parents to appreciate me," try the techniques a couple of times anyway. You might think this idea is stupid, or it won't work, or your parents won't believe you, but you will never know for sure unless you give it a try. Remember, it's the little things you do in life that make a difference.

Everyone deserves to have a wonderful life. I don't think kids should have to be the ones who do the work to clean up the relationships with their parents. But since a lot of kids don't have great communication skills with their families, it's up to them to make the relationship work.

By showing your parents examples of how to be in a good relationship, you can change it completely so it doesn't have to be about "kissing up." It can be about trust, successful communication, and respect. In order to get your relationship to be like that, you may have to work at it. By appreciating your family and getting them to appreciate you, you are one step closer to having the relationship you want.

### *Personal Goals*

1. Teach your parents how to be better parents by setting examples.

2. See how many times you can acknowledge your parents in one day without looking too obvious.

3. See how many times you can get your parents to appreciate you by doing something for them.

4. Use the "magic words" as often as you can.

5. Find helpful things to do that will get you on your parents' good side.

6. Try agreeing or compromising with your parents whenever you can.

7. Don't abuse "the power of the kiss-up."

8. Find friends or other adults to confide in when life at home is hard to deal with.

9. Keep practicing these new skills.

10. Be patient. Some parents take longer to learn and figure things out. You can't teach your parents in one day!

## When We Are Talking
(author unknown)

When you look at me, I know I have your attention.

When you stop what you are doing to listen, you are telling me that my ideas are important to you.

When you surprise me by letting the phone go unanswered, I know that sometimes I can come first for you.

When you nod and make comments about what I'm saying, I know you are taking my ideas seriously.

When you make sure each one of us kids gets to have his or her turn to talk before another one starts, we all feel listened to.

When you let me finish my own sentences, you are helping me learn to think things through.

When you listen to my meaning rather than correcting my pronunciation or grammar, I really feel like talking to you.

When you sit down on a chair or on the floor, rather than towering over me, I feel more confident.

When you really listen, I learn to talk.

When you really listen, I learn to think.

When you really listen, I know I'm loved.

# CHAPTER 4

# The Power of Words

## *PARENTS:*

### *Communicate Fairly*

Parents and children seldom speak the same language. Mother and father cannot always decipher the cries of their infant. Toddlers speak fluent gibberish, preadolescents speak incessantly, and then suddenly, when they are teenagers, they speak a language of their own. When different meanings and lots of slang are thrown in, adults are hard-pressed to understand the lingo of their kids. Armed with skills for improved communication, parents can teach their children to cope with the problems and challenges of life while keeping the lines of communication open.

## Open the Lines of Communication

When talking to a little child or a taller-than-you teenager, it is important to speak to your children the way you would want someone to speak to you. Because kids can go out of control at the slightest provocation, when talking to them, the adult must remain clear, calm, and to-the-point. State your needs using clear statements that do not blame, shame, judge, or criticize. This includes being a good listener.

Good communication and listening skills involve constantly remembering that what is important in the mind of a child is not necessarily important in the mind of an adult. Parents must continuously make an extra effort to acknowledge their kids' feelings and listen from their kids' point of view. Nine-year-old Zack told me:

> Adults always use words they think we understand. My teacher says things like "you have to toe the line." I didn't even know what he meant when he first said that. When he tells the class to act responsible and be independent, I know what the words mean, but I don't know what he wants me to do to be those things. I'm too scared to ask him, because I know he'll just yell at me for not paying attention, or he'll make fun of me in front of the whole class.

Be specific, be clear, and explain yourself when talking to kids. Zack's teacher could say, "I need this class to toe the line. What that means to me is to have each one of you pay attention during class time, and get the required work in on time. Who would like to share what you can do to 'toe the line' in class?" Encourage kids to ask questions and clarify what they have heard.

So many people are terrified of speaking up or asking questions, so I encourage kids in my seminars to ask for what they want. I say to them, "If you don't ask, you don't get!" Nobody knows what you want or what you need if you just sit there and let the world silently pass you by.

Open up the lines of communication and give kids an opportunity to express themselves in a safe environment.

---

Leading yet not dominating, this is the Primal Virtue.

—*Lao-tzu*

---

## Create Trust So They Will Talk

One mother told me about a situation that came up in which she was able to create a safe environment for her daughter. Marina received a phone call from her fifteen-year-old daughter's math teacher. "Your daughter was caught cheating on a test yesterday, and frankly, I'm concerned about her grades. She's going from an 'A' to a 'D' and I just wanted to let you know." "Thank you for calling me and letting me know what's going on," Marina responded calmly. "I would like to get together with you and my daughter to discuss this in person. Can we talk about this tomorrow after school?" Marina chose not to get into a lengthy discussion over the phone before knowing her daughter's side of the story.

Many parents are quick to condemn their own child before the child can defend him- or herself. After setting up the appointment with the teacher, Marina confronted her daughter. The two of them talked openly and calmly. Marina never accused her daughter of cheating, never belittled her or made her feel bad. The conversation went like this:

> **Mom:** Mia, your teacher called to tell me she caught you cheating on a test yesterday. She also said you got D's on your last two tests. I'm really sad that you didn't trust me enough to tell me about what happened. Before we see your

**teacher** tomorrow, I would like to hear your side of the story, so I know how to handle the conversation.

**Mia:** The teacher passed back our papers before the test. I thought I put them all away before the exam, but one was stuck on my lap under my sweatshirt. I knew if I just put it away, I'd get busted. If I said something to the teacher, she'd probably embarrass me and I'd get busted anyway. So I left it there. I'm sorry I didn't tell you, Mom, I was scared you'd get mad.

**Mom:** Honey, you can trust me. I may be disappointed in something you did, but I still love you and I'll help you to work it out. Tell me honestly, Did you look at your paper? Before you answer, I want to be honest with you. I cheated on a couple of my tests when I was in school. Of course, I'd never cheat today, but I think everyone may have done it at least once in their lives. I guess it's a fairly human thing to do. Kind of stupid, but human. So, tell me, did you really cheat?

**Mia:** (Knowing she could trust her mom) Yeah. Once the paper was there, I kinda looked at it a couple of times. But I didn't leave the paper there on purpose, I promise.

**Mom:** Why did you need to cheat? Have you had a hard time studying for the last few tests? The teacher said you got a bunch of D's instead of your usual A's. What's going on?

At that point Mia began to cry. She explained to her mother that she is really stressed at school. She has a lot of work and is having a hard time keeping up. She didn't tell her mom about the lower grades because she didn't want to disappoint her. Marina reassured her daughter that she was not a bad person, or a bad student for that matter. Marina promised her daughter that she would talk to her teachers to find out what they could do together to make school less stressful for Mia. Marina also reassured her daughter that she was on her side, and was available to help in any way she could.

Marina could have accused her daughter of being a liar and a cheater. She could have thrown her parental weight around by revoking privileges and grounding Mia. This reaction would have created a barrier of mistrust between mother and daughter. It is up to the adults to create mutual trust and honesty within the family unit. This can be done by following a few basic rules for everyday behavior.

*1. Be aware of the way you speak about your children when you think they are not listening.* Complaining about them to others, talking behind their backs, or comparing a "good" sibling to a "bad" sibling creates a feeling of disharmony and distrust in your family and between siblings. Your powerful, unspoken message can be absorbed just as deeply and become ingrained as strongly in the soul of your child as your outspoken message can.

*2. Think about what you say and how you say it.* Feel how the words, messages, or attitude you use would penetrate your soul if they were directed at you. How does it feel? It may be unrealistic to feel love and compassion for yourself and others at all times, but when you do feel good about yourself you can project that feeling onto your children. When they can believe in you, they learn to believe in themselves.

*3. Listen carefully.* Practice listening to what they have to say with both ears open. Give them your undivided attention by looking at them when they talk to you. Let them know that their feelings and needs are important to you. Acknowledge them when they express an opinion. You do not have to agree, but you can let them know you hear them. Show compassion and empathy for the issues in their life, no matter how frivolous it may seem to you. If you respond from your heart instead of your ego, your children will feel your love and compassion, and can grow up into adults who are empathetic and caring to those around them.

*4. Talk to your kids with respect.* Honor your children by demonstrating manners. Do not interrupt when your kids are talking; instead, show patience by listening to what they have to say. Say "please" and "thank you." Speak in a tone of voice that is considerate. Think about how you would feel if you were in their place. Say "I'm sorry" when appropriate. When your kids see that you are willing to admit to, learn from, and apologize for your mistakes, it makes it easier for them to accept their own mistakes. This promotes mutual respect, appreciation, and forgiveness, which are so important in all relationships.

If all parents treated their infants with love and devotion and responded with attention, compassion, and understanding to their simplest needs; inspired an open and loving line of mutually respectful communication with their young children; treated their adolescents with fairness, appreciation, and esteem, teenagers would emerge with a strong sense of self, an ability to articulate their desires, a loving, compassionate demeanor, and a reverence for humankind.

---

You can no longer deceive yourselves as you did before. You now have got the taste of truth.          —*Ouspensky*

---

## Keep Your Cool

No matter how much effort you put into good communication skills, at some point your kids will throw a tantrum or fly off the handle. After all, even though they may act as if they are from another planet, they are still human, and human beings are far from perfect.

Adults must do their best to remain calm in the eye of a "kid-storm." It is perfectly okay to show your vulnerability, your sadness, or your confusion, as long as you are not the one who is ranting and raving. This kind of behavior in adults can cause kids to get out of balance, which gives license to escalating emotions. If you start to "lose it," take a time-out for yourself. Say "I'm going to cool off right now. I will talk to you about this when I have thought about it some more." Then, leave the room *before* you act out or say something you may regret later. If you do lose your cool, remember that you are human, and human beings get angry. Be forgiving with yourself and with your kids. Apologize if it is warranted, then start over again.

If your children misbehave, they must be given the opportunity to learn from their mistakes. Punishment implies "submission" and "getting even." Discipline implies "punishment," "force," and "teaching them a lesson." The root of the word *discipline* is disciple, which means student or pupil. A parent's job is to guide the "student" toward self-discipline and inner guidance. As parents guide their children's behavior on a daily basis, their children learn to deal with the little issues in life, which gives them the knowledge, the ability, and the experience to deal with bigger issues later on.

## Give Logical Consequences

Instead of using force and violence while "teaching them a lesson," parents can use the art of natural, logical consequences for inappropriate behavior. Logical consequences should be direct and clear, with fair rules and achievable expectations. Children must be able to see the direct connection between cause and effect to be able to learn from the consequences of their behavior. Logical, respectful, and reasonable consequences allow kids to develop empowering cause-and-effect thinking skills which enable them to think for themselves.

Here are two examples of natural, logical consequences:

• Mom asks for all the dirty laundry on wash day. Teenager "forgets" to put her dirty clothes in the clothes hamper. Mom does the laundry. When teen says, "Mom, where are my clean socks?" Mom calmly responds, "I don't know. I did all the laundry that was in the hamper." Teen replies, "But, Mom, I need clean socks." Mom simply says, "Then you'll have to get your laundry done yourself, because I have already done the laundry for the week."

*By keeping calm and letting her teenager handle her own laundry, Mom simply follows through with natural, logical consequences. Her teen does not have to learn hatred and distrust. But she does learn responsibility, and the logic of cause and effect.*

• The kids are playing ball outside when a window suddenly shatters. Dad is furious because he asked them not to play there, having told them it wasn't safe. His first reaction is to scream and punish the kids, taking away all privileges for the next week. Instead, he takes a deep breath and says, "I'm really disappointed that no one listened to me. This accident could have been avoided. You kids will have to clean up the glass shards and get this window repaired." "But how do we do that, Dad?" the kids ask. "I'll show you how to pick up glass without getting cut. Go get the work gloves and a bucket from the garage. When that's done, I'll drive you to the hardware store and you can buy the materials you need to replace the window. Don't forget to bring your wallets."

*Dad does not have to act as if he enjoys this situation. But instead of punishing the kids for "being bad," he can give his kids an opportunity to learn from their mistakes, undo damage, and take responsibility for their actions.*

Logical consequences does not necessarily let kids off easy, but it allows them to repair a mistake with dignity and self-respect. It helps a kid to learn that when she grows up and is constantly late for work, her boss will not ground her for the weekend, break her toys, or take away all of her CDs. Her boss will fire her. This is a plain and simple example of cause and effect.

We have to remember that young children, preteens, and teens all struggle on a daily basis with the development of their self-esteem. Influenced by the media and peer pressure, they can go out of balance and have tantrums at the slightest provocation. Adults must do their best to keep their cool when it appears that their kids are out of control. This does not mean that you must have all the answers or remain in control at all times; it does mean that your kids will look to you for sanity and security in their lives. Be an example of respect and dignity. The old adage is true: Children learn what they live, and live what they learn.

I have seen adults chide, cajole, or even intentionally push their kids into a deeper state of anger or defeat by the remarks they make. Just recently, I witnessed a mother standing in front of a store with her hands full. Her daughter, who appeared to be about six years old, was standing next to her crying and crying. "Mommy, help me please. Mommy, don't do that, please," the child begged. As I walked by, I asked the mother if the child was okay. "She's fine, she just wants me to buy her some pumpkin seeds and I told her I wouldn't," the mother replied firmly. At that moment, the little girl stopped crying long enough to gulp in enough air to speak. She blurted out, "I am not fine. She said she would take back my new party dress if I didn't stop crying. Mommy, please don't take back my new dress." The mother gave me a "go away" look, so I said, "I'm so sorry" to the child and walked away knowing if I said anything else, I might just make matters worse for the distraught little girl.

What I really wanted to do was ask the mother how she would feel if she were a child at that moment. How would she want her ideal mother to respond to her if she wanted pumpkin seeds? Perhaps buying a snack for the child was inappropriate at that moment, but threatening the little girl with taking back her new party dress because she was sad or angry seemed even more inappropriate. The mother's actions created a sense of distrust, loss of control, and anger in the child. These kinds of power struggles happen on a day-to-day basis and cause the collapse of good communication skills, trust, and ultimately, the relationship between parents and their kids.

---

Those who cannot remember the past are condemned to repeat it. —*Inscription at the Dachau Concentration Camp Museum*

---

## Eliminate Threats, Bribes and Put-Downs

Sharona is a single mother who was feeling quite depressed. She works in the corporate world and was just turned down for a big promotion she was sure she would get. Her substantial raise would have provided some well-needed changes for her three children. A few days before finding out about the promotion, Sharona also had a fight with her ex-husband, and the energy around the house was not very comfortable. To top it all off, when she got her hair cut, her hairdresser cut her hair too short. Sharona continued to be depressed for a few weeks. She had feelings of sadness, remorse, and discontent. The stresses of her everyday life kept piling up, as they do for many people.

Imagine for a moment what it would be like if Sharona's ex-husband, parent, or friend had said, "Stop walking around the house with that attitude. You've got no reason to feel sorry for yourself. Be happy for what you have. And if you don't change your attitude, I'll take away the new dress you just bought."

Not many adults would stand for that type of treatment. Like the little girl in the previous story, Sharona needs understanding, compassion, and someone to listen to her feelings about the events that have transpired in her life. She needs to know that she can talk to someone and trust that they will listen without putting her down for her feelings. If her parent, partner, or friend tried to bribe or threaten her out of her feelings, Sharona would get angry and feel resentful. Threatening to take away the new dress she just bought has nothing to do with what Sharona is feeling. When adults or children are shamed, humiliated, or deliberately hurt by those close to them, their sense of self-worth is shattered, and their angry feelings begin to fester.

Avoid self-esteem shrinkers—threats, blaming, and put-downs just create confusion and resentment. Parents constantly use these poor types of communication skills to manipulate their kids. Toxic statements should never be used. Positive communication skills and compassion that build self-esteem and encourage self-appreciation work much better.

**Don't say:**
If you go to sleep now, I'll give you one more cookie.
**Do say:**
It's bedtime now, and I really would like some time to myself. Please get into your bed.

**Don't say:**
If you do that one more time, I'll slap you.
**Do say:**
I would like you to stop touching that because I'm afraid it might break.

**Don't say:**
Quit crying or I'll give you something to cry about.
**Do say:**
I'm sorry you feel so sad now. Would you like a hug?

**Don't say:**
You're such a slob. Clean up your room right now or you're grounded!
**Do say:**
We're having company tomorrow, and I would like the house to look nice. Would you like to clean your room now or after school tomorrow?

**Don't say:**
You can't go out every night this weekend, and that's final.
**Do say:**
I really understand that you want to be with your friends this weekend. Why don't you pick one night to go out, and then have a couple of your friends over on the other night? You can order pizza and hang out. Dad and I will stay out of your way.

Children can be highly emotional at any given moment. Teenagers' hormones can cause them to fly off the handle in the blink of an eye. By remembering this, an adult can be forewarned and act accordingly. When you are listening to teenagers talk about anything or complain about everything, take a deep breath to center yourself. Set the example by keeping your cool, and listen to what they are saying. Be kind, respectful, and empathetic as you listen. Do not offer solutions or help them deal with their feelings unless asked. Back off verbally, and be there for them emotionally.

---

By insisting only on the best behavior, parents repress and deny the dark side, the shadow that lurks in all of us, giving us depth and character and adding balance to our lives.
                                                        —*Judy Ford*

---

Children want fairness, freedom, and fun. With some compromise sprinkled in for tempering, children can learn the joy of having what they want within the limits their parents set for them. This is not spoiling; this is encouraging them to enjoy life as we wanted it to be for ourselves when we were growing up.

## Make Eye Contact

I was discussing the art of good communication skills in one of my seminars with a group of preteens. When I asked them if they knew what an "I" message was, a twelve-year-old thought I meant "eye" message and said, "It means looking someone in the eye when you talk to them. Yuck! I hate doing that. Why do adults always make us look at them when they talk to us?"

The rest of the class quickly chimed in. They said:

• "My mom always says, 'Look at me when I'm talking to you, young lady.' I hate looking at her when she's mad and I hate being called 'young lady.' It feels like such a put-down."

• "When they make us look at them, it gives them power or something."

• "When I'm told to look at my dad when he's talking to me, I want to look at the ground, not at him. It's hard to look at him when he's mad, because then he's kinda scary to me."

Eye contact is one of the many important components that make up good communication skills. You can set the example and look at your kids when you speak to them, even if they move around so much you can barely follow them. But do not expect them to look back at you. It is "Kid Behavior" that makes children and teenagers look everywhere but into your eyes when being spoken to. The confrontation is usually too much for them. When it seems you have all the power and control, your kids feel disempowered. That is when they tune you out, get angry, become aggressive, and look the other way.

Once you can understand and remember that this behavior is normal and acceptable in the "World of Kids," it becomes easier for parents to stop insisting that their kids look at them when they are speaking.

## Make Sure They Understand You

"Listen to me when I'm talking to you!" is a common phrase shouted by parents around the world. Kids may hear what you are saying, but because adults' and children's rationales differ, they may not understand what is being asked of them, or they just might not be paying attention. You can say, "I would like to know you are paying attention to me when I speak to you," or, "I'm not sure you really understand what I mean." By communicating clearly and asking directly, you will know if:

- you need to repeat what you have just said.
- you need to clarify what you have said.
- they are following you at all.

The first step in getting your kids to follow what you are saying is to talk instead of yell. Children have a miraculous way of tuning out what they do not want to hear, and yelling usually offends everyone. The second step is to ask gently and patiently as many times as is necessary instead of nagging. When calmly asked for the fifth time to set the table, Carole's eleven-year-old daughter finally heard her. She said,

She completed the task with her self-esteem intact, and I was happy to have a calm kid at dinner instead of an angry preteen who had just been yelled at for not doing what she was told the first time. The only hard part was making sure I didn't yell or say it in a nagging tone of voice. It takes effort, but the end result is worth it.

I have asked over two thousand teenagers what it would be like if they were listening to music in their room, when someone screamed, "Turn down your damn music. You're giving me a headache." Every single teen said, "It makes me want to crank up the sound even louder." Then I asked, "What if someone looked you in the eye, spoke gently and with kindness, and said, 'I have a really bad headache today. I know you like your music loud, but would you be willing to turn it down for a while until my headache goes away? I'd really appreciate it.'" The teenagers unanimously agreed that they would be willing to turn down their music. Sixteen-year-old Natalie summed up what they were all trying to say:

> When parents and teachers talk to us like babies or treat us worse than animals, we get mad and tune them out. They can't keep talking to us the way they do and expect good results. If their friends treated them the way they treat us, they wouldn't have any friends! Most kids don't want to fight with their parents; they just want to be understood, and they want things to be fair. All that adults have to do is talk to us with a little respect and treat us like we are decent people, and things would be so different. We can't be expected to show respect and kindness and all that stuff if they haven't shown it to us first.

Nagging, name-calling, blaming and put-downs all insult a person's intelligence. **No one in his right mind wants to please someone when he has just been insulted.** These types of messages create tension and resistance instead of encouraging cooperation and successful communication. When adults lash out at their kids, it is often because they are on "automatic pilot" doing what comes naturally, or perhaps doing what their own parents may have done. When we are disrespectful to our kids, we give them no reason to listen to us or to respect us.

## Use "I" Messages

When you use an "I" message, you say what you feel and what you want to have happen. *You* own the problem, feeling, or thought, and you speak about how you feel and what you need at that moment. An "I" message is a feeling, not an opinion. It is different from a "you" message. A "you" message sounds like:

- You are such a brat.
- How many times do I have to tell you to hang up your clothes?
- You never do what you say you are going to do.
- How could you be so careless?

*"You" messages are accusatory, critical, and blaming.*

"I" messages let kids hear what your concerns are in a nonthreatening manner. An "I" message sounds like:

- I feel really angry when no one listens to what I have to say around here. I want to feel like I am being listened to.
- I feel frustrated when the laundry hasn't been folded. All the clothes get wrinkled, and then I have more to iron.
- I want to know that I can count on you to follow through with what you tell me you will do.
- I would like everyone to put their Roller-

blades back where they belong. That way I won't trip over them on my way to work every morning.

*"I" messages do not blame. Instead, they talk specifically about the situation, how you feel about it, and what you want to have happen.*

---

• "I" messages are a positive way to deal with unacceptable behavior and set up clear boundaries.
• "I" messages help you to stay focused on the issue at hand, instead of attacking the person.
• "I" messages allow you to clearly state what you need.

---

If you have communicated your feelings and concerns and your child does not respond to your "I" message, try redirecting your question. You might say, "Who thinks the skates should be left on the stairs at night? Who does not?" When you ask the question both ways, you give your child the opportunity to get involved in a discussion without feeling threatened. Stick to the issue at hand. Parents must remember to say what they mean, and mean what they say. Take action with firmness, kindness, and understanding when necessary. Positive communication skills give you an opportunity to let your kids know that you trust their ability to make positive decisions.

An "I" message can sound something like "Oh, you spilled your juice. I need you to clean it up. Here, let me help you" instead of "Why did you spill that? You are such a bad boy!" Instead of saying to your teen "I'm disappointed in you, you left your dishes in the sink again. You're such a slob," try saying, "I don't want to clean the dirty dishes when I get home from work. I need to know I can count on you to do your own dishes. Please do them now so I can start dinner." Avoid name-calling at all cost. Use the words *good* and *bad* when talking to your dog. Do not use them for kids—it can effect their self-esteem. Children are known to misbehave or make mistakes; it is normal. As you deal with the issue at hand, remember it is the behavior that is wrong, not the child.

Instead of literally or figuratively pointing your finger outward in an "I told you so" type of finger wagging, point your finger at yourself. When you point your finger at someone, have you noticed that there are three fingers pointing directly back at you? Try to identify three reasons why you are out of control, and take a moment to look within yourself to notice your actions and reactions. What has set you off? Why are you yelling, nagging, or threatening? What emotions have been triggered in you? What can you do to improve the way you respond?

## Express Anger Safely

After learning how to use "I" messages, a father in my class began talking about the anger he had toward his son. He said, "Now I understand this "I" message stuff. As long as I point my finger at myself and own my feeling about it, I can say, 'Son, I think you're a lazy slob.' " He doesn't understand, that is not an "I" message. Mario was still pointing out at his son. An "I" message delivered in anger is usually a "You" message.

Instead of "You" messages such as "You did this," or "You did that," or "You make me feel angry," you must own your feelings by saying what you feel and what you need, without making someone else wrong or feel bad. If you are feeling angry, another way to express it might be, "I'm angry because there are still dishes in the kitchen sink." Be specific. This eliminates any blame, shame, or accusations. "I" messages convey a sense of respect which appeals to your child's intelligence and innate desire to cooperate.

Be sure you do not mix an "I" message with an accusatory remark such as, "I'm angry because there are dishes in the sink. I guess you're too lazy to clean up around here." A remark like that will put your child on the defensive no matter what else you say. Own the feeling, and speak from your heart without threatening or accusing. This makes it easier for the other person to hear what you are saying without feeling intimidated.

Anger often comes mixed with other emotions such as frustration, fear, and jealousy. These normal human emotions are often discouraged in children, particularly in young boys as they are told "Boys don't cry." Angry little boys and frustrated grown men often use both physical and verbal abuse to express themselves, instead of taking the time to channel their anger and use good communication skills to find balance. Little girls are often taught to be polite young ladies who must stifle their angry feelings. They are told acting out "is not ladylike." Girls and women need a safe, nonjudgmental forum in which they can talk things out to better understand themselves and the world around them.

Children often feel anger when they have not had the opportunity to express their frustration or grief. Anger is hereditary, it is contagious, and it can consume an entire family, turning family and friends against one another. Children and adults must all learn how to handle their anger in a safe, constructive manner.

---

Anger is just one letter short of "danger."     —*Della Reese*

---

*If you are angry or irritated with someone, do not take it out on your kids.* Be firm, centered, and nonintimidating when expressing your own anger or disappointment. You can say, "I'm feeling really frustrated about something that happened at work today. It's not about you, it's just a problem I'm having with my boss. I don't really want to talk about it right now, but I'll work it out after I've thought it over for a while. I'm going to take a hot bath so I can relax and stop feeling so cranky."

There may be plenty of times when you need to talk about how angry you feel. Remember, it is *your* anger or disappointment in a certain behavior that you are expressing. Do not attack the personality of the child you are speaking to. This will only lead to more tension, defensiveness, and resentment. Say "I get furious when the front door is left opened. I'm afraid the dog will get out and get hurt. I really want that door to stay shut." Be clear and to the point. State what you see, what you feel, and what you want done. The formula is easy and the message becomes clear.

## Write a Feeling Letter

In Journey's chapter 8, she shows kids how to write a Feeling Letter. It works for parents too. You can use this format any time you feel anger, pain, sadness, frustration, or betrayal. This simple yet powerful writing technique, designed by Dr. John Gray, is a step-by-step process that can move you from feeling rage to release in a very short period of time. Begin by writing this Feeling Letter with no intention of giving it to the person you are angry with. Let the process be for you—to heal any anger, pain, or frustration you may feel. Begin every line with "I" so you stay true to how you feel. By the time you reach the section on love you will experience the incredible transformation that is possible when you learn the power of forgiveness and the freedom to let go of negative feelings.

When you make a simple mistake or say something mean, be brave and apologize to your kids. You can say something like "I'm sorry I yelled at you guys. I'm working on not yelling, but it may take some more time before I really get it. Please be patient with me." A responsible apology goes a long way in setting an example for your kids and giving you the respect you deserve.

When expressing your anger or disappointment, use love as your guide. Take a deep breath, take a step back, and go into your heart. Before flying off the handle, do not forget to breathe. Identify the problem. Is the problem yours or theirs? What feelings were set off in you? How should this situation be approached? How would you want to be spoken to at this moment if the roles were reversed? Put yourself in their place and respond from there.

---

Books can inspire you to love yourself more, but by listening to, writing out, or verbally expressing your feelings, you are actually doing it.     —*Dr. John Gray*

---

As you practice writing Feeling Letters and exploring your emotions, you may surprisingly discover that you are upset for completely different reasons than you first thought. As you write out the feelings that come up, negativity tends to disappear. As suddenly as negative emotions come up, you can as suddenly release them. The experience can be freeing.

## Try Active Listening

Another technique for cool communication with your kids is active listening. When using active listening skills, one of the things you must do is show that you are interested in what your kids have to say by facing them and looking at them when they speak. Give them your full attention.

Young children respond well when you are at their eye level. One teenager told me, "My mom is always on the phone, so I can never get her attention. Sometimes I feel like I don't really matter to her." Another said, "My dad hardly ever looks at me when I'm talking to him. He's always busy with lots of things to do. Sometimes I think that his stuff is more important than me."

As you focus your attention on your kids when they speak, put yourself in their place as you try to understand where they are coming from. Remember, kid mentality is very different from adult mentality. You do not have to solve or fix their problems unless they ask; simply acknowledge them by looking at them. Nod your head and say "Uh-huh" and "hummm" when they are speaking. These little sounds let them know you are following the conversation and care about what they are saying. If you say "I understand," they may not believe you, so use that phrase only when it is really true.

Remember to avoid criticizing or making judgments. Don't offer advice or say "I told you so." Stay focused on what they are trying to convey, even if it is difficult to follow. Keep the lines of communication open with your children so they can trust you enough to keep the lines open with you.

## A Dozen Good Listening Skills

Effective communication is not limited to the use of "I" messages and active listening. A few preteens in one of my seminars told me that good listening skills are easily learned but do require continual practice. Here are the criteria they offered:

- Speak to us the way you want us to speak to you.
- Stop yelling.

- Stop nagging.
- Put down the paper or magazine when we speak to you so we know you're listening.
- Don't interrupt us; we hate it as much as you do.
- Let us know you understand what we're saying by acknowledging us.
- Don't get mad when we're brave enough to tell you the truth, or we'll stop telling you anything.
- Be a good listener.
- When we talk to you, you don't have to solve all of our problems; just be available for us.
- Let us ask questions without feeling like we're stupid just because we didn't already know the answer.
- When we share our ideas with you, don't put us down, criticize us, or act judgmental.
- Don't jump to conclusions; listen to the entire story before you get mad or ground us.

These kids were relieved to have an opportunity to express themselves, and they told me they wished they could tell their parents about these skills. If parents could willingly listen to the sound advice of their children, they would be well on their way toward an open, positive, loving relationship.

It can be incredibly difficult to put your own ego aside long enough to hear the advice your child has to give. Adults want to stop children in their tracks for their insolence and disrespect. It is not always disrespect that is taking place but a child's cry to be heard, to be acknowledged, and to be honored for who she is.

Take the time to ask your children what you can do to make things better. Ask them what will work for them. Seeking advice from your kids can be a monumental step for a parent to take; it can miraculously bridge the gap in communication between you and your children.

There are numerous other techniques that can be helpful when speaking to people of all ages. At the end of this book, I have listed many good resources for further study in the Recommended Reading List.

## When They Don't Talk

As adolescents embark into the uncharted territory of the teenage years, it is normal for them to clam up around adults. Now you find yourself with a prepubescent adolescent or a tongue-tied teenager who will not open up and talk to you. In the land where children originally came from there is a secret rule that is not overtly advertised: "When you are a teenager, do not tell adults your secrets for fear of betrayal."

One parent told me, "My teenage son never talks to me, he just goes to his room and closes the door. Have I done something wrong? I don't know what to do." This is not a direct reflection of your parenting skills: some personality types never share their feelings. They do, however, deserve as much respect and understanding as any other kid. Some girls like to talk—hence the telephone permanently attached to the ear of a teenage girl—whereas some boys tend to reflect on things before talking about them. They will retreat to their room or wherever they can to be left alone.

If you assume an attitude of control by attempting to change your child's behavior through lecturing, coercing, yelling, or trying to control their beliefs, you end up feeling frazzled, intimidated, stressed, and angry. Your kids often end up with a mixed bag of feelings which include frustration, anger, and defensiveness. Feeling defensive may stimulate them to find more covert ways of doing whatever you said they should not do.

If you assume an attitude of neglect by ignoring your kids, denying problems exist, or allowing them to do as they please, you end up abandoning yourself and shutting the door on your kids. They feel unloved, ignored, rejected, and confused. Some parents find it much easier to ignore their problems, but children are not problems. They are living, breathing, feeling people who thrive on closeness and emotional honesty. They deserve to learn about the important things in life from their parents.

Parents and their kids grow emotionally closer when parents create an atmosphere of contact without control. By communicating with their kids in a loving, nonjudgmental way, parents can keep the relationship alive instead of letting it die. This approach reduces anxiety and fear, creates trust, and brings a sense of closeness and emotional honesty into the relationship.

If your child has shut down or you think she may be doing something you do not approve of, put your arm around her and talk to her. Let her know how you truly feel deep inside. In their book *Positive Discipline for Teenagers: Resolving Conflict with Your Teenage Son or Daughter*, Jane Nelson and Lynn Lott suggest saying "Listen, I'm not into this. I don't really know much about it, and I don't really like it. I don't think I approve of it. But I want to know what it's like for you. I want you to help me understand what it means to you." The authors go on to say, "Relating to our teens in this way takes awareness, skill and practice. Fear and lack of practice might tempt us to slip into our old controlling or neglectful behavior. But faith in ourselves and in our kids plus practice can help us make emotional honesty a part of our lives."

You may have to create or renew a sense of mutual trust between you and your kids before they feel safe enough to open up at home. They need to feel secure knowing whatever they say will be accepted, not rejected. Remember, you do not have to agree with what they say, but you do have to be available to listen with an empathetic ear. Gang membership is at an all-time high because kids are looking for a place where they can fit in and feel accepted; where they can be heard and understood. They are looking for a sense of family.

Be honest with your kids. They do not need to know all the intimate details of your life, but teenagers especially want to know what is true about you and the world. They want to know whom you respect and what you hope to accomplish in your life. They do not always need a lecture to impart life's lessons. For example, as my son and I watched a child scare a flock of birds, we began a conversation on the art of gentleness and ways to be respectful to all creatures great and small.

Gently weave what you want them to know into your daily interactions. This enables them to understand where and how they fit in. As you become more familiar with the way your kids communicate, you can establish a more open, effective, understanding relationship with them. It makes life much easier. Have faith in yourself and your children.

## *Personal Goals*

1. Create a trusting home environment where your kids feel free to talk openly and honestly.

2. Practice using "I" messages.

3. Use active listening skills with your kids; stop what you are doing and give them your undivided attention.

4. Do not offer advice or solutions unless you are asked.

5. Make all consequences logical, reasonable, and rational.

6. Practice listening whenever your kids speak to you, with the sole intention of respectfully understanding what it is they are going through.

7. Next time you are angry, do not lash out. Write a Feeling Letter instead.

8. When your kids are emotional, remain calm and just listen and be supportive.

9. Be firm, centered, and nonintimidating when expressing your own anger or disappointment.

10. Give your kids the kind of attention you enjoy receiving.

## KIDS:

### What You Say and How You Say It Counts

Sometimes, people don't realize how their attitude and the words they use affect people. The words you use can make someone feel better, make someone sad, or make someone angry. The way you say certain words can also get you into trouble. Life would be much easier if everyone learned how to communicate better.

Poor communication skills are often the cause of fights between parents and kids. Have you ever heard your own parents complain about your attitude? You have probably heard things like:

- Don't give me that attitude.
- Don't talk to me in that tone of voice.
- Cut the attitude.
- Don't you dare talk to me like that.
- I don't want to hear that attitude again.
- How dare you look at me that way.
- If you don't lose the attitude right now, you're grounded.

### Attitude Counts

In one of the communication classes my mom and I taught together, we asked a group of ten- to sixteen-year-olds if they knew what their parents meant when they were told they had a bad attitude. Every one of them said they knew exactly what their parents meant. Most of the time, we know exactly what our parents are talking about even if we claim not to understand.

It's pretty amazing how the tone of voice we use can completely change someone else's mood. Here is an example of what might happen when you speak with a bad attitude:

> *Dad:* Did you do your homework yet?
> *You:* No.
> *Dad:* Well, why not?
> *You:* Because I didn't feel like it.
> *Dad:* I suggest you get started.
> *You:* I suggest you leave me alone.
> *Dad:* Hey! Don't talk to me with that attitude unless you want to get yourself in trouble!!

By choosing your words carefully, you can avoid getting yourself in trouble. Here's how it might sound:

> *Dad:* Did you do your homework yet?
> *You:* No.
> *Dad:* Well, why not?
> *You:* Because I didn't feel like it.
> *Dad:* I suggest you get started.
> *You:* Do you mind if I start in a little while.
> *Dad:* Why don't you start now?
> *You:* Can I do it in thirty minutes? I promise I'll do it without you having to remind me. I want to show you that you can trust me.
> *Dad:* You deserve a chance.

---

I am convinced that life is 10 percent what happens to me and 90 percent how I react to it. And so it is with you . . . we are in charge of our attitudes.

—*Charles Swindoll*

---

If you say you're going to do something, be sure you follow through. When you keep your word, your parents will learn they can trust you, and they will feel comfortable giving you more freedom.

## The Tone of Your Voice Counts

Have you ever realized how often the tone of your voice changes? It sounds different when you talk to your friends, when you talk to a teacher, and when you talk to a baby. Your voice also changes when you are mad and when you are happy. If your voice sounds rude, that is usually when adults say you have a bad attitude. The reason for the mean tone in your voice might be because you are upset about something that happened at school. Since adults hear things differently than kids do, they take what you say personally, and think you're being rude to them. That's when you get in trouble.

Concentrate more on the tone of voice you use when you talk to your parents. That way you won't get yelled at because they think you are being rude. You have to be careful, though. Just because you may have had a bad day does not mean you have the right to be mean to others around you. The techniques in this chapter will show you how to avoid getting busted for having a bad attitude.

If you are really upset and you're having a discussion or an argument with your parents, the tone of voice you use when you say something is sometimes much more important than the words you use. Then again, sometimes the words you say are more important than how you say them, so you have to be careful.

Leslie is fifteen. She said,

> When my mom calls me a bitch it really pisses me off. Instead of yelling back at her and calling her a bitch, or screaming that I hate it when she calls me that, I learned how to tell

her how it makes me feel when she calls me names so I won't get in trouble. Now when she gets mad, she usually remembers not to call me names. If she forgets, I remember to let her know how it makes me feel.

This might take quite a bit of practice, but calmly telling your parents how you feel about something instead of screaming at them can really make a difference in how they relate to you.

## Your Words Count

You probably have been in a situation where a group of nasty words suddenly popped out of your mouth. You may have said what you were thinking before you realized the damage it would do. Or you might have been in a situation where someone said something that offended you. It doesn't matter exactly what the tone in their voice sounded like; it was the words they used that hurt. Even if the person said "I'm sorry. I didn't mean to say that, it just slipped out," it probably didn't matter to you whether they meant to say it or not. The fact is they said it and it upset you. Sometimes we don't realize how wrong or painful some of our actions or words are until we experience the disrespect ourselves.

These situations end up hurting other people and getting you into trouble. That is why it is so critical to think carefully about what you are going to say and how you are going to say it before you actually let it out. You might be thinking "Why should I think about what I'm going to say? Words can't hurt someone that badly." The truth is, some people are more sensitive than others, and mean words can deeply hurt them. The cycle of bad communication skills has to end somewhere. By using the skills in this book, you will have the power to end this cycle and make your communication skills better at home, as well as with your friends.

## Showing Respect

Everyone wants to be treated with respect. Parents like being treated with respect just as we do. It makes them feel appreciated. When they feel appreciated, they usually feel more generous. If you are rude when you speak to adults, they get upset and feel disrespected. They get angry and are not generous at all, and then you don't get what you want.

This goes for teachers as well. Elizabeth's teacher yelled at her for talking in class. The next day, Elizabeth gave her teacher dirty looks all through class. The teacher was so threatened by those dirty looks, she called Elizabeth's mom to tell her about her daughter's "poor behavior." This created bad feelings for everyone. Elizabeth was upset, the teacher was angry, and the mom was furious because her daughter was disrespectful. If you have a problem with an adult, you can talk to a friend or talk about it with a guidance counselor, but being disrespectful to adults will just get you into trouble.

---

Children need love, especially when they do not deserve it.
—*Harold S. Hulbert*

---

Adults will respect you if you show them respect, too. It works both ways. Don't fight or argue over every little thing they say or do; it's hardly ever worth the consequences.

## Active Listening

To avoid miscommunication, you can try active listening. It's a cool technique for communicating effectively with your parents. It may be a difficult concept for some of you to understand, so keep practicing. You need to be alert, ready to focus, and most importantly, ready to listen. The key to proper active listening is acknowledging the person's feelings. It is not about whether you agree or disagree, or if you understand. It is about letting the person know you heard what she said and you acknowledge the way she feels.

Two other important concepts of active listening are to repeat back what you have heard, and turn your body and look at your parents when they talk to you. You want them to know that you heard what they said, so you repeat back like a parrot. The conversation may sound silly, but once you try it, it will be easy to get the hang of it.

Here is an example of a typical situation *without* using active listening skills:

> *Mom:* You never walk your dog anymore.
> *You:* It isn't my fault, I keep forgetting.
> *Mom:* Well then whose fault is it? You'd better start making yourself remember if you want to keep that dog.
> *You:* You can't take my dog away from me just because I forget to walk him sometimes!
> *Mom:* Oh yeah? I'm the parent. I can do whatever I want, even take away the dog.
> *You:* I can't believe you're doing this to me! You're the worst mom in the whole world! I hate you so much!

Now look at an easier way of working through this situation with the help of active listening:

> *Mom:* You never walk your dog anymore.
> *You:* I know, I keep forgetting.
> *Mom:* You'd better start making yourself remember if you want to keep that dog. I can't believe how irresponsible you are sometimes.

*You:* It sounds like I've let you down by acting ir-
responsibly, right? I'm sorry I forgot. I'll do it
right now.

*Mom:* It would be nice if you would try harder so
you can remember to walk the dog.

*You:* I'll try.

All the dialogues in this book may sound really stupid
when you're first experimenting with them. But each one
brings you one step closer to getting the freedom, respect, and trust you deserve from your parents. When you
use active listening skills, you don't have to agree with
what your mom says; you just have to listen and acknowledge her feelings, and make sure you follow through with
what you say you're going to do. The technique is really
simple.

While using active listening there are several things
you have to watch out for and not do:

### • *Interpreting*

Interpretation is when you try to explain what the person
*really* means when he says something. When using active
listening skills, never interpret what the person is trying
to say. This technique even works with your brother or
sister.

For example, your sister says, "Today we performed
our skits for the class, but my partner was sick so she
wasn't there. My teacher made me do it anyway. I was
the only one in the class who had to perform all alone. I
was really embarrassed."

Don't respond with "It's really no big deal." That is
*your* interpretation of what she might be feeling. What
you should say is "It sounds like that made you feel really
uncomfortable." By saying that, you're just acknowledging her feelings, which is all you need to do.

116

## • *Body Language*

When focusing on body language, you have to watch the way you listen with your body. This includes the expressions you make on your face, your body posture, and where your eyes are focused. If your parents know you're really listening (which does not mean you have to agree with them), they usually simmer down.

You can show you have no interest in what someone is saying, or you can show that you care by the expression on your face. Your body posture can show you are bored and ready to fall asleep, or alert and interested. When your eyes aren't focused on them, it shows you're distracted and not listening. Making eye contact shows you're there for them.

## • *Fooling the Eye*

Even though we came from a far-off land that parents aren't aware of, both parents and kids like to be acknowledged and respected when we have something to say. When your parents are talking to you, try to show some interest so they think you're listening to them. Sometimes parents say, "Look at me when I'm talking to you." But the truth is, a person doesn't have to look someone in the eye in order to hear what he is saying. Sometimes being forced to look at your parents while being criticized or yelled at can be very annoying. Here's a trick you can use so you can look at your parents without actually having to look them in the eye.

The way this works is to look at something on their face and trace it with your eyes (without looking too obvious), so they think you're looking directly at them. Look in the direction of their eyes and trace their eyebrows or their nose, or count their freckles. Try to listen to as much of what they are saying as possible, so you can respond if you have to. In other words, do not tune out completely. If you make it look like you are actually having eye contact, your parents feel that you are respecting them. According to adults, this can look like maturity on our part, and that makes them respect us more.

### • *How You Acknowledge Feelings*

We all feel differently about the things we go through. One person might laugh about something while the other person might run off crying. Be careful when you say "I know," or "I understand," because there may be times when it's not really appropriate to say those words. You can never *really* know how the other person is feeling, even if you have experienced the same thing. It's better to say things like "Really," "Uh-huh," or just nod your head.

Active listening can definitely come in handy, but you can't use it all the time. If you are outside and your mom tells you to put on a jacket, it would be really weird if you said, "Gee, Mom, you're really worried that I'm cold." Pay close attention to the right and wrong times to use this new technique.

The best way to teach your parents how to use active listening is to show them. Try it on them whenever the time seems right. Hopefully your parents will catch on, and after a while they will want to improve their listening skills with you. Active listening doesn't solve problems, but nothing is ever completely solved until everyone's feelings have been heard.

---

If a child lives with approval, he learns to live with himself.
    —*Dorothy Law Nolte*

---

## Get Your Parents to Do the Talking

Sometimes it can be really annoying when your parents want you to talk about your feelings, how your day went, or what your plans are. Have you ever had one of those days when you didn't feel like talking about yourself? At that moment, the last people you want to share your thoughts with may be your parents.

Here are a few tricks you can use to get the attention off of yourself:

• If your mom picks you up from somewhere, ask how her day was as soon as you enter the car. Try to remember if she had certain appointments or errands and ask her how they went. She might be really happy that you thought of her for a change and she might forget to ask about your day. As she starts talking about herself, remember to use your active listening skills and watch your body language.

• When you ask your parents questions about themselves, you make them feel like you're interested in them, and you might not have to talk about yourself as much. But be ready to respond just in case they ask you questions anyway.

• If one of your parents insists on getting answers, just give short, polite answers and then try to change the subject delicately. For example, your dad might ask you how your day went. You could answer with "It was fine. By the way, Dad, do you know what we're having for dinner tonight? I'm starving." If that doesn't work, try to find one or two positive things to say about something that happened at school so your dad will be satisfied. For example, you could say something like: "Well, I passed my English test," or "I finished my art project."

Make sure that when you change the subject, you don't let it sound like you're hiding something from them or else they will wonder what you're trying to hide. The point is not to be rude or to put on an act; the point is just to get your parents to do the talking when you don't want to. There are so many things you can do while your parents are talking that will lessen the chance of a fight and, at the same time, have them gain more respect for you. When adults think kids are listening and showing an interest in what they are saying, they think we are more mature. When our parents think we are more mature, we get more freedom, more choices, and more respect.

## Telling the Truth

Another way you can create crystal-clear communication with your parents is to always tell the truth. If you have a good relationship with them, you won't need to lie.

If you lie to your parents, it's possible that they could find out. To avoid punishment, most kids lie again to cover up the last lie. By doing that, you end up getting yourself into deeper trouble. If your parents discover that you have been lying, you get in trouble for what you have done *and* for the lie that you told. They immediately lose trust in you and you lose privileges. Lying can get really confusing. One way to avoid the confusion is to stay out of trouble in the first place.

Kids lie because they are afraid of the consequences, or they don't want their parents to know what they are doing. They think they might get in trouble if they tell the truth. If you tell the truth right away, you might not get into as much trouble as you would if you were caught lying.

After your parents find out that you lied to them, it will take a long time for you to gain their trust back, which would mean less freedom. Don't blow your chances. Just tell the truth and admit to your mistakes when you make them. Remember, for some weird reason, adults love it when you look them in the eye. It makes them feel respected. Look at them, tell the truth, and hopefully your life will be easier!

In certain situations, telling the whole truth might not always be the right thing to do either. I am not saying it is okay to lie, but you can soften the truth so no one gets hurt. For example, if your mom comes home with a new outfit that you really hate, you don't have to lie or tell the whole truth. Instead of saying "That is the ugliest outfit I have ever seen," you can avoid hurting her feelings by saying "Well, it's not one of my favorite outfits, but if you like it, then it's okay."

If you want to go to a friend's house and your parents won't let you go, it might be tempting to lie and go anyway. Instead of lying, talk to your parents and try to reason things out. Use the skills from the other chapters in this book to help you get your point across. Use your active listening skills when your parents talk to you, and remember that what you say and how you say it counts!

---

Truth gets you high, lies bring you down.

—*Ram Dass*

---

## Be True and Honest to Yourself

Be true to yourself. Don't fool yourself into believing you have to act or speak in a certain way to be accepted by others. Instead of feeling guilty for doing something or getting mad, admit to your mistakes and stand up for yourself. Believe in YOU. Staying true and honest to yourself and to the people around you allows you to grow and learn about yourself, and the people in the world around you.

It's as important to be honest with yourself as it is to

be honest with others. When you're honest with yourself, it means you know and respect who you are. You will gain more respect from others if you treat yourself with respect. Don't forget to be aware of the tone in your voice when you speak to someone.

What you say and the way you say it have a huge impact on the people you talk to. When talking to your parents, try to be aware of your attitude since parents pick up on the slightest insult. Always watching what you say and when you say it can be a drag, but when you do, you can avoid fights in your family. When all else fails, remember to love yourself no matter what.

---

### *Personal Goals*

1. Treat your parents with respect and see what a difference it makes in your life.

2. Make sure you use a "positive" attitude.

3. Watch the tone of voice that you use.

4. Use words that are helpful, not hurtful.

5. Use active listening skills so everyone feels heard.

6. When using active listening skills, have as much eye contact as possible.

7. Be considerate of other people's feelings.

8. Get the attention off of yourself by getting your parents to do the talking.

9. Be true and honest to yourself.

10. Respect yourself and those around you.

---

# CHAPTER 5

# Who's in Charge?

## *PARENTS:*

### *Avoid Power Struggles*

Power struggles create a separation between who is right and who is wrong. Parents and siblings who do not want to lose their place of power will do everything within their power to win. Family members end up against one another, instead of for one another. This can lead to feelings of separation, rejection, and loneliness. Raising children does not have to be about power or struggle. Resolving conflicts with kids can be handled with dignity and respect for all.

## A Kid's Eye View

Wherever I turn, I hear parents complaining that their kids talk back, act disrespectful and unruly, and do not do what they are told when they are told to do it. On the other hand, kids I have worked with in my seminars have repeatedly said, "I just want some respect from my parents." "My parents decide everything for me; I never

have any say about my own life." "Adults are so hypo-
critical; they say 'don't interrupt,' but they interrupt us
all the time, or they say 'don't swear,' but they swear all
the time. It's so unfair."

• Twelve-year-old May said, "My mom always uses my age against me. She'll say
things like 'You can't do that because you're
only twelve.' Then she says stuff like, 'You
have to set a good example because you're
almost thirteen.' It drives me crazy! Adults
can be pretty weird."

• Ten-year-old Kurt said, "My dad always
comes in my room and tells me not to watch
stuff on TV. He gave me the TV in my room,
and now he just comes in and grabs me by
the arm and starts yelling. Why can't he just
talk to me?"

• Jennifer is thirteen. She said, "My mom is
always correcting my English. I don't speak
as badly as most of my friends. I hate when
my parents make fun of the way we talk.
Can you imagine what would happen if I said
something bad about their friends?"

• Caterina's little brother slipped and fell
while roller-skating. He cried for two hours.
She said, "My dad didn't believe he was hurt,
so he just kept telling him to stop crying. He
kept telling him he was okay, and that he
wasn't hurt. My brother had to go to a school
event that night, and when his teacher saw
him, she told my parents to take him to the
emergency hospital. We found out that his
arm was broken in two places. My dad never
believed him when he said he was hurt. Can
you believe that? Now, when my dad gets

sick, that's a different story. He's like a big baby and we have to take care of him. I just don't get it, but I know it's not fair. Sometimes I really hate my dad."

Some adults have said:

• "My daughter was talking on the phone yesterday, and I told her to hang up. She told me to wait a second, so I hauled off and slapped her. That taught her not to sass me again," I overheard one mother say quite proudly to her friend.
• "I can't believe mothers these days, giving choices to their two-year-olds. These kids are only two. Who the hell gives them the right to make decisions? Their mothers need some sense knocked into them, if you ask me," said a salesperson in a store.
• "My son seems like he's always grounded because he never cleans his room. I just make him stay in there. Maybe he'll clean it up someday," I heard another parent remark.

This imbalance of power between parents and their children is insidious. It can be so blatant that it causes immediate conflict. This imbalance can also be so subtle that the family does not realize it is even taking place.

## Who Holds the Power?

In my seminars, I hold up my hands as I use an imaginary balancing scale as a euphemism for the imbalance of power in the parent-child relationship. As the scale tips higher on one side, it automatically lowers on the other side. There I stand with my hands in the air, one hand hovering much higher over the other hand cowering underneath. "Who is on top?" I ask. Parents and kids all respond the same: "The adults have more power over the kids." "How does it feel?" I ask the ten- to sixteen-year-old students who delight at the opportunity to speak their minds without fear of repercussion. The responses are always the same: "bad," "lonely," "unfair," "sad," "hopeless."

When I ask the parents how it feels to have the physical stature, the brute strength, and the years of experience to exert that power, they typically respond, "We have to tell them what to do because otherwise they would never learn," "Who is gonna do it if we don't?" and finally, "That's a parent's job." Just exactly what is the parents' job, and whom are they working for?

---

Nothing is more important to our shared future than the well-being of our children.      —*Hillary Rodham Clinton*

---

## Why We Have Power Struggles

Because newborns cannot do anything for themselves, their parents must do everything for them. A baby is at the mercy of his or her parents; adjusting to their sleeping habits and their way of life. Babies depend on the safety net their parents provide.

As babies grow into children with developing minds of their own, their parents seem to forget their own experience as children. As soon as a child develops his or her own will, the battle begins.

This battle can be extremely difficult and painful to

live with. Children say hurtful things, and teenagers can be vicious. They can be demanding and disrespectful. Their unexpected outbursts and temper tantrums can sap parents of all the energy they have left.

A few years ago, I experienced this with my own daughter. Late for school one day, she asked me if she looked okay as she was running out the door. "I guess so," I said with a shrug, still tired from a sleepless night. Journey hurled her backpack onto the floor, stomped up the stairs and said, "God, I hate when you do that, MOM [emphasis on the *Mom*]. Now I have to change, and I'm late." "What did I do?" I asked in astonishment, having no clue how I may have participated in this outburst. "You shrugged your shoulders and said you didn't know if I looked okay or not," she snarled back as she slammed her bedroom door. I was so taken off guard by this un-expected morning tirade, I began to cry.

When Journey reemerged from her room a few minutes later, she said good-bye to her brother, purposely ignoring me as she marched out the door. I immediately said, "Journey, I'm really upset about what happened. I feel hurt that you aren't going to say good-bye to me. What I did was try to tell you that I didn't know if the style you had on is nice or not, because I didn't know kids wore shoelaces for belts! I feel so sad when I get treated with disrespect. I feel I deserve more respect, and I would like to be talked to with thoughtfulness." My daughter turned to me and sheepishly said, "I'm sorry Mom."

Fortunately for us, we have this communication thing fairly well worked out, and we use the techniques as often as possible. But at that moment, what I really wanted to do was storm into her bedroom and scream at her for being so rude and disrespectful. I wanted to punish her for having such a bad attitude. "Someone has to put this kid in her place," I thought, for a fleeting nanosecond. When you are furious and your kid is acting as if she knows it all, your gut reaction may be to yell and scream, to threaten and bribe, to use brute force, or to shut down and just walk away from the entire situation. If you are a parent who has felt this kind of anger and frustration with your kids, you probably can identify with this feeling that emanates from so deep inside.

And yet, during my daughter's morning tirade, I realized that if I made just one shift in my perception, I could change my perspective to avoid toxic thinking. I could change my negative thoughts to create a new experience. I could speak to her with love and forgiveness even though I still felt hurt. The key here is forgiveness. I realize that whatever I can do to add kindness to my relationships and kindness in the world, will send far-reaching ripples that may touch the lives of others.

Because I am the parent, it is up to me to set the example. If I am overbearing and threatening, my daughter will rebel against me even more. I find that using my power wisely is not always easy, but I have had years of practice that makes it easier most of the time. I must constantly remind myself to be respectful when I let my kids know they have hurt my feelings or overstepped my boundaries.

Offering acknowledgment and support to a hormone-infused, out-of-control teenager while you keep your cool is one of the most difficult aspects of parenting. Sometimes you have to disengage yourself so you can cool off, cool down, bite your lip, and not get caught up in the game.

Here are a few rules to follow when you are upset:

• Take a deep breath, grit your teeth, and suppress any urge you may have to verbally or physically abuse your child. (Sometimes this is difficult to do, but it must be done!)
• Use a few carefully chosen words that clearly state what you want your child to hear or know at that moment.

- Focus on accountability rather than being judgmental and critical.
- Do not attack or threaten; instead, use thought and restraint when speaking about your feelings.
- Speak in supportive ways: Use "I" messages and active listening skills.
- If you cannot be supportive, choose another time to express your feelings.

---

It is wiser to choose what you say than say what you choose.
—*Anonymous*

---

Without the awareness that we are *supposed* to relate to life from different perspectives, and without the tools for dealing with some of the gut-wrenching situations our children expose us to, parents and their children will continue to grow at odds with each other. Parents see things one way; kids see them another way. The parents' "Do what you're told" and their kids' "That's not fair" mottoes are chanted daily in most households around the world. When adults clearly recognize and respect the separate realities between themselves and their children, they can dramatically reduce the imbalance in the relationship which creates struggle and disharmony. With this insight into the nature of why children act as they do, parents can find a healthy balance that works for everyone.

## Avoid Power Struggles

In the land where kids come from there are no laws, just "kid behavior." For example, if someone tries to make a kid do something she does not want to do, it is perfectly acceptable behavior for her to whine and cry until she gets her way or until she's left alone. In reality, one of the easiest ways to lessen the number of power struggles with your kids is to give them choices within appropriate limits as often as possible. Start when your kids are young. For example, you might say, "Do you want to wear the red sweater or the green one?" The fact is, they have to wear a sweater, but which one they wear is up to them. You allow your children to make choices within the boundaries you have set up for them. Your children feel empowered, you have what you want, and everyone is happy. This creates a win-win situation.

As they get bigger, let your kids participate in the development of house rules. Beth did not want her boys to play ball in the house. At a time when they were all gathered together for a family meeting, she said, "I get concerned when balls are thrown in the house, because I'm afraid something might break. What should we do about this?" As she and her boys brainstormed possible solutions, her youngest son, Matthew, said, "Maybe we shouldn't throw balls in the house." Beth happily said, "I'd feel really comfortable with that. Thanks for thinking of it, Matthew." Later, Beth told me, "When Matthew's friends come over and start rolling that ball around, he always holds the ball and says, 'Let's go outside and play ball.' When I let my boys in on decision making, they are pretty good at upholding the rules." Beth knew what she wanted, but if she had laid down the law, her sons might have conveniently forgotten what Mom had said.

- Beth stated a problem she was having and asked her sons to come up with ways to help solve the problem.

- Through brainstorming together, Beth gave her kids a chance to "come up with the idea," giving them the opportunity to take responsibility for their own behavior.
- When she praised Matthew for thinking up the idea that worked for all of them, he felt proud of himself.
- When included in family decision making, the boys were proud to uphold the household rules.

Another problem common to most families is getting kids ready for school in the morning. A mother in my parenting class told her story. Denise is the single mother of fourteen-year-old Nick and eight-year-old Heidi. Every morning she struggles to get herself to work and her kids off to school on time. She said, "Nick is pretty good about getting ready once he gets out of bed, except that he always tries to sneak in a few extra minutes of sleep every morning. Sometimes that ends up to be an extra fifteen minutes which we just don't have. Heidi is worse. She takes her time, fusses with her hair, changes her clothes at least three times, usually has at least one temper tantrum, and makes us all late. I feel like a drill sergeant as I keep asking them, 'Are you up yet?' 'Did you brush your teeth?' 'Did you feed the dog?' 'Is your lunch ready?' 'Are you ready to go yet?' 'Only five minutes left.' By the time we run out the door, I'm frazzled, and my day has only just begun!"

---

What is stubbornness but determination seeking soil in which to root.                                   —*Dawna Markova, Ph.D.*

---

131

One way to beat the early-morning blues is to sit down with your kids and create a simple morning checklist. If possible, work with one child at a time so you can focus on his individual needs. Have him write down all the things he has to do in the morning, and then add whatever he may have left out. Be reasonable in your requests, taking into consideration your time constraints and which chores are really necessary. Picking up clothes or making the bed may easily be solved by closing the bedroom door until after school. Denise tried this technique and reported back to the class. "My kids and I created a checklist, and it's working so far. Some of the things we put on the list are:

• Mom and Heidi prepare lunches the night before, Nick puts in snacks in the morning.
• The night before, both kids decide what they will wear the next day. Heidi gets two outfits to choose from because she always changes her mind. But she can only decide between those two outfits.
• Nick walks the dog, Heidi feeds the dog, Mom fixes breakfast.
• We all take responsibility for putting our own dishes in the dishwasher and wiping our corner of the kitchen table (we have two sponges in the kitchen to prevent fights)."

Denise concluded, "I don't nag anymore. The kids know what they have to do and how much time they have to do it. Every so often I say, 'How are you two doing?' As my kids check off their morning lists, it gives them a sense of responsibility and pride in their simple accomplishments. My life is easier now, too."

## Give Them Opportunities to Make Decisions

When parents forget that kids see the world differently than they do, they only make things worse by trying to control and manipulate their kids. Always telling kids what to do, how to do it, and when to do it never gives them the chance to form their own ideas and develop their own inner strength. When we always give advice laced with criticism, we do not give our kids a chance to appreciate themselves.

In order to avoid power struggles, give reasonable choices within limits that work for the entire family. Provide your kids with reasonable opportunities to plan activities and organize their chores. This makes each child feel important, in control, and involved in the family. By offering choices, you give them a chance to listen to their own inner voice and provide them with the ability to start making decisions at a very young age.

As they become teenagers, tempted by peer and cultural pressure, they will have learned to listen to themselves. Peers pushing drugs or alcohol will not be an extension of Mom or Dad always telling them what to do, how to do it, where to do it, and what it should feel like if they do it right. When you teach them to trust themselves by giving them the opportunity to make reasonable decisions on their own, they develop their own inner strength.

There may be times when your kids are unable to make wise choices on their own. That is when you must base a decision on your gut instinct ("I'm the mom/dad, that's why!"). Remind them often that no matter how much they bargain or try to rationalize, you simply may not agree with what they want to do. If your kids know that you are fair and on their side, they will not growl as much when you say NO! Although, they *will* growl. Be prepared for door slamming, yelling, and lots of sulking.

Remember, in that imaginary faraway land where kids originated from, two of the basic rules of living are:

- Resist authority when it does not suit you.
- When you do get your way, you can choose to be happy or sad. Your mood swings are completely up to you.

Mood swings and intense feelings are normal, especially for teenagers. Teenagers do not have to turn to drugs, alcohol, food, or suicide to erase the feelings they experience in their lives when they have been raised by parents who encourage them to feel and embrace the myriad of emotions that do come up. Seventeen-year-old Peyton agreed. She said,

> I have never done drugs, smoked cigarettes, or tried alcohol. I have no need to. I don't want to numb my feelings; I want to embrace them. They are a part of me and I want to know myself fully. The reason I feel like this is because my parents raised me to feel whole and complete. They always included me in decisions that concerned my life, and they treated me with respect. I never had really strict rules put on me, and no matter what, my parents always listened to me and acknowledged my feelings. I was never, ever told to stop crying, or shut up, or not feel what I was feeling. They always offered comfort and understanding. I've grown up to trust myself, to love myself, and to respect myself. I really owe it all to my mom and dad.

When I spoke to Peyton, I was overjoyed to meet a teenager who is articulate, intelligent, self-assured, and well mannered. The truth is, all teenagers have the ability to feel capable and act intelligently when given the opportunity to believe in themselves and make their own decisions.

We all know that life is not perfect; therefore, we must learn how to successfully cope with disappointments in life. When kids are allowed to feel their disappointment and respond to situations as they arise, they learn how to be responsible for their own feelings. Let them experience and express all those feelings and emotions as they come up. You do not have to fix those feelings. Your job, simply, is to be there for them offering love, compassion, and guidance.

While parenting may never be an easy task, it is a constant one. From moment to moment, from situation to situation, from day to day, as my children stretch the limits, push my buttons, and test the water, I must ebb and flow with their ever-changing tides. It seems that each situation warrants a new look at their behavior and my feelings about that behavior. As my husband and I set up the limits for our children to follow, it is within those very limits that they have room to choose and to express themselves. As they continue to grow and push those limits, we do not always have to be the rule setters and our children do not have to be the rule breakers. By working hard at communicating honestly and clearly, it is possible to create situations that everyone in your household can feel comfortable with, while building a future based on love and respect.

## Allow Mistakes

Allow your children to make mistakes. Help them to understand and learn from their mistakes without shame, guilt, or embarrassment. As a child, I was wisely told by my mother, Eileen, "It's okay to make mistakes; that's why there are erasers on the ends of pencils."

In my teen seminars, I have asked thousands of adolescents to raise their hands if they have ever broken something accidentally. Usually all hands are raised. Then I ask how many got in trouble for breaking something accidentally. Only one or two hands usually go down. The variety of punishments inflicted by parents for making a simple mistake is astounding. These punishments range from screaming and yelling to getting grounded or beaten.

If you broke something in the kitchen, would you like your spouse to call you a clumsy moron, then yell at you to pay attention? If you make a mistake at work, how would it feel to have your boss put you down and embarrass you? What tone of voice do you respond best to? How does it feel to be vulnerable? Think for a moment about how you would like to be treated if the tables were turned.

We constantly admonish our kids with questions like "Why didn't you go to the bathroom before?" "Why did you spill that?" "Why did you do that?" "What's wrong with you?" These are simple questions that carry huge accusations, and are often answered with "I don't know." Humiliation, blame, and shame are not motivators; they build generalized resistance to authority. Empower your child by understanding their needs and respecting their time schedules. Help your child to understand why going to the bathroom before leaving the house may be advantageous. If you are going bike riding you can say, "There won't be any bathrooms along the bike path. We should all go to the bathroom before we leave." To avoid more dinnertime spills, show your child how she can avoid spilling her juice by gently moving her glass to a safer spot on the table. Stop using words that hurt. Start using words that help. It takes a lot of courage to act in a patient, loving, and heartfelt way, and to remember that no one is perfect.

When you were growing up, you may have made some

stupid mistakes or done a few things you regret. As an adult, you can look back at those events in your life and be grateful you survived or outgrew those stages. As much as you may want to prevent your own kids from making the same mistakes you made, or getting involved in behavior you do not approve of, the truth is you cannot stop your kids from making their own mistakes and taking risks. They may make mistakes you do not like, but they will make mistakes because they are learning. Kids need to learn that they can fall down and get back up again. They also need to know you will forgive them for being imperfect, for doing something wrong, or for not giving you the love and respect you may deserve. Once you master the art of forgiveness, you can transcend resentment and anger, and experience loving emotions once again.

---

If I could say just one thing to parents, it would be simply that a child needs someone who believes in him no matter what he does.
                                                        —*Alice Keliher*

---

## Deal with Angry Feelings

A few years ago, I was upset with my daughter's behavior. I said to her, "You are being so childish." Journey responded, "I *am* a child, Mom!" At that moment I realized that it is normal and acceptable for a kid to act like a kid. Children find it very offensive when we say "Stop acting like a baby." I had to remember what it felt like to be smaller and younger, with very little power or control over my life.

Because parents and kids have separate realities, when an adult gets angry, the child only sees the angry adult. They hear the loud voice and feel the anger. They suddenly forget the issue at hand. No matter what you say or do, the child thinks, "You're mean!" There will be times throughout your career as a parent when you do feel mean, angry, disgusted, taken advantage of, annoyed, or just plain furious. It is perfectly okay to let your child know how angry you are without having to explode into a violent rage.

On the other hand, by acting overly patient, kind, considerate, and ignoring your own feelings, you could end up exploding over a "crime" that was disproportionate to your anger.

When you are angry, remember to contain your anger as much as possible. Containment allows your children to feel safe in your presence, not threatened or fearful. Be respectful; do not call your kids names or put them on the defensive. You can let them know you are angry without scaring them. Say what you see, what you feel, and what you want done. Here are a few examples:

- "When I see all the dishes left in the sink, I get really mad. Please put the dishes in the dishwasher."
- "I'm furious! I need to go somewhere, and the car hardly has any gas in it. Please fill up the tank after you use the car."
- "I spent all morning polishing the kitchen floor. Now it's covered with muddy footprints. I'm so fed up! I want you and your friends to take your shoes off before you come inside."

Put your foot down and be firm whenever necessary. Set your limits and boundaries by stating them respectfully and clearly. This helps your kids to see their mistakes and learn from them. Please remember, you do not have to use insults or threats to make your point. Do not call them names, do not hit them, just let them know where you stand. And never reprimand them in front of their friends or anyone else, as this just creates embarrassment.

I have seen so many adults treat children of all ages with disrespect and cruelty. We must all remember that every human being—both big and small—responds to kind words and gentle voices. When you treat your son or daughter with equal human worth and dignity, you teach them self-respect and inspire them to respect others.

## Make Curfew Reasonable

A typical power struggle between parents and their teenagers takes place over curfew. There are numerous theories on what time kids should be home. One extreme says:

> • Don't give them any curfew; if you have raised them right, you can let them decide for themselves.

This unrealistic approach does not work, because in reality, we all have limits and rules that we must abide by. Unfortunately, life is not always fair, and kids need help with that notion. They need boundaries. They need to know within what perimeters they can spread their wings and fly. If they have no curfew, no rules, and no limits within which to function, they go out of control. There is chaos and confusion, and they flounder like a fish out of water.

Another theory is:

> • Parents should decide upon and enforce the time their kids come home.

This extreme does not allow kids to make reasonable choices or be responsible for their actions. It creates an atmosphere of order without freedom. It sets them up for rebellion, and they soon begin to sneak out and "break" curfew.

We use a different technique in our family:

My son is ten. During the summer, he likes to ride his bike up and down the street, stopping to visit his friends. My husband and I had some concerns, so we talked it over with our son. We told him we want him to come home one-half hour before dinner so he can help set the table and prepare for our evening meal. At first he balked at the idea, but after we discussed it together and came up with reasonable conclusions that we all could live with, he willingly comes home on time. He learned the art of negotiation, and we avoided a power struggle by:

- giving him a reliable wristwatch.
- listening to his feelings and his needs.
- calmly discussing how we feel about the situation.
- brainstorming solutions.
- coming to a mutual agreement that works for all of us.

My husband and I sat up many nights discussing what we would do when Journey began to date. We talked about our fears, our concerns, and our beliefs. The first time Journey went out with a group of friends, we decided to ask her what *she* thought her curfew should be. Our conversation went like this:

**Mom:** Journey, before you go out, I want to discuss curfew.

**Journey:** What time do I have to be home tonight?

**Mom:** What time do you think would be reasonable?

**Journey:** I don't know. We're just going to a movie, and we might stop off at a friend's house, so I don't know how long we'll be.

**Mom:** I want to know what time to expect you so I don't sit up worrying all night.

**Journey:** You don't have to worry, Mom. I'll be okay.

**Mom:** I know I don't have to worry, but I love you and I can't help it! I think it's a mommy thing. I would like you to think about two things. One is: how late you can reasonably stay out while still being able to get up in the morning without feeling exhausted all day. And two: I am going to wait up for you. I know I don't have to, but I will sleep better when I know you are home safely. So, knowing that I don't like to stay up late, and knowing that I have an all-day seminar to lead tomorrow and need a good night's sleep, what time do you think would be fair for both of us?

**Journey:** Okay. What about 1:00 A.M.? Is that okay with you?

**Mom:** I think that's a little late considering I have to work in the morning. Can you come home a little earlier tonight?

**Journey:** How about midnight then?

**Mom:** Midnight sounds fair. I trust that you'll be home on time, so I can get to sleep, okay?

**Journey:** Okay, Mom. See you later.

By discussing calmly, giving our daughter reasonable choices she can handle, providing her with an opportunity to problem-solve, and giving her a chance to show compassion for our feelings, we are building a bridge of trust and mutual respect. That night she walked through the front door at 11:59 P.M., tiptoed into my bedroom, and whispered, "Mom, I'm home." I thanked her for being on time, and she made sure I realized she was scoring points by coming home a minute early. By showing consideration and cooperation, she does earn points, and by being flexible and fair I earn her trust.

A common question parents ask me about curfew is: What do you do if your teen comes home late? Bryan is sixteen and has his own car. One Saturday night he drove a group of friends to the movies, getting home past curfew. He told us his story:

> On the way home, one of the girls really wanted to stop off at Burger King. I guess she didn't eat dinner before we all went out. It was just a quick stop, then I drove everyone home. I was about thirty minutes late when I walked in the door. My dad went nuts! He was screaming at me for being late, telling me I was inconsiderate and irresponsible. Man, I drove all those people around and got everyone home safe. I never drink and drive, and I'm a careful driver. My dad grounded me and took away my car for two weeks. He wouldn't even give me a chance to explain why I was late or anything. I tried to help someone out and I got screwed. Man, my dad really pisses me off. He's totally unfair.

Bryan's father could have said, "Son, I've had a long, hard day today. I was afraid something happened to you, and I was getting really nervous waiting for you to come home. I'm wondering what you could do next time you are going to be late so Mom and I don't worry?" This opens up an opportunity for father and son to talk together, to understand each other's feelings, and to work together as a team to find positive solutions. Dad could also set an example for his son by calling home every time he is going to be a few minutes late. This mutual give and take, coupled with trust and honesty, is the basis for a loving relationship between parent and teenager.

When children misbehave or step outside of the family boundaries, parents can choose to be reactive or proactive. You *react* to a situation by lashing out, yelling, or letting your emotions and ego get in the way. This creates anger, frustration, and a feeling of separation for everyone involved in the line of fire.

A proactive response would be free of shame, blame, and humiliation. Proactive parents take time to listen and discuss, to work things out, and to let their kids know how they feel. There are five quick steps you can follow to help you stay focused:

1. If you start to *react,* tell yourself to "stop."
2. Take a few deep breaths.
3. Think about what is happening at that moment.
4. Notice how you are feeling.
5. Take as much time as you need to get clear about your own ideas before you speak.

Let your kids know how you feel by using "I" messages. Say what *you* feel and what *your* needs are. Help your children become independent thinkers by asking them "What can we do to make this work? What should we do if it doesn't happen?" Allow yourself to come back to your child's world; find out what is going on with her. Ask questions that help her create her own thinking process.

## Be Fair

Children thrive in an environment where parents are consistent and fair. Yet, how many parents have said to their children, "Let's go, I'm leaving," without any warning? The parent's anger builds as the child continues to play, and the outraged parent then yells, yanks, or hits his or her child into obedience. Even dog-training classes teach a more humane approach.

If you were watching a baseball game on television at a friend's house and your friend came up to you and said, "Let's go, I'm leaving right now," would you immediately turn off the TV and get up to go? You might say, "Let me just watch this last inning," or "Hold on, I can't go yet." As adults, you would work this out so you both feel okay about your conflict of interests. Children usually are not given this chance. With children, it helps to let them know in advance that you will be leaving soon and will give reminders at various intervals. I give my kids a ten-minute warning, a five-minute warning, and a three-minute warning. This allows them to finish a task, a game, or a conversation before I leave. Once you say you are leaving, try your best to stick to your time schedule, and let your child know if your time frame changes.

A father of a ten-year-old boy told me:

> I am human, and sometimes it is so hard to control my temper when my son is acting up. I want to be fair, but it isn't always so easy. Last night my son went into a rage for something I thought was very stupid, but evidently was very important to him. He was a raving lunatic, and there was no reasoning with him. My wife and I were extremely upset by his attitude and decided to go into our room to get out of his ver-

bal line of fire. We stayed in our room while our son screamed and yelled outside our door. It sounded like he was throwing things around his room until he finally fell asleep. When he woke up the next morning, we were still feeling angry and disappointed. Our son looked sad and was still mad at us for not understanding how he felt the night before. When he half apologized for acting out, I told him he needed to take full responsibility for his actions. I told him his behavior was unacceptable, and that we will continue to remove ourselves from his outrageous actions if it continues. Of course, that made him mad all over again.

What the father could have done at the moment his son took partial responsibility for his own behavior by "half apologizing," was to:

- Thank his son for taking responsibility for the way he acted.
- Put his arms around his son and hug him.
- Gently remind his son that both Mom and Dad will continue to remove themselves from the line of fire when necessary.
- Not say anything else about the previous night until they all cooled off and could see things in a different light.

By doing this, the son would have been able to focus on the fact that he did take some responsibility for his actions, and he would have felt loved and acknowledged. This encourages the child to take responsibility next time.

> Significant problems cannot be solved at the same level
> of thinking that created them.     —*Albert Einstein*

By being fair and respectful, you can sidestep continual power struggles. Life is not always fair, and this is a lesson best taught by parents who love and care for their developing child.

## Take a Parental Time-Out

Taking a time-out is a useful concept. To take a time-out is to physically move away from the situation—to calm down and cool off. Putting a child in the corner or forcing him to stay in his room is often overused by parents as a punishment that does not always teach the appropriate lesson meant for the misbehavior.

Sandi is the mother of two teenage sons. She said,

> When my son was younger, he wouldn't take time-outs, because he wouldn't stay in his room. I'm not a believer in locking a kid in his room, because I think that's abusive. But I was at my wit's end because he kept coming out of his room and screaming at me. One day, I had a revelation: I'll take a time out! I decided to get out of his way. I didn't leave the house, but I did let him scream and yell, while I practiced deep breathing in my room.

When you are confronted with a child who is out of control or you find yourself losing your temper, you can remove yourself from the situation by taking your own time out. The trick is to do it in a calm way. This is not always easy, but when you do not shout at your kids when they misbehave, you remain the one in control—which prevents them from being the boss with all the power. Kids cannot handle an overabundance of power, they do not know how to use it constructively. What they can handle and what they need is a sense of balance and reasonable control over their lives. They may test you and push you to your limit, but they still need you, and they count on you to be there for them.

Take time to gain perspective and show your kids an effective way to deal with anger. Since this is a new technique for many parents, you must teach yourself to remain calm when the situation gets out of control. That is the key that makes it work. **You need to take a break.** Point your finger at yourself when you speak to help you own your own feelings and let your kids know you are human. Say something like "This isn't working for me. I'm really uncomfortable with what's going on here. I need some quiet time right now, so I don't take my anger out on you. I'm going to my room; I'll talk to you later"—which is very different from saying "Stop calling me names," "Shut up," or "Who the hell do you think you are? Go to your room." A few things you can do for yourself are:

- State your boundaries clearly and calmly.
- Let your kids know how you are feeling.
- Speak clearly without getting angry.
- Go into your own room and take a time-out. Lock your door if necessary.
- Make sure your house is child-safe so your child cannot get hurt.

While you are in your room gaining perspective on the situation, you can:

- write your feelings in a journal.
- meditate.
- call a friend and talk about what is going on at the moment.
- take a hot bath.
- get some physical exercise.
- have a good cry to let off steam.

Another mother said, "When I did this with my own son when he was younger, he would scream and cry and knock on my door. It was not easy for me to sit in my room with my child screaming outside my door. In between his sobbing, I would say *very* calmly, 'I'll come out when I'm ready and as soon as the yelling stops.' I would repeat that several times. He would eventually stop and say, 'Mommy, I'm not yelling anymore. Will you come out now?' When I finally came out, I gave my son a big hug and we went about our day. There were no guilt feelings, no shame, and no residual anger."

A four-year-old dictating when Mommy could come out of her room? One might say he had all the control. What she gave him was reasonable power regarding cause and effect. The child knew his behavior had to stop for Mommy to come out. When children have reasonable responsibility in their court, it helps them to realize that they are part of the equation, part of the family dynamic. When they understand this concept, it helps to even out the power play that arises in most families.

When a temper tantrum or angry fit is over, do not nag your kids about it or reprimand them by saying things like "Are you sure you're done?" or, "Was that necessary?" Simply bring them back into the family unit as you move on with your day. In the aftermath of a blowup, open up your heart to your child, and imagine how you would feel and what you would need from your ideal parent if you were a child in that same situation.

## Let Them Go to Their Room

Many parents say, "I can't give my child a time-out because he has a TV, Nintendo, telephone and stereo in his room, so it's not a punishment." Some older kids do not seem to care if you send them to their room. They storm off and slam the bedroom door. The sound of a slamming door can send parents into a fury.

Jan, the mother of a thirteen-year-old daughter, said, "Janna has a stereo, a TV, and a telephone in her room. She's a pretty good kid, gets good grades, and is studying to become a ballerina. But when she screws up, I can't send her to her room. She has everything she wants there, so it doesn't seem like a punishment. I don't know what else to do."

Another mom said, "I can't send my son to his room either because he has too much fun in there, so I prescribe hard labor. I usually make him follow me around all day and do all the chores he hates. One time he went to a friend's house and didn't tell me where he was going. I was so worried. That weekend he had to clean out the attic and scrub the grease off the garage floor as his consequence."

Scrubbing the grease off the garage floor would be a logical and reasonable consequence if the boy had spilled grease in the garage, but having to scrub and clean because he went to a friend's house unannounced is not reasonable or logical.

To achieve a clear understanding of what is expected, there are a few things a parent must do:

- Sit down together and clearly spell out the rules that work for everyone, so your kids clearly understand them. Let them participate in the rule-making process.
- Discuss the importance of leaving a note

so everyone knows who will be where.
- Have them leave the telephone number of where they are going to be.
- If they still go out without letting you know, not being able to go to a friend's house the next time may be a reasonable consequence for your child.

If you do send your child to her room to cool off, there is nothing wrong with her having a good time there. Create a win-win situation by simply saying "I want you to go into your room and cool off for a while. Come out when you feel ready." This kind of statement allows you to call the shots, while providing your child with a sense of dignity and self-control. It allows everyone to take a little break before things get too out of hand. Children should be allowed to go to their room to take some time out from misbehaving, or to cool down before an explosion actually occurs.

Parents must change their own thinking about punishment and deprival. Do not make them suffer for what they did; help them to learn from their mistakes. Christina is twelve. She said:

> My little brother always gets into my stuff, and he bugs me when I have friends over. He's such a little pest and he makes me really mad. If I yell at him and tell him to get out of my room, he tells on me. He gets me in trouble all the time. One time he was bugging me so bad, I hit him. Boy, did I get in trouble for that! My mom screamed at me for setting a bad example for my brother. She said I should know better. I had to apologize to him, then I got grounded for five days. I had to stay in my room

and couldn't talk on the phone. My dad sided with them, and he was mad at me too.

Realizing that kids and adults interpret things differently, I asked Christina how she felt about her experience. She responded:

> I feel like my life is so unfair. My little brother gets to do everything, and I am just supposed to always set a good example for him. Sometimes that feels like a lot. I mean, my mom spanks my brother, but I can't hit him, NO WAY! That's sort of confusing, you know what I mean? Plus, when I got in trouble, nobody asked me what happened. There was a reason why I hit him. He was being such a little brat, but that doesn't matter. I'm the one who gets in trouble all the time.

Christina's experience is fairly typical among siblings; kids bicker and argue, they tease and they test one another. Christina's response is typical among adolescents; they do not want to apologize to the sibling who is provoking them, and they express frustration and anger according to the examples they have been given.

Christina and her little brother need to have some cool communication skills to use, instead of resorting to violence. This kind of sibling interaction can be avoided if brothers and sisters learn love, respect, consideration, and compassion at an early age. Parents must demonstrate these skills for their kids by parenting in a loving way. Using skills and techniques from this book, parents can teach their children to speak to one another with compassion and understanding. They can encourage their children to become centered individuals who are respectful of others and who exhibit self-control.

Instead of yelling at her daughter and immediately grounding her for five days, Christina's mom could have stopped what she was doing to deal with this very serious infraction. I have listed some steps to follow if you find yourself in this type of situation:

- Firmly say, "There is no hitting allowed in this house!" (You can only say this if it is true for the adults as well.)
- Find out what your child is angry or upset about.
- Help your child identify her feelings by saying "I see that you are really mad at your brother right now. What happened?"
- Listen without interrupting.
- Try to understand the problem from your child's perspective.
- Give your kids specific examples of what they can do when they are really angry, like:
  1. punch their pillow to safely release anger.
  2. use their words to express their feelings.
  3. draw or paint an angry picture, using their nondominant hand to let go of control.
  4. write a Feeling Letter (see chapter 8 for Kids).
  5. go to their room and listen to music to unwind.

When you show your children how to channel their feelings of aggression or anger, they learn that they are not bad, their feelings are legitimate (from their perspective), and they have positive options for dealing with negative feelings (and in Christina's case, hitting is not one of them!).

Kids need an opportunity to move away from negative feelings and come out whole again. Boys and girls must be allowed to step away when they need space. Going to their room and relaxing may be exactly what they need at that moment. On the other hand, some kids need to talk when they have problems. Those kids with access to a telephone will call anyone who will listen. One fifteen-year-old girl told me, "Once when my parents were mad at me, I had to stay in my room. I was so mad I wanted to explode. So I called a teen hot line and someone on the other end just listened. I didn't have to give my name and I could just talk. I felt so much better afterward." Give your kids the opportunity to find positive things that help them feel better.

Give your kids a chance to redo something that wasn't done right the first time. Do not threaten or bribe them; that only scares children into obedience and lowers their self-appreciation. Sometimes you have to just let go and let them discover society's responses to inappropriate behavior, like getting suspended from school for swearing at a teacher, or spending the night in jail for drunk driving. This can be terrifying for parents because no one wants to see his or her child fall down and get hurt. The older they get, the more you are forced to let go and stop managing their behavior. As your teenager drives off to a party in the family car for the first time, all you can do is hope she will be safe. You have to let go and trust that life itself will protect them.

Remember to choose your battles carefully. Do not fight over every little thing you do not approve of; save your thunder for those moments that seem like life-or-death issues. Wearing the same socks three days in a row or having a messy room never killed anyone. Think about what really matters in your relationship with your child and what really matters in life.

---

Complete permissiveness can be as harmful as total strictness.

---

## Letting Go

There will come a time when you cannot control your children anymore. You can no longer manage their affairs, tell them what to do, or how to do it. They will not let you fuss over them or hug them in public: you have been fired as manager; now you must find ways to be rehired as a consultant in your teenager's life. This does not mean you should stop loving them; parents should never revoke their love, no matter what. However, you have to accept the reality that your children will make mistakes, just as you did when you were growing up. Hopefully, they will learn from their mistakes and stay safe and sane in the process.

Parents must set appropriate boundaries, as they teach their children to be responsible citizens. All you can do is provide them with strong, healthy family values, and hope that they have learned them. Hopefully, all the values you have imparted over the years will come forth at the right and appropriate time.

When children are little, you can control their environment. When they are big, they choose their own path and create their own lives, and you cannot stop them. You can choose to grow as a parent, as you let your kids choose their path with your guidance, or you can struggle to remain in control as they break away with a vengeance. Each child has his or her own path to follow.

Hard times, heartbreaks, challenges, and struggles provide them with opportunities rich with growth and potential knowledge. Loosen up, love them, and give your children the chance to experience the things in life that will make them have more depth and understanding as human beings.

---

Treat people as if they were what they ought to be, and you help them become what they are capable of being.

—*Johann Wolfgang von Goethe*

---

## *Personal Goals*

1. Love your children enough to say "No" when appropriate, and mean it when you say it.
2. Do not try to solve all of your kids' problems.
3. Step back from minor squabbles.
4. Give help and advice only when asked.
5. Let your kids play an active role in decision making.
6. Give your kids a chance to have opinions and ideas, then respect them.
7. Validate their thoughts.
8. Allow time for negotiation.
9. Avoid intimidation; it will only inspire rebellion.
10. Be on the lookout for good behavior. Train yourself to find it.

# *KIDS:*

## *Play as a Team; Don't Yell and Scream*

When people fight, they usually say things they don't really mean. If your mom calls you names and shouts at you, your reply would probably be to yell and swear at her. The only problem is, if your mom calls you a brat and you tell her to f___ off, you get grounded. Since adults are the ones with all the power, we're the ones who always end up getting in trouble. It takes two people to start an argument, but it only takes one person to make it stop. Believe it or not: if there is an argument going on, you can be the responsible one to make it end. Kids and teens have tons of power; you just need to know how and when to use it so it works.

If you are fighting with your parents, it is important to calm things down by talking about how you feel and listening to how the other person feels. This will work a lot better than yelling and swearing at each other. If you get angry or defensive, your parents get even angrier. Don't yell; talk softly and let them know that you don't want to fight. When you act calm, they see how loud they are yelling and eventually they may realize that they are out of control.

## Get Their Attention

If your parents do something that upsets you, try not to yell at them. Yelling at your parents only makes things worse. You need to talk it out with your parents using the strategies you have learned in this book, and let them know what is bothering you. The first thing to do is to make sure it is a good time to talk to them about your problem. Even though we talked about this in chapter 1, here is another example of how to find out if your parents are willing to listen:

> *You:* Dad, I have to talk to you. Is now a good time?
>
> *Dad:* Sure. (He continues with his work.)
>
> *You:* Dad, I need your full attention; otherwise I feel like you aren't really listening to me. Should I wait until you're done?
>
> *Dad:* Maybe now isn't the best time. How about in fifteen minutes?
>
> *You:* Then will you listen?
>
> *Dad:* Sure.
>
> *You:* Okay. I'll be back.

---

With a little patience and acceptance, we learn to discover a gift hiding behind every difficulty.

—*Barry and Joyce Vissell*

---

## Make Sure the Mood Is Right

Before you start talking, find out if the person you are talking to is in the right mood to listen. It might be a bad time, and that could lead to a fight. Once you get his undivided attention, sit down with him and talk about whatever is bothering you.

The way to find out what kind of mood your parents are in is simply to ask. If you see your mom sitting on the couch reading the newspaper, even though it looks like she is free, she might be in a bad mood. Do not ask, "Mom, are you in a bad mood?" If she is in a bad mood, pointing it out will only make it worse.

What you say is, "Mom, something is bugging me. Is now a good time to talk to you about it?" If she says no, leave it at that and ask her again later, without sounding like you're nagging. If you realize that you have asked her many times and every time her reply is "No," try saying something like "Mom, when would be a good time to talk to you about my problem?" That way you can set up an "appointment" with her. When parents are in a bad mood, it's usually harder for them to listen. When you set up an appointment with your parents, you have a better chance of catching them when they are ready to listen.

## Reason with Your Parents

Once you get your parents' full attention and you make sure the mood is right, you can start to reason with them. For example, let's say your dad tells you to clean your room. You tell him to go away and leave you alone. He calls you a brat for not listening, and you both start a screaming match. Sound familiar?

After you have both cooled off and the mood is right, stand up for yourself and tell your dad that you don't like it when he calls you names. Be careful how you say it. Remember to ask him first if it's the right time to talk. Say something like "Dad, I want to talk about the fight we had earlier. Is this a good time for you to really hear me?" If he says it's not, ask him when it would be a good time. Remember to schedule an appointment if you have to. If he does agree to talk to you, tell him how you feel when he calls you a brat. Be really clear (adults like that). You could say, "It makes me really mad when people call me names. Would you just remind me to clean my room one more time before you get mad at me?"

Another example of how to reason with your parents might be:

• Mom screams, "Get your stupid papers off the table!"

• Instead of getting mad and saying that your papers are not stupid, but she is, or telling her that you'll clean it up later, just clean up your papers so you don't have to go through a huge argument.

• This is not about giving in or wimping out. You have the choice to fight with your parents and make your life difficult, or you can make things simple. The choice is up to you.

---

Don't hold on to anger, hurt or pain.
They steal energy and keep you from love.
—*Leo Buscaglia*

---

You have to reason with these people. It is the only thing that works for them. The next time you are in a situation where your parent says something that really makes you mad, just remember to keep calm and try to work through it. If you are the one person in your family who stays calm while everyone else is screaming, your parents will eventually realize that they are the ones always causing problems. They will realize that you are more mature than they gave you credit for, and you will easily gain the respect you deserve.

## Use "I" Messages

This is another one of those important techniques that will make a difference when you talk to people. An "I" message is when you point your finger at yourself and say what you feel and what you need, instead of using a "you" message and pointing it at someone else. "I hate you and I want you out of my life" is a "you" message and a put-down. It isn't a correct "I" message.

Imagine you were just in a huge fight with your little brother and you run into your room. Your mom comes in to see if everything is okay, and you say, "Leave me alone. I hate my brother so much." Certain responses make adults mad, and this is usually one of them. What you have just done is told your mom what to do by saying "Leave me alone." By saying "I hate my brother," you just make your parents angrier because they want you to get along with your siblings.

When you can remember that adults understand things differently than we do, and give different meanings to things we say, it gives you a kind of power. You have the power to make a difference in your life by using techniques from this book that will work for you. Try saying "Is it okay if I try to cool off?" Your mom might say something in response. If you repeat yourself in a *regular* voice, *without* a bad attitude, chances are she will understand and leave you alone. Do you see the difference? One way seems more like a command—and everyone knows that parents hate being ordered around by their children—and the other way is about you. You aren't blaming anyone, you aren't ordering anyone around, and you aren't insulting anyone. You're just saying what you feel and what you need. That definitely works much better than a command.

"I" messages also come in handy if your parents always nag you and you want to tell them to stop. Using an "I" message can help avoid fights because you are owning the problem, instead of throwing it back on the other person. Remember to speak calmly, and don't use an attitude! Here's a dialogue using "I" messages:

> **Mom:** I'm sick of telling you to put your things away. Can't you do what you're told?

**You:** I don't like being nagged, Mom. I'm putting my stuff away right now.

**Mom:** If I don't keep telling you, it never gets done.

**You:** When I get nagged, all it does is make me angry and then we end up in a fight.

**Mom:** Then do what you're told to do in the first place and I won't nag you.

**You:** I think I need gentle reminders to get my things done. It would be really helpful to me if I could be reminded without being yelled at. Would that work for you?

This may sound extremely corny, but to avoid having your parents think you have a bad attitude, you must speak in a way that doesn't make them mad. The tone in your voice really counts, too.

"I" messages work wonders because no one gets offended or upset, as long as you use them correctly. When you own your feelings and take responsibility for yourself and your actions, you end up with power and control over your life. When you are not threatening or blaming your parents, they don't have any reason to get mad at you or ground you for saying something rude or nasty, or talking back.

---

Look before you leap . . . Think before you speak!

—*Anonymous*

---

## Bite Your Tongue

When kids talk back or yell at their parents, it usually leads to a fight and they end up with consequences or getting privileges taken away. Sometimes it is so much easier to just "bite your tongue," do what you're told to do, and tell your parents about your feelings at another time. "Biting your tongue" means you don't talk back, you don't say anything mean or hurtful, and sometimes it just means shutting up. I know how hard it can be to "bite your tongue," but sometimes it really does help. The point is not to give up your soul and let your parents take over; the point is to have peace within your family so you can have more freedom in your life without the threat of being grounded.

If your parents said something that upset you or offended you, and you decide to talk to them about it, make doubly sure no one is in a bad mood before you begin your conversation. If you had a fight, be sure you wait until everyone has cooled off and no one is angry anymore. That is when it is the easiest for adults to give you their undivided attention. Sometimes your parents might need a little more time to cool off than you do.

When you do talk to your parents, you may find yourself starting to say something that you know will get you in trouble. "Bite your tongue," and don't say it! You have the power to decide if the consequences are worth it. The choice is yours. You have to speak up when it is necessary, but think about what you are going to say first.

## Take a Break

If things get too hot during a fight and you realize you don't want to argue anymore, ask the person you are fighting with if you can take a break so you can cool off for a while. It will be easier to get your point across after you have both cooled off.

---

Progress can happen when everyone is calm and clearheaded.

---

If you are in a fight that has gone way overboard and you and your parents are too worked up, it is up to you to find a way out. The best way for you to cool off would be to take your own time-out! That means spending some time alone for a while to think things out.

Some parents wouldn't approve of their children leaving in the middle of a discussion. Here is what you can do to get some time to cool off. Without yelling or talking in a defensive or angry voice, calmly say things like:

- Do you think I can take a time-out right now to think about all this?
- May I please go think about this for a while, and then if it's okay with you, we can talk about it later?
- It seems like we aren't getting anywhere by yelling at each other. Do you think we should take a break for a little while?
- Would you mind if we wait until we've both cooled off before we discuss this any more, so we don't keep yelling at each other?

Hopefully using one of these sentences will allow you to leave the room so you can calm down. If your parents say that you cannot leave, point out the fact that it would be a lot easier to discuss things after everyone calms down. You have to be careful with your exact words and the way you say things, because if you speak with too much authority, your parents will make you stay and listen to whatever they want to say. The best way out is to say things in a nonthreatening, calm way. It will also make your parents respect you more for cooperating. If your parents say "We'll talk about this right now," do your best to stay calm and focus on what you say and how you say it. Use active listening, "I" messages, and keep remembering that adults see things differently than we do.

If you are having a really hard time with someone, be sure to find positive ways to express your feelings so you don't have to hold on to all of your anger. You could talk to another family member, a special friend, a school counselor, or call a help hot line which you can find in the Yellow Pages of the telephone book. If you get in a fight, nothing gets solved unless you stop and take a break.

## Don't Yell and Scream

You need to pick your fights sensibly, especially if your family tends to get in a lot of them. If someone says something that makes you mad, decide whether it's worth causing a major fight and getting yourself in trouble. If it's not that big a deal, then let it slide. Avoiding fights can keep you from getting grounded, getting lectured, or being punished.

You may think avoiding fights is impossible to accomplish, but that's because you aren't used to it. Try staying out of your parents' way if they are in a bad mood; don't do things that purposely get them mad; and if your little sister is bugging you, leave the room instead of starting a fight. If you try these techniques a couple of times, they may work for you.

If you really feel that you are not willing to be nice to your parents, think of how it would feel to avoid fights and have your parents trust you and give you more freedom. Wouldn't that be cool? This kind of freedom might mean:

- Your dad won't follow you around or spy on you.

- Your mom won't listen in on your phone calls.
- Your parents won't ask for all the details before you go to a party.
- You can stay out later than usual.

If you don't want to be yelled at, try not to yell at your family. If you yell at your mom, she is probably going to yell back and maybe even punish you. Personally, I think it would be a lot easier if you stay calm and in control.

---

So be sure when you step
Step with care and great
   tact,
and remember that Life's
a Great Balancing Act.
                    —*Dr. Seuss*

---

Yelling and screaming usually include insults and angry feelings. By playing as a team, you can work together to get things solved. By talking about how you feel and what you need, you can get through to the other person and let her know what bothers you and how you would like it to be changed. You have to treat others the way you want to be treated.

## Play as a Team

When you play as a team, you avoid angry words and arguments. One way to play as a team is to use the techniques I talk about in chapter 3. When you get your parents to appreciate you, or you take the time to show your parents that you appreciate them, you create a win-win situation in your family so everyone is happy. I know that may sound weird, but keep reading. If your parents are in a good mood they are usually nicer to you and you get to do more things. They might let you go to the movies, stay out late, or let you do something with a friend when they would normally have said no.

The best way to get your parents in a good mood is by doing things for them. I have a little trick I use to get my parents in a good mood: I offer my help when they are doing something. The trick is to offer help when the chore is almost done. For example: If your dad is doing the dishes, keep an eye on him to find out when only a few plates are left to be cleaned. Then go up to him and ask if he needs any help. Since he is almost finished, it is most likely that he will say no. Be ready to do the rest of the dishes just in case he says yes. This will work for just about any chore one of your parents may be involved with. Here are some examples:

- washing laundry
- folding laundry
- washing the car
- washing the dishes
- putting groceries away
- cleaning the windows
- cooking/ baking
- setting the table before meals
- cleaning off the table after meals
- taking out the trash
- helping a sibling with homework
- mowing the lawn
- vacuuming the house

Parents love it when you participate. Once in a while you'll have to offer to do the entire chore before they even start to do it, so they don't think you just offer your help when it's "already too late"; otherwise they will think you're taking advantage of them.

You can prove to your parents that you're capable of being responsible and helpful when you continue to do things for them without being asked. The way parents respond to your participation usually makes them want to do things for you in return. They start to believe you have become more responsible and mature, which makes them think you deserve more respect and freedom. That's when you start to see how all that helping out around the house was definitely worth it.

Remember that sometimes you have to do things for your parents when they least expect it and when you aren't trying to get something in return. If you get in the habit of only doing things for your parents when you want something, they'll eventually realize what you're trying to achieve. By helping out when your parents least expect it, you'll have better luck the next time you ask for something, and chances are they will most likely be proud of you for helping them.

It doesn't matter if your parents find out about this technique. Both of my parents know about it, and I pull it off on them all the time without their realizing it. Be part of the team instead of playing against your family.

## Dos and Don'ts of Apologizing

If you make a mistake or say something wrong, don't blame others. Take responsibility for your mistakes. Apologize when you can. Saying you are sorry can make an angry adult feel calmer. An adult can be very understanding and a lot easier to talk to when things are calm. Even though the word *sorry* is just a word, saying it at the right time can make it sound like you really care, and you might not end up getting in as much trouble if you show you really mean it.

Listen to how it might sound if you don't apologize.

*Dad:* I can't believe this is the fifth time I have had to ask you to clean up your plates!

*You:* I keep forgetting.

*Dad:* You'd better start remembering because you sure are beginning to get very irresponsible.

*You:* If you didn't give me so many other chores to do, I wouldn't have so much on my mind, and I would be able to remember more.

*Dad:* Don't you dare start blaming this on me! This is your responsibility and nobody else's. If you can't show more responsibility, you're going to get grounded.

*You:* Leave me alone.

*Dad:* That's it. You're grounded!

Here is an example of saying sorry at the right time:

*Dad:* I cannot believe this is the fifth time I have had to ask you to clean the dishes!

*You:* I keep forgetting.

*Dad:* You'd better start remembering because you sure are beginning to get very irresponsible.

*You:* I'm really sorry I keep forgetting.

*Dad:* I need you to start taking more responsibility and remembering to clean up after yourself without having to be told.

*You:* I'm sorry you're angry, Dad. I'll clean up now.

I know this may sound ridiculous to some of you, but there definitely is a way to talk to adults that works. You can say these things without completely giving in to your parents. In the last example, it sounded like you apologized for not cleaning up after yourself. Your words were "I'm really sorry I keep forgetting." You may not really be sorry at all, but you're probably sorry you forgot to clean up because now your dad is making such a big deal out of it. When you say "I'm sorry," your dad hears the words, while in your own head, you understand your own meaning. Even though you're saying that you're sorry for forgetting to clean up, in your own head, you know you're sorry because of the fuss your dad is making. Once again, you avoid starting another fight.

Sometimes it's worth it to apologize. When you say you're sorry, silently focus in your own mind on what you're *really* apologizing for. Then say out loud what will make your parents happy. Without giving up your own beliefs, you show respect to your parents and responsibility for your actions, which leads to less fighting.

---

I know you believe you understand what you think I said, but I am not sure you realize that what you heard is not what I meant.                                    *—Anonymous*

---

Apologizing is an art. If you use the word *sorry* in a bad way, it can blow up in your face. Don't say "Okay, I've said I'm sorry. Can I go now?" Instead of an apology, it sounds like you're being rude. Adults aren't stupid. When you say "I'm sorry," say it as if you really mean it or they won't believe you! Otherwise, your parents will think they have to punish or lecture you so you will not repeat your action.

## Choose to Make a Real Difference

Many of the techniques and skills that are mentioned in this chapter may not be things you want to do. When I was little, I wanted to be a tap dancer more than anything in the world, but I didn't want to take lessons. I wasn't willing to work hard to achieve my dream; I wanted it to come easily and effortlessly. I wanted to become a professional tap dancer overnight.

I have talked to hundreds of kids who want to have fewer fights with their parents and more freedom and respect in their lives. But that can't happen overnight. Just like becoming a professional tap dancer, you have to work at it. Even though some of these techniques may seem impossible for you to say or do, if you keep practicing, you will see a difference in your life.

You might not want to play as a team, preferring instead to yell and scream. Perhaps you actually think fighting with your parents is a fun thing to do. Fighting doesn't make anyone feel good about themselves, and nobody can make your life miserable except you; you have more control over your life than you realize! Use your new skills to stop many of the fights that happen at home, and see how you can make a real difference in your life.

### *Personal Goals*

1. Treat others the way you want to be treated.
2. When a problem comes up, find the right time to talk to your parents about it.
3. Practice using "I" messages when you talk.
4. If someone in your family starts yelling, calmly talk about how it makes you feel without yelling back.
5. Take a break from potential arguments whenever possible.
6. Avoid fights by "biting your tongue."
7. See how your family reacts when you are the first to apologize.
8. Help out whenever you can and watch how many benefits come back to you.
9. Practice using all the new communication skills you've learned to make life better at home.
10. Be a part of your family instead of fighting against them.

## Of Children
### by Kahlil Gibran

Your children are not your children.
They are the sons and daughters of Life's longing for
　itself.
And they come through you but not from you, yet they
　belong not to you.
You may give them your love but not your thoughts.
For they have their own thoughts.
You may house their bodies but not their souls.
For their souls dwell in the house of tomorrow, which you
　cannot visit, not even in your dreams.
You may strive to be like them, but seek not to make
　them like you.
For life goes not backward nor tarries with yesterday.

You are the bows from which your children are sent forth.
The archer sees the mark upon the path of the infinite,
and He bends you with His might that His arrows may
　go swift and far.
Let your bending in the archer's hand be for gladness;
For even as He loves the arrow that flies, so He loves also
　the bow that is stable.

# CHAPTER 6

# Room to Grow

## *PARENTS:*

### *Give Them Space*

It is our job as parents to prepare our children to cope with the laws of the world, and children must learn to function within the limits of society. However, as they get older this can no longer be done by telling them what to do or how to do it. If parents continue to manage and direct the lives of their adolescents, they will be met with resentment by kids who push their parents away. Parents must let go and give their kids more space.

Giving your teenager space, or "letting go," actually begins when they are quite young: when you leave your baby with a sitter for the first time, or let your toddler walk all by himself, or when you send your child off to her first day of preschool. Letting go also means giving up control. We can do this effectively by gradually letting go little by little as they make their own way in the world. Parents need to find a balance between holding on too tight and not being involved enough. As children grow, it is characteristic for them to assert more independence.

## Give Them Elbowroom

As children approach their teenage years, they may become defensive and secretive. This is a normal, natural process as they strive for their own independence. They must pull away in order to become whole and complete as individuals. With a good foundation, and an understanding and supportive family, youngsters can develop into healthy, wise teenagers who grow up to be healthy, balanced adults.

As they grow, let them express feelings of anger, guilt, sadness, and confusion. When children are unhappy, they may sulk or act out—if they want to be left alone, give them space to release anxiety. Do not nag, blame, shame, criticize, judge, or offer "I-told-you-so's" when they return to the family unit. Teach them not to hold grudges by welcoming them in with no strings attached. Move on and give them the opportunity to begin all over again.

> • Children need guidance and support.
> • Children need positive opportunities to learn from their mistakes.
> • Children need to be loved in spite of themselves.

Be there for your pre-teen or teenager without giving advice and pushing your beliefs onto them, or you might push them away completely. Love them unconditionally as they grow, or they will look elsewhere for love and acceptance.

> • Learn to listen with your eyes and your heart.
> • Respect your child's need for withdrawing.

- To give them privacy, knock on their bedroom door and wait to get invited in before entering.
- Do not snoop or pry.
- Do not solve their problems unless you have been asked to do so.
- Do not ask too many questions, but make yourself available to answer any questions they may have.
- Be an ear; really listen to what they have to say.
- Be supportive.
- Create a relationship of trust and honesty that allows your child to come to you with any question, concern, or problem.

---

Our children give us the opportunity to become the parents we always wished we'd had.  —*Dr. Louise Hart*

---

Children distrust anyone who betrays them. When they truly believe "You just don't understand," they will begin to build a barrier between parent and child. As children grow and spread their wings, the barrier of distrust will continue to grow and fester. When your teenager begins searching for trusting relationships and the meaning of life, make sure he finds meaning and trust when he talks to you.

## Let Go As They Grow

When my daughter started high school, I felt as if she had sprouted wings and was flying away. "I'm not leaving for college, Mom," she reminded me as I dried my teary eyes. Picking her up from school one day, I looked around at the other kids. What impressed me the most at school was the size of the students walking around; the girls looked liked women, and many of the boys had mustaches, hair on their legs, and hormones. I could not see their hormones, of course, but I am sure they were raging. My baby is going to spend the next four years with all those "big" people. As she walked out the door that morning, I had to keep reminding myself that she had become a young woman.

It must be time for me to loosen those proverbial apron strings. Sometimes they feel bound too tight. As I try to cut through them with my easygoing attitude, understanding, compassion, and sense of fairness, I find myself also wanting to pull the reins back in again.

As my daughter begins to experience a shift in development and behavior, I must also shift my style of parenting. By understanding and appreciating our differences and our essential shift in roles, I can let go of running her life and instead move into the role of counselor, guide, and mentor.

## Become Separate

As my daughter and I both get older, I see so many similarities in us. Like a baby who imitates Mommy, my teenage daughter often moves and speaks like me, reprimands her younger brother in the same manner and tone of voice that I so often use, and keeps her room in the same disarray I keep my office. When I am angry at my husband, I take on a certain kind of demeanor. When my daughter is angry with her brother, her tone of voice rivals mine. She is the young beauty that I once was. To look at pictures of me in my teens and twenties is to see the image of my daughter.

As she grows and begins to pull away, I notice that while she is so similar in her psychological-emotional makeup, she also can be very critical of me. It is common for parents to be scrutinized under the watchful eye of their "adult-in-training." They say things like "Mom, you should stand up straight." "Dad, don't do that, it embarrasses me." "Mom, those shoes don't go with that dress." "Dad, do you have to laugh so loud?" Parents do not like to be ordered around.

When this happens with my daughter, my anger builds at her "insolence." I am quick to take on the role of a typical-parent-who-knows-everything and you-can't-talk-to-me-that-way attitude. Journey then tries to remind me about fairness and justice and good communication skills, and she apologizes for telling me what to do.

It is often so hard to stop myself and really listen to her. I want to think I am in control, even though I am actually momentarily out of control when my anger surfaces. It is painful to have her be that occasional mirror that reflects my flaws. The fact that I occasionally carry my own mirror—checking my own moves and motives, wondering if I did or said the right thing in certain situations—makes me feel even more vulnerable.

As Journey analyzes my every move, she will continue to pull away from me and form her own ideas and belief system. As they say in most self-help programs, she will "take what she wants and leave the rest." I must prepare myself for this. I must allow her to grow gracefully into the person she is becoming. It involves letting go. It involves stepping aside from my need and desire to control every situation. It is time for me to allow my daughter to be an "adult-in-training" instead of the little girl who believed her mommy was her fairy godmother incarnate.

## A New Parental Job Description

I have a new job now; instead of taking care of my little girl, I must become a consultant to my teenager. I can now act as guidance counselor only when my counsel is asked for. I still may be able to magically soothe her ruffled feathers when a boy cancels a date, or the "perfect" bathing suit doesn't really fit right, but I can no longer just show up and tell her how to act, what to eat, what to wear, or anything that involves making decisions for her. It brings me enormous sorrow to have to retire as her fairy godmother. I loved buying clothes for my little girl. I loved brushing her hair and deciding whom she could play with after school. I enjoyed buying her books and signing her up for classes I thought she would love. I miss those days.

Many parents find that the moment when they are no longer able to hold on to their changing child is often when they become invisible or lackadaisical in their parenting. **That is a huge mistake.** Don't give up; they need you now more than ever. In fact, now is when they need you the most. They want to know that you trust them and their ability to make wise decisions. They want to know you are there for them, even if they act as if you do not exist.

What they do *not* want is your advice or your opinion or your critique of them or their friends. What they do require is respect, and the opportunity to express themselves fully. Be a good example. They want opportunities to discover who they are and what they believe in. Like the flowers in a garden, children have an inherent desire to bloom. Till the soil, plant the seeds, fertilize and water, nurture well, then stand back and watch your seedlings blossom, grow, and thrive.

## Recognize the Loss

As children grow up and become more of who they are, they need their parents less. It is from this place of loss, which can manifest as anger, or just not being needed in the same way, that many parents begin to have problems with their adolescents. The constant bickering and differing of opinions continues to grow and spread like a cancer until the relationship has been so badly damaged, the teenager no longer trusts or respects his parents, and the parents sadly give up hope, or completely withdraw their love and support.

Just as parents start to sense their kids are growing up and they are "losing them," the adolescents begin to see their parents as real people complete with faults and imperfections. Up until then, they viewed their parents as Godlike, and this new realization can be very frightening for most kids.

I interviewed a teenager in one of my communication skills classes. Sixteen-year-old Nicole discussed how her mom used to act and how she sees her now:

> My mom used to be really cool when I was little. I really looked up to her. I thought she was so beautiful, and I wanted to grow up to be just like her. But then she got sick and she gained a lot of weight. I guess I got mad at her for not being perfect anymore. When she gained weight she didn't look pretty anymore, and she just didn't move around like she used to. I guess I changed too when I started growing up, because I started thinking differently, and making my own decisions. My mom got better, but we started disagreeing and basically fighting about everything. She kept telling me I was too skinny and I was showing off. She put me down all the time. She wanted me to be her baby, and I'm not a baby anymore. I hate when she tells me what to do or embarrasses me in front of people. I guess I built up a lot of resentment toward her, and now we aren't very close.

On the other hand, one of the mothers in my parenting class expressed her concerns about her eight-year-old daughter:

Ever since Kara was a baby, we have been very close. But now I sense her starting to pull away. She talks to her friends and doesn't tell me what she's talking about. She no longer wants me to read her a bedtime story. I expected this sooner or later, but it feels like it's happening too soon. I feel really sad about this. It feels like a place in my heart is wounded. I don't want her to grow up and not need me anymore. And I don't want to push myself on her because I don't want her to hate me either.

This parental wound can run very deep. When your child first starts to pull away, the wound begins, and it continues to deepen as your child grows. Feeling, acknowledging, and understanding this sense of pain and loss is an important aspect in raising children, and is important in being able to reason fairly when dealing with adolescents and teens. When you can recognize where your feelings stem from, you do not have to disperse your negative feelings on innocent people. It is not fair to ground your teen from going to a party because you are feeling the pangs of separation.

---

Do not look back in anger, or forward in fear, but around in awareness.
—*James Thurber*

---

Adolescents, on the other hand, may experience anger when they realize their parents are real people with problems and feelings of their own. Michael Riera (*Uncommon Sense for Parents with Teenagers*, Celestial Arts, 1995, p. 29) writes, "In anger, one is active and seemingly in charge, instead of being in the more passive and potentially humiliating state of vulnerability. And teenagers, more than any other age group, will go to extremes to avoid humility and vulnerability. If parents can accept this fall from grace as inevitable rather than a personal attack, then they can learn a great deal about themselves. After all, some of this adolescent feedback hits the bull's-eye. It is also a clear sign that the parent-adolescent relationship needs to become more consultant and less managerial. If this shift can happen, family relations become fertile ground for the teenager to learn compassion and acceptance."

As children go through the stages of growth and development, it is normal for them to pull away. If you have a relationship steeped in anger, your child may pull away even more. You can find harmony and balance with your kids when you act as consultant or mentor, instead of acting as an overbearing, do-as-I-say, authoritative manager.

## Recognize Their Budding Sexuality

As pubescent hormones rage out of control, parents often have a difficult time accepting the physical changes occurring in their budding adolescents. This seems particularly difficult for mothers and daughters. It is the mother's discomfort with the fact that her baby is not a baby anymore. These young girls are now becoming sexual beings. When mother and father see this change occurring in their daughter—the budding breasts, the pouty lips, the shapely figure—they may have a difficult time identifying with what they see, which creates an unspoken, unidentifiable anxiety and anger deep within.

In many Third World countries and indigenous cultures, puberty is a stage of life that is acknowledged and celebrated with ritual. Preparation for the mating dance is a time-honored event in certain cultures where twelve- and thirteen-year-old girls are expected to marry and have children in keeping with the natural rhythm of their bodies. The foundation of our culture mandates that adolescents ripe with changing hormones must suppress these instincts and abstain from sexual behavior. Unfortunately, not all adolescents suppress these instincts.

Sherisa is the mother of a fourteen-year-old daughter. She said,

> I was furious with how my daughter was dressing. She looked like she was going to pick up someone in a bar or something. Then I saw all the girls at her school dressing like that and tried to figure out why. After talking about it with my therapist, I realized my daughter and I were fighting about clothes for nothing. She was just into the current fashion, and to me this was about sex and how sexy she looked. I was scared for her, and scared for me. Maybe a little jealous, too, because I don't look like that anymore! Taking her sexy clothes away and grounding her wasn't changing the way she dressed. I have to find a different way to approach her, gain her trust again, and find a way that lets us both feel good about this situation.

Our culture encourages the "model image." Young girls strive to look like the sultry model on the cover of a magazine. One thirteen-year-old girl in my seminar complained, "Guys like girls with cleavage. They watch TV shows like *Baywatch* that have all these beautiful girls on them. Even my dad reads *Playboy*. My mom wants plastic surgery for her face and thighs, and I probably will too." Our culture provides women and men of all ages with an abnormal viewpoint of the "normal" body, and a quick, surgical way to change what they do not like.

Most adult women dress for success, dress to please, or dress to entice. Their young counterparts do the same.

Not all women, or men, for that matter, show off their bodies, but most people try to look their best for a date, a job interview, to attract the opposite sex, or to get attention. Clothing is simply one of the first ways teenagers explore their changing roles.

Try to remember what it was like when you were a teenager. Did you have long hair or wear bell-bottoms? Did you wear a big peace sign around your neck, or flowers in your hair? Did you burn your bra in the 60s or wear see-through shirts in the 70s? Did you dye your hair green in the 80s? Every generation has a fad of its own that links it and gives it a sense of belonging.

What our sons and daughters need is a strong sense of themselves *before* they reach puberty, so they can trust their own instincts and find ways to feel good about themselves without always looking outside themselves for approval.

## Talk Openly About Sex

Along with growing up, making decisions, and accepting responsibility for one's actions, adolescents also deal with the issue of sex and sexuality. It is not something most parents want to talk about, yet it is often the underlying issue that most affects adolescents and their parents.

While it may be awkward to talk about sex with your kids, **you have to talk about it.** Be clear, honest, and upfront. Answer questions that are age appropriate. The old "Birds and Bees" story does not work for teenagers today.

Here are a few guidelines to follow:

- As you begin your conversation, do not assume anything about their sexuality, and do not rule anything out.
- Let your kids know what you think about teenage sex. They need a clear understand-

ing of your moral and religious values to formulate their own.

• Be realistic in your approach; remember what it was like when you were a teenager, and think about how your own teen may be feeling now.

• Discuss the importance of your child's taking responsibility for her body and her actions.

• Give her all the information available on safe sex, sexually transmitted diseases, and birth control. (Better safe than sorry!)

• Talk with your teen about the psychological, physical, and emotional aspects of giving oneself so completely in a relationship.

• Keep those lines of communication open so your adolescent feels trusting enough to come to you for facts and advice, instead of receiving misguided information from others.

Ultimately, parents have little control over what happens, and that can be frightening. In today's world, one night of unprotected sex can lead to more than teen pregnancy; it can lead to sexually transmitted diseases that can be fatal. The best you can do is make sure your teenagers are well informed. Teach them to understand how their bodies function sexually, and teach them to respect their bodies. Loving and trusting your kids no matter what, even when you are anxious about their behavior, is the best message you can convey.

## Teach Your Children Well

When teenagers have not learned respect for themselves and others, it shows in their behavior. A group of teenage girls discussed what it is like "in the real world." They said:

- "Some guys are so disrespectful, they whistle and make catcalls at me and my friends. It's so disgusting. Do they think that turns us on?"
- "There is a guy at school who's so rude. He pushes all the girls into their lockers and snaps the back of our bras when we walk down the hall. What gives him the right?"
- "How come guys call us 'honey' or 'baby'? It feels so demeaning."
- "I told this one guy I didn't want to go out with him. Now he calls me 'bitch' every time he sees me. He's telling his friends I'm a slut. I think that's sexual harassment or something like that."
- "I broke up with my boyfriend after one year of going out together. Now he calls my house all the time, follows me around at school, and talks to my friends about me. It feels really creepy to know he's kind of stalking me. Doesn't he have any self-respect?"

So many men have taken a blow to their identities because they did not have a vulnerable male role-model to identify with. At a time when the number of deadbeat dads and absentee fathers is at an all-time high, boys need their fathers. Even if dad is not available, young men need a male role-model to demonstrate how they can respect others, but above all, they must see how men show self-respect. They need someone to model the positive behavior they should exhibit. This male role-model could be a teacher, a counselor, a family friend, a relative, or someone from an organization such as Big Brothers/ Big Sisters.

I am not suggesting that mothers completely give up their adolescent sons to the male domain, because the mother–son relationship is equally as powerful. However, in my work with single mothers and families, I have seen many moms either pull away from their sons because they were uncomfortable with, or did not understand the inherent differences in the way men and women relate; or gave up because they spent countless years trying to get their sons to talk and share their feelings. I believe mothers have a responsibility to help their sons understand and respect the basic male–female differences of relating, and to help these young men find balance in their lives.

Both fathers and mothers must set good examples for their sons. Spitting on the ground, treating their friends with disrespect, being unkind to animals, using power and control to dominate others are negative behaviors that are not essential to masculinity. If all boys (and girls) were raised with a sense of self-appreciation and respect for the world around them, mothers and fathers could relax as their teenagers begin interacting with the opposite sex. Children deserve to be raised with a sense of autonomy *and* connection to family, friends, and to society.

---

Children are likely to live up to what you believe of them.       —*Lady Bird Johnson*

---

## Respect Their Cave

One of the many ways adolescents discover themselves is by withdrawing to think things through from their own perspective. Teenage boys and girls retreat to the cave of their room. They need to be left alone. They turn up their music to tune out. Teenage girls tend to talk on the phone. Just like their adult counterparts, they need to talk to remember their problems or to forget about them. They need to talk it out to understand themselves on a deeper level. By retreating into their caves, kids can assimilate what is going on in their lives and then forget about it as they move on.

In one of my seminars, twelve-year-old Maya said:

> My mom can talk on the phone for hours. She even cooks dinner while she's talking. She tells all her problems to her friends and to my aunt. One time, she stayed on the phone for over three hours! But every time I want to talk to one of my friends, my mom says, 'Three minutes, Maya.' If I ever get grounded, she takes away the phone. She can't live without it, but she expects me to. I don't get a chance to talk about my life with my friends, but my mom gives me major chances to hate her for being so unfair.

Kids can get very stressed out at school. Classwork, homework, projects, grades, and peer pressure can be extremely overwhelming. Going to their room to relax and unwind is a necessary and healthy reaction to anger and stress. It provides them with a way to let go of anger and stress instead of letting it grow and fester inside.

In his book *Men Are from Mars, Women Are from Venus,* Dr. John Gray discusses one of the biggest differences between men and women: coping with stress. Gray says:

> Men become increasingly focused and withdrawn while women become increasingly overwhelmed and emotionally involved. At these

times, a man's needs for feeling good are different from a woman's. He feels better by solving problems while she feels better by talking about problems. Not understanding and accepting these differences creates unnecessary friction in our relationships.

Gray continues:

When a man is stressed he will withdraw into the cave of his mind and focus on solving a problem. He generally picks the most urgent problem or the most difficult. He becomes so focused on solving this one problem that he temporarily loses awareness of everything else. Other problems and responsibilities fade into the background. At such times, he becomes increasingly distant, forgetful, unresponsive, and preoccupied.

Children may demonstrate both male *and* female traits, thereby confusing their parents. Both girls and boys may become focused and withdrawn, or overwhelmed and emotional all at the same time. They dash to their room and slam the door. The music begins to blare, the parent begins to fume. "Turn that damn thing down," Dad bellows. The music gets cranked up higher. Emotions reach an all-time high.

Like Gray's "Venusian" who needs to talk about her feelings to feel better, some children also need to talk to feel better. If they are ready and willing, then parents can take the opportunity to listen without interrupting, correcting, judging, or solving. Let them ramble on if necessary; this freedom helps them to express worries, frustrations, concerns, disappointments, and joy. Through our listening and support, our children find caring, understanding, and their own identity.

One of the many ways adolescents discover themselves is by withdrawing to think things through.

Respect their differences, and remember that they need to retreat. Create a home environment that encourages and respects their need to cool off and figure things out.

## Compromise

We must have healthy boundaries and rules within our homes that each family member can live by. Allowing children to participate in the creation of those rules gives them an opportunity for decision making, team playing, and active participation in their own lives.

Everyone must compromise to a certain extent because a child's perception of limits and rules will differ greatly from those of his parents. In all decision making, it is important for the parent to remember that kids originally came from a faraway land where life was perfect. The things that are important to them will not always have the same importance to their mom or dad. While men may be from Mars and women may be from Venus, parents must remember that the place kids originally came from has its own rules, ideals, and belief systems. However, these differences do not justify abusive, inconsiderate, disrespectful behavior by parents or their children.

Fifteen-year-old Kathryn was grounded for four months because she climbed out of her bedroom window one night to go to a party at a nearby friend's house after her parents had told her she could not go out. She said:

They didn't give me any good reason for not going; they just said I couldn't go. They weren't willing to compromise or work anything out. They pretty much always say no to things I want to do, especially anything new. When they found out I was gone, they got really mad. I got grounded from the phone, baby-sitting, and hanging out with my friends. My parents also cemented my bedroom window shut, took the doorknob off my bedroom door, and made me sleep in their room for a few weeks. My parents treat me like they hate me now and I feel like they'll never trust me again. I did one thing they didn't like, and they took away my life. I feel like I have nothing to live for anymore. I wish I could die.

Parents must remember that relationships take years of nurturing, caring, compassion, and respect to make them work. A teenager who is already angry and untrusting needs opportunities to believe in you and to believe in herself.

A dialogue to prevent sneaking out in the first place might have sounded like this:

> *Kathryn:* Can I go to a party at Tony's house to-night?
>
> *Parents:* What kind of a party is it?
>
> *Kathryn:* Just a bunch of people are going to hang out.
>
> *Parents:* Will his parents be home?
>
> *Kathryn:* I don't know.
>
> *Parents:* Will you please find out?
>
> *Kathryn:* I'm fifteen now. Why do parents always have to be there?
>
> *Parents:* We feel more comfortable if a responsible adult is somewhere in the background. We're concerned about drugs and alcohol.
>
> *Kathryn:* There are drugs and alcohol at a lot of the parties these days. I'm really careful, and

you know I'd never do that stuff. Plus, if the party does have any bad stuff, I'll just come home. Can't you trust me?

**Parents:** We trust you, Kathryn. It's all the other kids we're not sure about. It's hard just to let you go anywhere you want. You're a great kid. But everything's happening so fast: parties, dating, driving. You're growing up so fast, it makes us a little nervous. See if Tony's parents will be home. If not, we'll talk about this some more, and see what we can work out.

As families create rules, limits, boundaries, and set up curfews, teamwork and compromise will go a long way toward bridging the gap that causes kids to rebel and overreact. Working together with your kids to create safe situations that work for everyone creates mutual respect and trust.

If you do have to say no, expect anger, door slamming, and hard feelings. This is a normal reaction from these strange aliens disguised as teenagers. Give them time to cool off. Let them vent their disappointment and anger in their room. If they give you the cold shoulder, remain the example of strength, love, and forgiveness.

---

Being a teenager is a temporary condition.

---

I asked a group of parents with kids between the ages of ten and seventeen about the kind of issues they compromise on in their household. These families all have hard-and-fast rules they do not compromise on such as: basic family values, issues regarding drugs and alcohol, and physical violence.

The responses to the things they do compromise on were as varied as the families themselves:

• We bargained on curfew. Our fifteen-year-old son wanted to come home at 1 A.M., and we said midnight. After we all talked about our limits and boundaries and what was important to us, my husband and I decided that 12:30 A.M. was our limit, and our son was fine with that.

• I think rules should always be age appropriate. Our son is nine. He wanted to buy those really baggy jeans. I immediately said 'NO!' Of course, he shut down and got mad at me. I calmly started a discussion on what we each believed was appropriate clothing for school, grandma's house, and going to a friend's house. I found out that he didn't want those really baggy pants, just loose ones that he could move around in. By giving him a chance to talk, and listening to what he said, I found out what he really meant, and he listened to what I had to say too. It was great because now we understand each other.

• My thirteen-year-old has beautiful hair. At the end of summer, she wanted to dye her hair green. I nearly died when she told me that. I knew that if I didn't give in, she'd probably do it anyway. So we talked about why she wanted to do it, and for how long she wanted to keep it that color. I told her I was worried about the impression she would make on her teachers when school started. I offered to buy her a good product to use so she wouldn't ruin her hair, if she agreed to wait until two months after school started so her teachers wouldn't have a bad impression of her right off the bat. We found a way to compromise, and it worked for both of us. It's not always so easy, but it sure beats her rebelling against me. At least now she thinks I'm fair. It really wasn't a life-or-death situation anyway.

• Our issue is always about clean rooms. My sixteen-year-old daughter keeps her room like a pigsty. When we talked about it, she said she didn't care about her room. I told her I cared about how the rest of the house looked. She was willing to keep her junk out of the rest of the house, and I agreed she could just keep the door to her messy room closed. The day we do our major housecleaning, she also puts her stuff away in her room. It's a compromise that keeps peace in our family that we all can live with.

These families all found ways to talk together, to listen to one another, to value the opinions expressed, and to come up with solutions that everyone could live with. This gives kids a way to be heard and feel respected. When they feel heard and respected, and realize that they have reasonable control over their lives, their need for power struggles and troublemaking quickly diminishes.

## Give Them Your Time

The pursuit of giving your children room to grow and letting go does not happen all at once. It is a gradual process that takes place over time. Little children need to be able to make simple, specific choices, so when they grow up, they can make positive and safe choices as they become almost completely independent of their parents.

As your children become teenagers, do not leave them to their own resources just because they now have minds of their own. Include them in your life, even though they may be excluding you from the details of their lives. Share your thoughts, let them know what you do each day, and where you will be.

Words are not enough; show you love them and care about them by your actions. Help them through troubled times of peer pressure, school stress, and hormonal hurricanes by being supportive. At this stage, it is important to remember not to tell them what to do. "Be there" with your unconditional love, emotional support, and a willingness to let go and let them grow.

We must give our children the freedom of thought and action, while remembering we do not own their bodies or their minds. We must give each child the opportunity to choose his own way, wherever it may lead. If children are raised with self-respect, a strong sense of self-appreciation, and an understanding of what is morally right, we provide ourselves with the opportunity to feel trust and pride as our children make their own way in the world.

Give your children a solid foundation of trust and self-respect from the beginning, and allow the necessary space to let them grow into who they are becoming. Remember, children come through us, not to us. We must provide the cocoon for our children to grow. Then, like a butterfly, we must let them loose to fly, while always providing a safe haven for them to fly back to, no matter what!

## *Personal Goals*

1. Ask your kids to help problem-solve when difficulties arise.

2. Have open discussions at mealtime and let everyone safely share their opinions.

3. Become the "mentor" instead of the "manager."

4. Work on letting go of control.

5. Respectfully ask your kids what they think about certain issues or ideas.

6. Teach your teenagers about safe sex and self-respect.

7. Listen carefully without making them feel guilty or offering your opinion (unless asked).

8. Teach your children to show respect for the opposite sex.

9. Be willing to compromise.

10. Do not give up on your teenagers; they need you now more than ever.

# *KIDS:*

## *Breaking Free*

When children are young, they count on their parents to take care of them. They look up to them and try to copy everything their parents do. Some little kids even go through a stage of wanting to be just like their parents. Little kids generally follow the examples their moms and dads set for them. Most parents teach their kids:

- how and when to talk
- how and where to walk
- what and when to eat
- what to wear here and there
- manners, both good and bad
- what to think about anything
- what to feel about everything

Children learn things from their parents just by watching them. They learn to trust them and to depend on them. When a baby is too little to feed himself, Mom or Dad feeds the baby. When a child is just learning to walk, her parents hold her hand to make sure she doesn't fall. Most parents always try to be there for their kids as much as they can.

As we get older, we slowly pull away from our parents. This is an automatic process and a completely normal thing for us to do. We begin to create our own life and make our own decisions. Growing up can be hard because sometimes the decisions we have to make are not that easy. Growing up can be hard on our parents, too. It seems like some parents have a hard time dealing with the fact that, eventually, we all have to grow up.

## Life Was Different When We Were Younger

When you were younger, your parents always told you what to do. If you picked up an old candy wrapper that you found lying on the sidewalk, your parents would tell you to put it down. They would tell you never to pick things up off the yucky ground. They were in charge, no questions asked. Of course you had your little tantrums and screaming fits; that is considered normal behavior in that magical land where kids originally come from.

Just when parents start to get the hang of:

- changing your diapers,
- feeding you,
- teaching you how to talk,
- helping you learn to walk,
- protecting you from everything that comes near you,

They "suddenly" wake up to find you have grown. Now they have to:

- deal with your new "attitude."
- stand back as you make your own decisions.
- allow you to stay out late.
- accept friends of yours they may not even know.
- watch you drive a car.

Eventually most parents learn to let go and give you more freedom, but you have to give them time. Some parents learn slower than others, and some parents have a harder time letting go. But the nicer you are to them, and the more mature and responsible you act, the faster they will catch on to the fact that you need space. Then you will have more of the freedom and fun that you have been waiting for all along.

---

Learning how to live a good life takes a lot of practice.
—*Alex Packer, Ph.D.*

---

## Time Flies When You Are Growing Up

Imagine having a puppy that you love more than anything else in the world. He always plays with you and obeys when you tell him to: sit, lie down, get up, stay, or shake. You never have any problems with him. He is the most playful little puppy you have ever met. As your puppy becomes a big dog, however, he stops listening to you as much as he used to. When you tell him to come, he ignores you and walks the other way.

This is basically what parents experience as we grow up and start to break away from them. One of the hardest reasons for them to let go of us is because it happens so fast. We know that growing up and having our own freedom takes a long time, but most adults disagree. They say things like "Oh, my baby is growing up so fast!" or, "Time flies too fast," or, "It seems like just yesterday when I changed your diapers." In the eyes of an adult, time goes by really quickly.

My grandfather told me the reason adults think time passes by so fast is because the older you are, the more time you have to compare to. Time is relative. That is why parents feel as if we become teenagers practically overnight; but to us, it seems like it takes forever.

It seems like the more we want control over our own lives, the more our parents want to keep protecting us. We have to find a place in between living in our own world and our parents completely running our lives. That way everyone will be happy.

## Parents and Their Rules

Sometimes parents have such a hard time letting us go that they get worried about what might happen to us once we start making our own decisions, going to parties, dating, and driving. Because of this, parents usually make up a bunch of rules that they think will keep us safe. I interviewed a fifteen-year-old girl who chose to remain anonymous. She said,

> My mom has always said she's tried to be a good mom. She's a single mom, and works really hard to support me and my sister, but she's always acted like she's never trusted me. She has always told me what to do my whole life. If I ever did anything wrong, she'd just scream at me. I spent most weekends taking care of my little sister because my mom worked and we couldn't afford a baby-sitter. I wasn't allowed to talk on the phone or have a friend over to keep me company, so I had to sneak phone calls so I could talk to my friends. I felt lonely most of the time, but my mom just kept telling me what to do and how I should feel appreciative about everything. She told me how I should dress, how I should act, and even how I should walk. I guess the older I get, the more I resent her. She never took the time to know the real me.
>
> She has so many rules and schedules we

have to follow. I wish she would just have fun once in a while. Now, I want her to get off my back. I'm not such a bad person, I don't think. But I guess I've changed. Now my friends tell me I'm a show-off. That's just because I started smoking, wearing makeup, and I also told everyone I'm not a virgin anymore. My mom would die if she knew all this stuff. I guess you could say I'm not her baby anymore. She can't tell me what to do now.

I think this situation could have easily been prevented. It would have helped if the daughter and her mom had a more open relationship. An open relationship would have allowed them to talk about their problems. For example:

- If the daughter felt that taking care of her sister every weekend wasn't fair, she would be able to talk to her mom about it, and they could work together to find a solution that works for all of them.
- If the mom believed she couldn't trust her daughter for some reason, they would be able to talk about that together, with each of them taking turns to talk about her feelings, while the other one listens. They could work together to find ways to gain each other's trust again.
- In this relationship, if the daughter told her mom she was lonely, the mother would have told her not to feel that way. If they had a more open relationship, the daughter could have told her mom that she was feeling lonely because she was never allowed to

be with her friends. She and her mom could come up with ideas to solve the problem so they both feel good.

If you have a parent who has many unfair rules, doesn't trust you at all, screams at you for everything, and grounds you at the drop of a hat, you need to take matters into your own hands. The mother in the last situation doesn't know how to parent her two daughters any better than she already does. She believes that the only way she could keep her daughter out of trouble and the only way she could teach her right from wrong would be to tell her how to live her life.

What you have to do if your parents do not let you make enough of your own decisions is to communicate with them. If you want your parents to have more trust in you, it is up to you to prove to them that they can trust you. All kids know that when they act mature, responsible and trustworthy, they gain more freedom and respect from their parents and the other adults in their lives.

---

Eventually most parents learn to let go and give you more freedom, but you have to give them time.

---

## The Way Some Adults Judge Us

As preteens and teenagers start to do more things on their own, their parents are always worried about what stupid thing their children are going to do next, or what kind of trouble they are going to get themselves into. Adults hardly ever trust teenagers and usually do not try to get to know the real person inside. They usually judge teens by their attitude and their appearance. So if a kid wears baggy clothes and has purple hair and a nose ring, adults automatically think that means trouble.

The manager of a clothing store told me, "When we see groups of teenagers come in the store, we call out the guards to keep an eye on them. These kids always steal us blind, so we have undercover security patrolling around to make sure these kids don't stick clothes or other items in their backpacks, or in their jackets." She also said, "We've had groups of girls come in to try on underwear. They take all the underwear out of the boxes and put them on under their own clothing, then they walk out of the store. We can't afford to trust any kid who walks into our store."

Kids continually blow it for themselves. By acting irresponsible, lying, and cheating, we lose the potential trust we possibly could have gained. We need to show people that teenagers are capable of being polite, responsible, and trustworthy, so we can gain the trust of the adults around us. By acting stupid and doing things that are illegal or that will upset the "adults in charge," kids keep themselves in the chains they are trying to get rid of.

If you are one of those people who do not steal, it must make you mad to have to pay for what other kids are doing. In some stores, kids can't even bring in their backpacks. Things like this cause the "good kids" to suffer as well.

I asked a few teenagers what they had to say about this. Here are some of their replies:

- Isaac said, "I feel like wherever I go adults don't trust me just because of the clothes I wear. It's totally unfair."
- Siobhan said, "I would never steal; I'd be too scared of getting caught. But it's not fair because all the kids who do steal completely blow it for the rest of us."
- Aleisha said, "I stole some candy once. I

didn't think much about it; I just did it. Then I stole a pair of really cool socks. I got caught, and the store sent me to their security room. It was so scary. My parents were really cool about it, though. They helped me a lot, because they didn't yell at me or ground me. They took me home and we talked about respecting other people's property and stuff like that. I actually listened to them, and they helped me understand what it would feel like to me if someone took something of mine. I'd be really mad if somebody ripped me off. I realized stealing is not a cool thing to do. If I can't afford something, then I guess it just isn't meant to be mine. Anyway, I don't want to end up in jail. I swear I will never steal again."

Aleisha was really lucky that her parents were cool about the situation. Sometimes we can learn a lot when we actually listen when our parents talk to us. When our parents talk to us about what we did wrong (not necessarily a lecture, just a conversation), we are able to understand and even ask questions. If your parents are not so cool, you have to learn to be responsible for yourself so you can make things easier in your life. If you can learn to take responsibility for your actions, you won't have to be so dependent on your parents.

## Try to Understand

As kids begin to understand why parents and other adults act the way they do, it becomes easier to accept the idea that it is normal for adults to think, feel, and communicate differently than we do. After all, in that faraway land where kids came from, life was perfect.

When we forget the basic truth that our parents are different, we end up angry and frustrated. This anger and frustration can lead to misunderstandings and family fights. Then kids hate their parents and try to rebel. I have seen a lot of people I know do everything they can to rebel against their parents. It usually includes things they know will make their parents mad. For example, they:

- don't try very hard in school.
- experiment with drugs and alcohol.
- hang out with people they know their parents would disapprove of.
- run away.

You may think rebelling is the way to break free from your parents. What you don't realize is that you will be the one who will suffer the most from doing stupid things.

## Some Solutions

Now that you're entering the adult world, you have to learn how to fit in. There would probably be less rebellion on your part if you had a little more freedom. But the more you rebel, the less freedom you have. Kids want more freedom to do what they want, more fairness and understanding in their relationships at home, and more opportunities for fun in their lives. These are the three basic things kids want from life.

In order to have more freedom from your parents, you need to show them you're responsible enough to deserve it. All through this book, I've shown you many ways to accomplish this. Here are some reminders:

- Do things around the house without being asked.
- Offer to help your parents when it looks like they could use some assistance.
- When you and your parents are fighting, stop and take a break.
- Do and say things to make your parents feel appreciated.
- Understand that adults think differently than we do, and that is why they act and react in such a different way.
- If you're asked to do something, do it immediately before someone gets mad.
- Say "please" and "thank you" (the "Magic Words") as often as possible without sounding too corny.
- If you need appreciation from your parents, instead of rebelling and being rude, show your parents examples by appreciating others around you.

Sometimes doing these things can be a drag. I know I've said it before, but when your parents see that you're acting more mature and responsible, you end up with more freedom, fairness, and fun. That's just how it works with adults.

## Be Unique

Everyone wants to fit in and be liked by others. Some people want it so badly that they would be willing to do almost anything in order to be accepted by their peers. Some people are so desperate to be accepted that they would willingly change their current lifestyle and do things they wouldn't normally do just to get people to like them. But the truth is, you have to like yourself and who you really are (not who you are trying to be) before anyone else will really like you.

---

This above all: to thine own self be true.
—*William Shakespeare*

---

I asked a group of teenagers why they dyed their hair such outrageous colors and wore such unusual clothes. The two main responses that I received were:

- "To be unique."
- "To be different from my parents."

One of the reasons so many kids dress weirdly, dye their hair different colors, and pierce a million different body parts is because it gives them a sense of being different from their parents. Being different and forming our own ideas is an important part of growing up and separating from the adults in our lives.

I interviewed a deputy sheriff from northern California. I asked her, "What's the first thing you think when you see a teenager with baggy clothes, dyed hair, and his body pierced in many different places?" She said,

Usually the ones who dress like that are really trying to stand out. They are screaming out to be noticed. I know they aren't all bad, and it almost doesn't matter what they are wearing. Whether you are wearing baggy, torn-up clothes, or skintight expensive clothes doesn't really matter because everyone is capable of stealing and anyone can be doing drugs. Some kids just want to be noticed and they don't want to get in trouble for it, so all they do is dress differently. They are the ones who find safer ways of being unique and expressing themselves.

When you think about it, it's kind of funny, because everyone goes to the same clothing stores to get clothes they think are unique, and everyone dyes their hair different colors in order to be unique. But everyone is doing the same thing, so it isn't being unique. To really be unique, you have to learn to be yourself and feel a sense of individuality inside yourself.

---

To be nobody but yourself in a world which is doing its best to make you just like everybody else means to fight the greatest battle that ever was or ever will be.

—*e.e. cummings*

---

If you want to be different and unique, it is important to find safe ways to express yourself so you don't hurt anyone. Instead of turning to drugs, alcohol, or an unhealthy lifestyle, you can express yourself by:

- finding what you like to do, and doing it!
- following your dreams.
- getting involved in sports, music, art, or acting classes to express your creative side.
- not following the fads but creating your own.

It is also important to find a few good friends who will like you and care about you no matter what. If you don't choose your friends carefully, who will you have to be there for you if your friends are all stoned and couldn't care less about whatever you need? Find friends who appreciate you for who you really are. You might react to this advice the same way you react to a fly on your nose; you just flick it off. But one day, you just might need a friend to be with you, to listen to you, and to help you. So try to make friends with at least one person who you know will be there for you when you need him or her.

Michael Pritchard is a well-known stand-up comedian who has been working with kids for over twenty years. He travels all over America talking with kids and performing at schools and on television. I was lucky enough to interview him in the comfort of his living room. Michael said,

> Everybody is looking for a sense of individuality, and they look for it on the outside for the external. But that's not where it is. Uniqueness is on the inside in the calmness. When people are wise to the fact that when things are crazy, be calm; and when things are calm, be crazy. That's uniqueness. I was talking to a boy who said, "High school is a place where kids spend all their time trying to fit into a group that doesn't exist." Say to yourself: This is me. This is who I am. And I am a gift not just to me, but to you.

Michael also said, "Learn to accept yourself. Learn to really believe that you are here for a special reason—and that on the road of life you will only have one constant companion, so make sure that you are good company for yourself."

Michael shared a story about a girl he had met named Carly:

> Carly said that when she was thirteen, everyone made fun of her and picked on her including her mother, her stepfather, and the kids at school. She decided she was going to try to find something that she would like to do. She went to the music teacher and asked him what instrument she could play. Even the music teacher was hard on her. He responded with "Well, obviously someone your size wouldn't look good behind the violin." Carly said she was so angry, she decided to learn how to play the violin. She built a room for herself in the basement so she could play whenever she wanted to. Eventually she became so good at playing the violin that she was given a chance to audition for the best musical conservatory in America. She decided she would play a piece from Bach. When the bow hit the third note, she knew she had won the scholarship. But that wasn't really important to her. She said she looked over at her stepfather, and he had tears in his eyes. She didn't know if he was ashamed that he had never said anything encouraging to her, or if he was finally proud of her for something. But that wasn't really important to her either. She said, "The thing that was important was that I had found a reason to love myself."

If you have a hard time loving yourself unconditionally, look deep inside yourself and find things you like to do. Be proud of yourself for your accomplishments and the person you are inside. We all have to love ourselves in order to get through the ups and downs of life. It's really important to find a reason to honor yourself and love who you are. Try to find something about yourself that teaches you that you are a very important part of life.

By changing who you are in order to be like others, you betray yourself. You're not being you; you're trying to be someone else. You have to learn to be yourself and love yourself before anyone else can like you.

## What Some Adults Think About Kids

I have been told that when parents describe us, sometimes they make us sound like monsters. Parents who have teens give warning threats to parents with younger kids: "Watch out when your child becomes a teenager," or, "You just wait until your child is older, then you'll see."

At the same time, kids are talking to their friends about how "All of a sudden, my parents are being really strict. My mom keeps yelling at me about everything now," or, "My parents just made all of these new rules. It seems like they think I don't know how to take care of myself and they can't trust me anymore."

Our parents have been told all kinds of evil stories about us: from the terrible twos to the troublesome teenager. As we get older, our parents practically expect us to turn into wild monsters and totally fall apart. It's up to us to prove all of those "old wives' tales" wrong.

We have to be careful not to buy into their stories. Since many parents expect their kids to become all those horrible things they heard about, it can be very easy for kids to believe those thoughts and actually become those things without even realizing it. In other words, be careful not to mess up and do all the things parents are warned about. By showing them that we are still normal people, and by using better communication skills, we can gain back any freedom, trust, and respect we may have lost along the way.

If you act responsibly, hopefully your parents will realize that you're more mature than what people told them to expect from your age group. They will finally realize you're not a potential monster but a human being who is capable of dealing with responsibility, therefore capable of having much more freedom. If your parents can't see you for who you really are, you still have to take responsibility for yourself in order to make a difference in your own life.

## Holding On

Even though it's natural for kids to break away from their parents eventually, we have to be careful not to break away too soon. As teenagers, we still need them for many things like:

- shelter
- food
- transportation
- money
- protection
- love and support

If we didn't have the basic things our parents provide for us, it would be like falling from an airplane without a parachute. In other words, we need our parents to provide us with the basic things for our survival. Every child on Earth is entitled to all this and much more, including lots of love. But there are some kids who think life on the streets is better than the violent abuse they received at home. If this is your situation, then please try to get help from a local shelter, church, or home for runaways. You deserve love, too.

I think the biggest disease this world suffers from in this day and age is the disease of people feeling unloved.

—*Princess Diana*

Hold on to your parents for as long as you can. If you break away from them too soon, who will you have when you need someone to help you? Once you're willing to learn how to understand the way adults think and react, you will find that it will be easier to live with them.

Next time you fight with your parents, remember how different you are. They think one way; you think another way. They see life differently than you do. They can't help wanting you to be their little baby forever. But if you use good communication skills, act respectful, and let them know they can trust you, you can grow up without too much of a struggle, while still keeping a loving relationship with your family.

### *Personal Goals*

1. Break free without getting yourself in trouble.
2. Go easy on your parents. Letting go can be hard on them.
3. Realize that parents make rules to protect you, not to be mean.
4. Show that you are responsible enough to have more freedom.
5. Accept the ups and downs of life.
6. Pick your friends carefully.
7. Find safe ways to be unique.
8. Prove to your parents that they can trust you.
9. Stay true to yourself.
10. Be responsible for your own behavior.

# CHAPTER 7

# An Ounce of Prevention

## *PARENTS:*

### *Testing the Limits of Your Love*

Perhaps one of the most difficult challenges of parenting is when adolescents begin to challenge the attitudes and beliefs of their parents. You cannot force your child to uphold your belief system or respect your values, and tightly pulling in the reins can be teenage-rationale for choosing to engage in sex, drinking, or drug abuse.

Parents teach their kids to "just say no," but the truth is, kids have had more practice saying yes. We have spent our children's lifetime teaching them to say "yes":

- "Yes, Mom."
- "Yes, Dad."
- "Yes, I'll do that now."
- "Yes, I'll do what you say."

They have gotten into trouble for saying "no":

- "No, I don't wanna go."
- "No, I won't wear that."
- "No, I won't clean my room right now."
- "No, I don't wanna do what you say."


Adolescents are used to saying yes. They say yes to their teachers. They are expected to say yes at home. They say yes to avoid being left out. They say yes to fit in with their crowd. They have not had much practice at successfully saying "No."

The behavioral change that comes about in adolescence can bring confusion, vulnerability, and emotional pain for many kids. As Journey and I watched her childhood friends turn into teenagers, we sadly saw the slow demise of the once-happy, carefree kids who used to come over to our house to play. Now, so many of those kids are smoking, getting bad grades in school, beginning to experiment with drugs, experiencing suicidal urges, and admitting their parents have been slapping them for years.

Journey asked me, "What's happening to everyone, Mom? It's so sad. Their parents just don't understand." "What will it take to make the parents understand?" I asked. Her answer came straight from her heart: "It's so simple. They need to listen to their kids. They need to be more understanding. But most of all, they just need to be fair. Everyone is getting in trouble for stupid things, like chewing gum in class, or coming home ten minutes late. When their parents find out about the 'crime,' the kids get grounded, yelled at, or hit. It doesn't make sense."

What does make sense is keeping the lines of communication with your kids wide open. Become a good listener. Do not give up on your kids as they branch out and test the icy-cold water (and they will test it). Remember that individuating from parents is a normal, natural process for adolescents. Let go of being their manager, and become their mentor. During this process it is imperative for parents to let go of expecting results, telling their kids what to do and how to do it, and trying to solve all their problems. If you focus on remaining supportive and understanding, instead of threatening and controlling, you create a safe haven where your kids can come with their unanswered questions and concerns.

---

It is hard to be a parent today, but it is even harder to be a kid.                                   —*President Bill Clinton*

---

## Parents Can Help

Kids want fairness, freedom, and fun. They expect you to be fair, and they assume you will provide them with the necessary opportunities to feel carefree and have fun. Be spontaneous with them.

- Go running or bike riding together to get their energy out.
- Hang up a punching bag and let them work off steam.
- Go to an amusement park and ride a roller coaster for safe thrills.
- Climb to new heights in the safety of a rock-climbing class to build confidence.

When parents are too strict, kids end up with virtually no decision-making skills. They do not have the opportunity to think for themselves. When parents say "Think for yourself," it is often laced with "Do as I say." This causes confusion and conflict, and kids end up either surrendering or rebelling. When faced with peer pressure, they are unable to "just say no." Parents owe it to their kids to establish guidelines that inspire them to use common sense and think things through.

The father of a thirteen-year-old boy said, "I think I'm pretty fair, but if I picked my son up from a party and saw beer cans and wine bottles all over the place, I'd be really mad at him. I'd probably yell at him, ground him, and never let him go to a party again."

It is natural to feel very concerned about your child's behavior. However, if you yank your kid out of the party, assume everyone is guilty, ground him for being in that situation in the first place, and act as though you don't trust him, your child ends up feeling humiliated, angry with you, untrustworthy, and rebellious. This creates a setup for your child to live up to your negative expectations.

## Contain Your Anger

Whether your teenager was drinking or not, there is a better way to deal with this situation. Begin by learning containment: *parents must contain their anger*. If you lash out by screaming, yelling, hitting, or threatening your child, you can cause him to shut down and pull away from you. When you blame or attack him, his self-protective nature kicks in and he fights back.

Parents should think about the situation first before acting out. You can:

- Assess the situation as calmly as possible.
- Reserve judgment until you can find out the details and get the whole story.

- Assume your child is trustworthy instead of automatically condemning him.

This is one of those critical situations where you can choose to let your child explain what was going on, and listen to what he has to say, or you can make negative assumptions and accusations. If you react negatively, without hearing his side of the story, he could come away from this situation saying "You don't trust me anyway, so I might as well drink." Adolescents who feel the need to exert their power may take drugs, smoke, drink, have premature sex, or use over- or undereating to "get back at you," because these are the only aspects of their lives they think they can control.

When you practice containment, really listen, trust your child, and create a mutually respectful relationship, you establish an environment in which your child can maintain his self-respect. This provides him with the freedom to act responsibly in the future, instead of giving him a reason to hate you and childishly "get back at you." Kids need opportunities to learn to trust their own judgment, and to prove to you that you can trust them. In a situation like this, it can take tremendous discipline and forethought not to fly into a rage. You can say "I want to take a few minutes to think about this," which goes over much better than "I can't deal with your behavior." Take time to cool off. When you resume the conversation, both you and your teenager will be more relaxed. Find that loving place in your heart and begin anew.

## Let Them Learn

On the other hand, when parents enable their kids by continually bailing them out, fixing their problems, and not setting limits for appropriate behavior, kids never learn from the consequences of their actions or gain the wisdom and common sense they need to survive in the world. Kids remain emotionally stunted when parents contribute to their immature behavior by continually rescuing them and solving their problems.

For example, when your child is young you:

- continually bail her out when she doesn't turn in her book-report on time by making excuses to her teacher.
- pay for the window she broke instead of having her pay for it out of her allowance.
- let her get away with taking a little piece of candy from the store without paying for it.
- let her drink alcohol.

When they are older, kids can translate this kind of behavior to:

- "My parents will get me out of this."
- "Don't worry, my parents will pay for it."
- "I only stole one pair of jeans from the store."
- "It's okay, my parents let me drink when I was younger."

Instead of constantly fixing all their problems, parents must provide their kids with guidelines for healthy decision-making at a very early age. Give them opportunities to make decisions. No matter how insignificant it may seem to you, this decision-making ability empowers your child.

## Set Reasonable Boundaries

Children depend on their parents to teach them to deal constructively with life's issues. They need boundaries, and it is up to the parents to set fair, appropriate, and reasonable ones. You can begin by setting little boundaries along the way. When your children are young, simple boundaries that expand into bigger ones as your kids get older may include:

- Treating other people the way you want to be treated.
- Not taking your big brother's toys without asking his permission.
- Not hitting, pinching, or biting.
- Being kind to animals (i.e., pet the dog gently).
- Eating healthy food and taking care of your body.

As your adolescent begins to mature, continue to expand the healthy boundaries. These may include:

- Being kind to everyone in the house.
- Upholding the house rules.
- Not swearing (parents can model this behavior too!).
- Not smoking.
- Always telling the truth.

These are ideals. No one is perfect all the time. Doing the best you can gives you the right to ask the same of your child.

When your children do misbehave, you must follow through with *reasonable* consequences so they can learn and grow. In chapter 5, I discuss positive solutions for kids' mistakes or "miss takes" that give parents an opportunity to "teach their children a lesson" using guidance, love, and wisdom, instead of depriving them of dignity and respect.

Teens *will* make some unwise decisions of their own, regardless of what their parents want. Parents must make themselves available to their kids and create an environment where it is safe to talk by practicing containment, listening, respecting confidentiality, and being supportive without being judgmental. Ideally, this should start when they are young. In addition, parents must create an environment of love, safety, and trust so their kids feel fundamentally strong and intrinsically capable of making wise choices.

## Teens Speak Out

I spoke to a few teens whom many might consider rebellious. Randy is seventeen and appeared to be very self-confident. He proudly displayed his numerous facial and body piercings and tattoos. He said,

> My parents stopped caring about what I do a long time ago. They have no control over what I do, anyway. Hey, rebellion is a natural thing for kids to go through. Lookin' like this, it's one of the ways I control my own life.

If Randy had been given a sense of belonging at home and a feeling of self-reliance and self-discipline as a child, he most likely would not have the need to mutilate his body as a teenager as he continues to go through the natural process of separation and forming of his own identity. Imagine how different Randy might be if he felt empowered, strong, appreciated, and loved. He also told me,

> When I was a kid, my parents always yelled at me if I screwed up. If I screwed up at school, they smacked me. I didn't have no say about nothin'. They never said they loved me. I never got the stuff I really wanted. Now I'm old enough, so I do what I want—for me.

---

What is destructiveness but creativity looking for a place to happen?                              —*Dawna Markova, Ph.D.*

---

Another teen told me, "My parents said they loved me, but I never got hugged; I just got yelled at." Child neglect can lead to abuse. Verbal abuse can be insidious. It does not leave a physical mark, but the pain and damage go very deep. Verbal abuse and neglect, like physical abuse, cause low self-esteem, emotional pain, and ultimately, rebellion.

Angie is thirteen and belongs to a gang. I asked her what she worries about most.

> I don't worry about much. Guns and dying maybe, but I feel safe in my gang. I don't like to go home. My parents, they just don't understand nothing. They hit me and my brothers and scream and yell and stuff like that. So I always hang with my friends. They give me the

attention and security I need. We take care of each other. And my boyfriend gives me all the love I need.

Like any child, Angie deserves to feel safe and secure in her room, at home with her family. Angie deserves to have parents she can talk to, whom she can trust and laugh with, and who will trust her. No child of any age should be on the street worrying about guns and dying. All children deserve to be in the safe, loving embrace of their mothers or fathers.

## Four Hugs a Day

"Four hugs a day, that's the minimum. Four hugs a day, not the maximum," sings Charlotte Diamond, singer and entertainer for both children and adults. A hug, a gentle stroke on the back, a kiss on the cheek, a tousle of the hair, all say to your child "I love you." Make a point of saying the actual words "I love you." Do not assume your child knows you love him, he does not know unless you tell him.

Physically acknowledge your children on a daily basis. Most children find comfort in a reassuring embrace. It tells them they are safe. My kids still love to cuddle. Be sure you touch your child in a loving, gentle way *at least* four times a day.

Some parents claim their babies do not want to be held or their young children refuse to be hugged. If the adult has trepidations, the child will sense this and may respond by pulling away. Do not force your children to be hugged; give them space if they want it. There is an artfulness in demonstrating affection; approach gently, with love.

Other parents have complained that well-meaning friends and relatives have encouraged them to *not* hold and cuddle their kids. A young mother approached me after a parenting talk I gave in Florida. She was confused about picking her baby up all the time. Moira said, "When my baby cries, my heart cries out to hold her. I just want to pick her up and soothe all her fears, but my mother-in-law screams at me every time I do. She says I'll spoil the baby rotten. What do you think about this?"

Human beings in emotional or physical distress deserve to be consoled. Cherish your child through loving, gentle touch and kind, consoling words. If your baby cries, go to her. Pick her up and hold her close. If your child is "just looking for attention," give it to her. If your teenager is upset, don't solve her problems; just acknowledge and listen to her feelings. It is up to you to defend, protect, and cherish your children. By demonstrating love and affection, you fill your kids up with "love-esteem," which is a sense of self-love and self-appreciation. When kids have this "full" feeling of self-worth, it is easier for them to hold others in high esteem.

## Give Verbal Hugs to Teens

In our culture, we have learned to equate touching with sex. Sex is just one of many forms of physical expression. Nonsexual touching conveys soothing messages of love, comfort, and acceptance. Most young children love to be hugged and cuddled; it helps them to feel lovable, provides a sense of security, and promotes self-esteem. If we want them to grow into loving human beings, our children must first experience and know that loving takes place in their home. When your teens are filled with love, self-acceptance, and self-appreciation, they will not have a burning desire to search for love in all the wrong places.

Building self-esteem in your children is your best insurance against behavior problems.

—*Dr. Louise Hart*

If you have a preteen or a teenager who does not want to be touched by you, give him a wink or a loving look. Offer encouragement whenever you can. Find some area in his life where you trust him and verbalize your approval. You must do this often to prevent your teen from reaching out to drugs or alcohol to fill an unfulfilled need within his soul.

• Let him know you accept and appreciate even the smallest, positive things he does.
• Tell him you love him before he goes to sleep at night.
• Whisper "I love you" in his ear when his friends are not looking.
• If he does get in trouble, look at the bigger picture—the incident (major or minor) is just an infinitesimal fragment of who your child is. Forgive him, love him, and let him move on.

At times, it can be extremely difficult to express verbal or physical signs of love and acceptance when your teen is in a state of rebellion. By remaining calm, containing your anger as often as you can, and finding small ways to acknowledge and appreciate your kids on a regular basis, you let them know you still love them unconditionally. Unconditional love is the feeling we are all striving for in our lives: to be loved and accepted for who we are in spite of the mistakes we make along the way. When kids spend a lifetime waiting and hoping to be acknowledged, appreciated, and loved for who they are—not who you *want* them to be—they join gangs to find the family they have longed for, or they fill themselves up with synthetic substitutes.

## Teach Your Children About Drugs and Alcohol

When it comes to substance abuse, most parents silently pray, "Please don't let it happen to my kid." They cannot comprehend, or they simply refuse to believe, that their children can be involved in drug abuse or alcohol consumption. One mother in my parenting class could not believe it was happening to her teenager. Janet's daughter began smoking cigarettes to fit in with her peers. Cigarettes quickly led to marijuana "to feel good" and amphetamines to lose weight. When her daughter showed up at school unable to hold her head up, the school counselor called Janet.

> I had no idea my daughter was doing that stuff. I always told her she was pudgy and tried to get her to eat healthier foods, but she wouldn't listen. I guess that's why she tried the diet pills. I grounded her for six weeks. She had to stay home and couldn't talk on the phone. I was so disgusted with her, I didn't even want to talk to her.

Grounding her daughter did not stop the inappropriate behavior. The next thing Janet knew, her daughter was sneaking out at night and snorting cocaine. Some teenagers get involved with drugs and alcohol to get back at their parents, to eliminate feelings of pain and confusion about growing up, or to fit in with their peers: in other words, to anesthetize their feelings.

We live in a society that prides itself on putting on a "happy face." We have to give our kids the message that it is okay to feel their pain without having to anesthetize themselves. They need an opportunity to learn how to deal with their emotions so they can learn appropriate coping skills. That is what helps them make good, healthy, appropriate decisions. This does not mean you have to abandon them.

- When you have faith in them, they learn to believe they are capable.
- When you trust them, they learn to trust themselves.
- When you believe in them, they learn to be independent and believe in themselves.

Instead of being the "boss" and telling them what to do, you must guide them. You can let them know you are there to help by saying "I'm here to help you figure this out if you need me." Some things you can say to encourage their decision-making skills include:

- "I know you're upset about what's happening. Have you thought about some ways to handle it?"
- "What are some things you might do?"
- "You've made some good decisions in the past. I trust you will make the best decision in this case."
- "I know you can figure that one out."

---

There are only two lasting bequests we can hope to give our children. One of these is roots; the other, wings.

—*Hodding Carter*

---

When critical issues of health and safety are concerned, it may be appropriate for you to become the "boss" again. For example, if your child is becoming anorexic, drinking and driving, practicing unsafe sex, or exhibiting violent behavior, then you as a parent have a responsibility to intervene. Get the help you need to help your child through this difficult passage.

## Create a Violence-Free Home

Children are not born bad, but they do grow up in a society that sometimes celebrates and often rewards violence. What's more, human beings are the only animals on Earth who abuse their children. Parents justify this by saying "Oh, a little slap isn't abusive." If you lose a huge business account due to your own negligence, do you deserve to be slapped by your boss? Does your spouse have the right to hit you if you forgot to clean the house or pay the mortgage? No human being (or animal for that matter) deserves to be hit, slapped, pinched, or forcefully grabbed. Domineering behavior of this nature does not allow a child or an adult to develop his or her own positive ideals, and it certainly is not the way to teach proper family values.

It may be difficult for some adults to show positive physical expression if they were raised in physically or verbally violent households. Children who do not receive security, affection, and loving touch at home usually find somewhere else to go where they feel listened to and accepted. If they fear punishment, children will lie, cheat, blame others, and use avoidance techniques to get out of a situation. They often seek early sexual or drug experimentation to fulfill a fundamental emptiness in their heart.

Jordan Riak has written an impressive pamphlet entitled *Plain Talk About Spanking* (PTAVE, 1996, copyright waived). His message is simple, yet powerful. I have excerpted a portion of his work here:

> Spanking is a euphemism. That is, it is a pleasant-sounding word for a practice that is anything but pleasant. We use it here because it is the most commonly recognized term in our language denoting violent behavior by adults toward children. "Hitting," "beating," and "battery" are more accurate and more honest words, but we have decided to stay with "spanking" here for ease of understanding.
>
> In an attempt to deny or minimize the dangers of spanking, many spankers have been heard to argue, "Spanking is very different from child abuse," or "A little smack on the bottom never did anybody any harm." But they are wrong.
>
> Some researchers claim that every act of violence by an adult toward a child, no matter how brief or how mild, leaves a permanent emotional scar. The effect of these scars is cumulative. To some extent we can demonstrate this from personal experience. Most of us must admit that the most indelible and most unpleasant childhood memories are those of being hurt by our parents. Some people find the memory of such events so unpleasant they pretend that they were trivial, even funny. You will notice that they smile when they describe what was done to them. It is shame, not pleasure, that makes them smile. As a protection against present pain, they disguise the memory of past feelings.
>
> A good comparison to spanking is arsenic poisoning. Everyone knows that arsenic taken

in sufficient quantity is lethal. Ingesting just a little, however, may have no obviously harmful effect. But who needs poison? The mere fact that a person is likely to survive is hardly proof that the experience is beneficial. Informed parents recognize that spanking their children is like lacing their food with a toxic substance. No good can result, and the risk is great.

But some parents will ask, "How can you claim to be a responsible parent if you don't grab the child who is about to run out into traffic and deliver a good smack, so that your warnings about the danger of the street will be remembered?"

In fact, being spanked throws children into a state of powerful emotional turmoil, making it difficult for them to learn the lessons adults claim they are trying to teach. Delivering a "good smack" may indeed serve an adult's need to vent rage, but at the expense of causing rage in the child. While the adult's relief is transitory, the effect on the child is long-term. Spanking does not teach children that cars and trucks are dangerous. It teaches them that the grown-ups they trust are also hurtful.

To be spanked is a degrading, humiliating experience. The spanked child absorbs not only the blows but also the message they convey: "You're worthless. I reject you!" That message powerfully influences the child's developing personality. It instills self-hatred.

*Lost Trust and Threats*
The experience of being spanked erodes trust, which binds the child to the parent. The

spanked child is less able to regard the parent as a source of love, protection, and comfort, which are vital to every child's healthy development. In the child's eyes the parent now appears to be the source of danger and pain. Some parents rarely spank or do not spank at all but threaten to do terrible things: "If you don't keep quiet while Mommy is on the phone, I'm going to sew your mouth shut." Or, "Somebody is going to cut your fingers off with a big pair of scissors if you don't stop touching everything in the store." Some parents find it easy to manage children by these means, at least temporarily.

At first, while children believe adults' threats, they obey out of fear. But they soon learn to sneak and tell lies in order to evade the terrible punishments they believe await them. Later, as they discover the threats are empty, they conclude that grown-ups also are liars.

When trust between children and their closest caretakers is damaged in this way, the children's ability to form trusting relationships with others is also damaged. This may render them incapable of ever achieving cooperation or intimacy with anyone. People who have been hurt in this way see all relationships as negotiations, as deals to be won or lost. They see honesty and trustfulness in others as weaknesses to be exploited exactly as it was once done to them.

*Force*
Spanking teaches children that human interaction is based on force: that might makes right. The more a child is spanked, the greater

is the likelihood that the child will become an adult who deals with others, not by reason and good example, but by force. The bully, the rapist, the authoritarian spouse who dominates, manipulates, and terrorizes his or her partner uses this kind of force.

Battering and battered spouses who spank their children are raising them to be batterers and victims exactly like themselves. The children learn from their parents' example that the way to vent frustration, express disapproval, and assert authority is by hitting someone smaller than themselves. This principle is demonstrated for the children every time they see their parents fight as well as every time they receive a whipping.

Children learn, once they are big enough and strong enough, that they can control others by threatening or hurting them. They learn that it is okay for husbands and wives to batter each other and for adults to batter children.

When children whose personalities have been formed in violent households grow up and produce children of their own, they find it very difficult to break free from the behaviors they have witnessed and experienced. The skills they apply to family life will be the poor ones bequeathed to them by their parents, and they are likely to perpetuate the cycle of violence through their own innocent children.

As spanking disappears from family life, other forms of domestic violence will also disappear. Not before.

*Physical Danger of Hitting the Buttocks and Hands*
Located deep in the buttocks is the sciatic

nerve, the largest nerve in the body. A severe blow to the buttocks, particularly with an instrument such as a piece of wood, could cause bleeding in the muscles that surround that nerve, possibly injuring it and causing impairment to the involved leg.

The coccyx, or tailbone, a very delicate bone at the base of the spine, is also susceptible to injury when a child is hit in that region. When children are required to bend over for beatings, their sex organs may be injured. Dislocation of the coccyx and genital bruising as a result of violent punishments are frequently reported by hospital authorities.

Spanked children do not regard their bodies as being their own personal property. Spanking trains them to accept the idea that adults have absolute authority over their bodies, including the right to inflict pain. Being hit on the buttocks, moreover, persuades them that even their sexual areas are subject to the will of adults. The child who submits to a spanking on Monday is not likely to say "No" to a molester on Tuesday. People who sexually molest or exploit children know this. They stalk potential victims among children who have been taught to "obey or else" because such children are the easiest targets.

Some people, in their attempt to justify battering children's buttocks, claim that nature intended that part of the anatomy for spanking. The claim is brazenly perverse. No part of the human body was made to be violated. Even being shaken can cause blindness, whiplash, brain damage, and actual death.

A child's hand is particularly vulnerable to damage from hitting because ligaments, nerves, tendons, and blood vessels are close to the skin which has no underlying protective tissue. Striking the hands of younger children is especially dangerous to the growth plates in the bones which, if damaged, can lead to deformity or impaired function. Striking a child's hand can also cause fractures and dislocations, and can lead to premature osteoarthritis.

### Spanking at Home, Performance at School

Most teachers will tell you that the children who exhibit the most serious behavior problems at school are the ones who are the most mistreated at home. Children who are spanked at home have been conditioned to expect the same kind of management by authority figures outside the home. For these children, the battle zone which is their home life extends to include school life. This sets them up for academic failure and dropout, and clashes with juvenile authorities and the criminal justice system.

In their attempt to erect a shield against what they perceive to be a comfortless, hostile world, these children naturally seek the company of other children with similar problems. "My parents and teachers don't understand me; my friends do," they say with cause. This is one reason street gangs evolve and why they are especially attractive to children whose self-esteem has been ruined by spanking, whipping, paddling, switching, humiliation, insults, threats, relentless criticism, unreasonable restrictions, and physical and emotional neglect.

We should not be surprised that many youngsters reject the adult world to the degree that they believe it has rejected them. Nor should we be surprised that adolescents, who throughout childhood have experienced violence, will use violence as soon as they are able. Unfortunately, the aggressiveness that many young people cultivate because they believe it is essential to their survival propels them toward failure or catastrophe. Our crowded prisons are proof of this.

Some teachers work tirelessly to redirect the aggressiveness that violence-ridden children have far too much of and instill trust, which such children have far too little of. But that is a monumental task requiring specialized skills and a level of dedication that not all teachers possess or can maintain for extended periods. It requires extraordinary resources unavailable to most school systems.

School dropout and juvenile delinquency would cease to be major problems wracking our nation if only it were possible to persuade parents to stop socializing their children in ways guaranteed to make them antisocial and/or self-destructive. In other words, to stop the spanking and start the nurturing.

This has been excerpted from:
Parents and Teachers Against Violence in Education (PTAVE)
P.O. Box 1033
Alamo, CA 94507-7033
http://silcon.com/~ptave

Infliction of pain or discomfort, however minor, is not a desirable method of communicating with children.

—*American Medical Association, House of Delegates*

## Spare the Rod, Cherish the Child

A child cannot be spoiled by too much love and affection. This is not the same as buying your child everything she wants or giving in to every demand your teen may have. Compassion, love, gentleness, and empathy are taught to children by parents and teachers willing to lead the way.

Do not lay guilt on them about your feelings or shame them for behaving in a certain way. Simply state your feelings about how you feel deep inside. You can do this by:

- being honest with your child.
- talking from your heart.
- sharing your fears.
- showing your emotions, including tears of sadness and joy.
- being willing to compromise.

Children are able to listen without feeling defensive when you respectfully speak to them in moments of calmness. When you create time to talk together—to share thoughts, ideas, and feelings—their outbursts and nasty behaviors will be fewer and far between. To be sure you do not overwhelm your children with your emotions on a daily basis, you must find a balance that works for you. Like a tree that needs sun and rain and room to grow, your child needs understanding and compassion to grow strong. Gentleness, kindness, understanding, and love keep them on track.

Drop your authoritative point of view, and let go of the duty-bound heaviness you may feel toward child rearing. Let your children know you are human. Be spontaneous, apologize for your own mistakes, and take yourself lightly. If you frolic together in a sense of freedom and joy, your kids will love to be around you. Family values may just outweigh peer pressure.

---

Love is such a powerful force. It's there for everyone to embrace: that kind of unconditional love for all humankind. This is the kind of love that impels people to go out into the community and try to change conditions for others, to take risks for what they believe in.
                                                    —*Coretta Scott King*

---

Kids will be exposed to sex, drugs, and alcohol; that is a given. There are so many reasons why kids use them. No parent wants to be the reason or the cause for their kids turning to these coping mechanisms. When adolescents' lives become pressured and they are faced with challenging situations, the last thing they may be feeling is love and self-appreciation. The way you respond to them at this critical juncture in their young, impressionable lives will make all the difference in the world. When you keep loving them, you can help them find their way back to loving themselves.

## *Personal Goals*

1. Structure a violence-free home.

2. Take time to get to know your child better, just as you would a friend.

3. Create a home environment where your kids feel safe to talk.

4. Listen without being judgmental.

5. Find fun things to do together as a family.

6. Set reasonable boundaries.

7. Support your teen for not drinking or doing drugs at parties.

8. If they do not want to be hugged because it is not "cool," tell them you will send them silent kisses and invisible hugs when their friends are not looking.

9. Have faith.

10. Treat each moment as if it were your last.

# *KIDS:*

## *Dealing with Risky Business*

Being a teenager can be really hard, and it's normal to be overwhelmed. There are so many decisions to make, so many confusing things to sort out, and so many new things to discover. Our generation has to face things that our parents didn't have to deal with when they were our age, like AIDS. Sometimes it seems like our world keeps getting worse. Even though life can be tough at times, you don't have to be miserable. You have to learn to trust yourself and believe in yourself, even if some people don't believe in you or treat you right.

If your friends push you into doing things that are illegal or not what you want to do, you're letting them control your life. Don't let other people pressure you into doing things. Never give away your own personal power. Make your own decisions, and don't be afraid to stick up for yourself and what you believe in.

### Why We Do What We Do

Several people have told me that they like causing trouble because they know their parents—and other adults—wouldn't approve of their actions. Some kids are so mad at their parents, for one reason or another, that they want to do everything they can to get back at them. Their way of getting back at their parents is to do things they aren't supposed to do.

Some kids:

- talk back to their parents.
- purposely do badly in school.
- sneak out.
- steal.
- drink.
- smoke.
- get stoned.
- have sex at an early age.
- pierce various body parts.
- get tattoos.

If these are some of the ways you choose to express the anger you have toward your parents, or other people, you need to know that there are other ways you can release your feelings. If you decide to stand out to get attention in a negative way, then you're just hurting yourself. If you decide to stand out from the crowd because it makes you feel good, and you aren't hurting anyone or anything, then that's okay. But if you're doing it just to prove something, or to really make your parents mad, then it is the wrong reason to do anything.

One way to stop "stinkin' thinkin'" (as my mom's friend calls it) is to believe in yourself. If you think it's impossible to believe in yourself, find positive things about yourself that you can be proud of. Find out what you're good at and get involved in it. If you aren't good at one thing, instead of getting upset or putting yourself down, try something else. Keep trying new things until you find something you like to do. We all have hidden talents; you just have to be willing to find yours without giving up on yourself.

No matter what you do, people tend to judge you when you look, act, or dress a certain way. I have heard kids say, "Why are you always picking on me for the way I dress?" (or act, think, or talk). Think about it; if you don't want them to pick on you, then don't do the things that cause negative attention.

---

We always put on a mask to meet the other masks.

—*T. S. Eliot*

---

I have met many kids who are confident about life and all the changes taking place around them. They don't need to find ways to escape from their feelings or have to follow the fads because they know how to express themselves in positive ways. I have met other kids who refuse to admit their feelings. Some of them hide their feelings so deep inside, even they don't realize how frightened and angry they are. They are so stressed out about their lives that they turn to anything that will relieve their stress, even if the relief only lasts for short periods of time.

## Deal with Stress

Everyone has stress at some time in his life, but not everyone knows how to manage it properly. Below are several different ways you can manage stress. They might not all work for you, but hopefully you will be able to find at least one idea that you like.

> • Close your eyes and imagine a beam of sunlight spreading warmth over your body. Let the warmth of the sunlight ease all the stress and tension in your body, allowing it to drift up and float away. Feel every muscle and every bone in your body relax. Then open your eyes and take in a deep breath. Hold it for a few seconds, then let it all out. Take a few more deep breaths if you feel you need to. This miniature meditation session can help to soothe and calm your brain. It

may not actually take away all your stress, but it might allow you to think more clearly.

• Planning out your schedule can help you when you have a lot of work to do and you feel overwhelmed. Prioritize the things you have to do by writing them down in their order of importance. It's usually a good idea to get the hardest and most brain-consuming thing over with first to get it out of the way. Don't forget to take little breaks to keep your mind clear and stress-free.

• Finish the projects you are assigned at school as soon as possible. Don't wait until Sunday night to do a major project that is due Monday morning. You'll find yourself with more stress than you can handle. As soon as you find out what you have to do, get started on it. Do a little bit each day or each week, depending on when it's due. Try to get it done before it's due in case you need to make changes. By finishing assignments in advance, you reduce your level of stress.

• One boy I know walks down to the neighborhood park every time he feels his stress level go up. He practices his karate moves or just sits and reads a book. Another guy I know spends hours playing basketball. He said it really lowers his stress level after school every day. Go running, ride your bike, or take a walk. Exercise and fresh air often help to eliminate stress.

Stress affects everyone. We need to learn how to channel stress and use that energy for something else. Sometimes being alone or focusing your energy on other things can help you get rid of stress.

You can do physical things like:

- go on a bike ride
- go jogging
- go for a walk
- play sports
- work out
- punch a pillow
- put on your favorite music and relax in your room

Releasing stress and anger is a healthy, natural thing to do. Find ways to express your anger and release stress so you don't have to bottle it up inside and then end up exploding later. Sometimes talking to a friend or someone you trust helps when you need to let your feelings out. You can also write about your feelings in a diary or a journal. If you find that you have too many things you have to do, you might need to plan some time to do nothing so you can just spend time relaxing.

Where kids originally come from, on that faraway star where life was carefree and fun, we were all free from stress. Stress used to be an adult problem, but in today's world, even little kids get stressed out. I guess the best thing we can do is learn how to deal with it.

## Smoking

Some kids think they need to smoke when they get stressed out. Some proudly say they are already addicted when they have just started to smoke. The truth is, they haven't been smoking long enough to become addicted, they only think they have. Some people my age say things like:

- "I'm so stressed out, I need a cigarette really bad."
- "I could use a cigarette right now."
- "I'm trying to quit, but it's hard."

As I am writing this, my friend's grandmother is dying of lung cancer because she smoked. My friend said, "I would never pick up a cigarette because watching my grandma suffer is so painful for me and my whole family. It's really hard to watch my grandma die, and I would never want to poison myself like that." Another friend of mine said, "My dad is smoking, so why shouldn't I?" Even though some of your parents might smoke, that is not an excuse for you to start doing it. When our parents were younger, no one knew how dangerous smoking was. There were no warnings on cigarette boxes because at that time, no one knew that tobacco and nicotine were addicting, deadly substances.

Since the discovery that tobacco and nicotine are dangerous, millions of adults have forced themselves to quit, because they now know that smoking can kill them. An article in the *Parenteen Newsletter* published by the Parents' Coalition of Bay Area High Schools (Volume III, No. 3, Spring 1997) reported, "Each cigarette contains more than 4,700 chemical compounds; 43 of those are known to cause cancer and 401 are poisons."

Something else you may not realize is that people who smoke cigarettes usually have hair and clothes that smell like an ashtray, and they have very bad breath! Every time they light up a cigarette, they are poisoning themselves in many ways.

The next time you think you need a cigarette, think

about all the people dying from problems due to cigarette smoke right this very second, and remember that there are more positive ways to deal with stress than doing things that damage your body. Find simple, safe, smart ways that work for you.

## Sex and Drugs

Some kids don't know how to relieve stress or deal with their problems, so they turn to drugs and alcohol for relief. In my research, I found an article called "New Info, New Dangers" in *Teen* magazine (September 1996, pp. 50–65) written by Maggie Keresey. She said that according to the National Institute on Drug Abuse (NIDA), "32 percent of eighth graders, 40 percent of tenth graders, and nearly 50 percent of high school seniors have tried some kind of drug at least once." The NIDA study also showed that nearly 40 percent of teens try marijuana before they graduate from high school. The average age for kids who try marijuana for the first time is 13.5.

If you find yourself in a position where someone is offering you drugs, try to think of something to tell them so they will leave you alone. You can say things like:

- I'm not into that.
- My parents are picking me up soon and if they smell anything on me, or notice I'm acting different, I'll be in a lot of trouble.
- I have a test tomorrow morning, and I have to be able to think clearly.
- Last time I tried that stuff, it got me so messed up. I'm not ready to try it again.
- My doctor said I'm allergic to that stuff and if I try it I could get really sick.
- No thanks. I'm the designated driver tonight.

Stand up for yourself and don't let other people
influence you.

Some people are allergic to drugs or alcohol. They can
have immediate allergic reactions after trying it one time.
I heard a story about a girl who went to a party and drank
nothing but sodas the whole night. She didn't get drunk or
do drugs, even though everyone else was doing all that.
She went home with a terrible headache and nausea.
Twenty-four hours later, she was dead. Apparently, someone had spiked her soda with a drug that her body was
allergic to. That had caused an innocent sixteen-year-old
girl, with her whole life still ahead of her, to die.

I can only hope that no one meant for things to go that
far. Maybe someone thought it would be fun. But at whose
expense? I've heard similar stories about kids who try
drugs willingly. They figure that their friends are doing it,
so why shouldn't they? They try the drug, and they die.
Once you're dead, you're dead; and at that point there
isn't anything you can do about it! Personally, I'd rather
suffer through peer pressure than risk my life by doing
drugs.

It's normal for people our age to be curious about
things. It's also normal to want to fit in with your group
of friends. But most kids and teenagers don't always
think ahead, and they don't worry about the long-term
effects of having sex too early or doing drugs and alcohol.
They say, "Why should anyone our age worry about that
now? It's so far in the future. We should just do whatever
we want while we're still young."

A few girls I know decided to have sex at age thirteen
because they thought it was "cool." They would smoke
pot or drink to loosen up, and then they'd have sex with
whatever guy was available.

• One girl I talked to said she didn't care about safe sex, because her "boyfriend was cool." Her boyfriend may be cool, but suffering through HIV and dying from AIDS isn't cool at all.

• Another girl I talked to decided to have sex at fifteen because she wanted to do everything she could to get back at her parents. She actually walked around her high school campus bragging that she wasn't a virgin anymore. She didn't realize that her reputation affects her, not her mom!

• I also talked to a sixteen-year-old girl who wants to get pregnant. She said, "If I have a baby, I'll have someone in my life who loves me for who I am." This is not a good reason to bring another life into the world. She has to love herself and get her own life together first, especially before she takes on the responsibility of an innocent baby.

As you get older, many illnesses develop from things you did when you were younger. There are so many sexually transmitted diseases around that I can't even count them all. And the effects of smoking, drinking, and getting high can be deadly. This isn't something you should just blow off and not pay any attention to, because you could end up suffering from the long-term effects of the things you do now. Here are some statistics I found in the *Parenteen Newsletter* (Vol. III, No. 3, Spring 1997).

- Today's marijuana contains from 8 percent to as much as 24 percent THC, the main psychoactive ingredient, compared to 2 percent in the 1960s and early 1970s when the leading studies were made on its effects. **One joint of the 1990s can equal 14½ joints of the 60s.** A group of kids today sharing just one joint can "get really plastered," the *New York Times* reported in November 1996.
- **A single joint contains the same amount of tar and other toxic substances as approximately fourteen to sixteen filtered cigarettes.**
- Marijuana smoke contains more cancer-causing agents than tobacco and is almost four times more deadly than cigarette smoking, cigarette for cigarette. **Studies show smoking five joints a week may be equal to smoking a pack of cigarettes daily.**
- Pot is a street drug and therefore inconsistent in its content and subject to contamination. Unlike cigarettes, no filters are used. **A 1997 study by the U.S. Public Health Service reported some marijuana contains residues of insecticides.**
- For motor skills such as driving, reaction time is reduced by 41 percent after smoking just one joint and by 63 percent after smoking two. **The effects can last for eight hours after smoking.**
- A study of **teenagers who smoked pot** at least six times a month found them more than **twice as likely to be involved in accidents** than those who did not smoke marijuana.
- The destructive consequences to the lungs and bronchial tissue (including ulcers, cancer, and emphysema) should be of special concern to preteens and adolescents, because **their young lungs are particularly vulnerable to the effects of the drug.**
- Smoking causes a temporary disruption in the delivery of the male hormone testosterone and slightly de-

creased organ size in males. **Heavy use lowers sperm count, decreases the level of sex hormones, and decreases sex drive and fertility.**

This information is not meant to scare you from growing up and becoming an adult; it is meant to scare you from doing drugs. I have seen what different kinds of drugs and alcohol do to people. Here is a true story that happened to some people I knew:

Three guys and one girl were driving in a car after a late party. The male driver was sixteen, one boy was fifteen, another boy and the girl were fourteen. All four of them were drunk. They were driving home at seventy miles per hour in a thirty-five-mile zone, when the driver decided to make a sharp U-turn. The car flipped over and rolled down a hill. The driver was not seriously injured and managed to get out of the car and run away. He left the other three people stuck in the car to die, because he was afraid he would get caught and get thrown in jail. Once they were all rescued, the fifteen-year-old was lucky enough to be released with just a few scratches and bruises. The fourteen-year-old boy was in a coma. He suffered a fractured hip and a broken ankle. The fourteen-year-old girl was pulled out of the car by the paramedics who had to use the "Jaws of Life." She was also in a coma. The bones above and below her eyes were crushed and she had to have plastic surgery. Her spine was crushed, and she had to go through weeks and weeks of rehabilitation.

You might think that going to parties and getting drunk would be a whole lot of fun. But when it comes down to it, do you think it's really worth it? About one week after the accident, the two people finally came out of their comas. The boy will never be able to walk normally again, and the girl's face will never look the same. For two kids who liked to party and drink all the time, this incident has changed their lives forever. The boy said, "You can all be sure of one thing, because of the accident, I will never be the same again." Unfortunately, some people have to learn the hard way.

So the next time you plan on going to a party and getting stoned or drunk, ask yourself if the potential consequences are worth it. It only takes one time. One time, and you could die.

---

It is really important for kids to realize that your drug dealer is not the kind of person who stays up late at night worrying about whether you get the right kind of drugs.

—*Michael Pritchard*

---

## When Your Parents Drink

We don't always have control over what happens to us in life, but we have complete control over how we choose to deal with what happens. For kids who drink, or whose parents drink or do drugs, help is out there. If you can't talk to your parents, talk to someone you know you can trust. Everyone knows at least one friend, minister, teacher, family member, or neighbor who they can count on. You can also go to Al-Anon meetings. Al-Anon is a worldwide, professional organization for people who are somehow related to alcoholics. They have separate groups for adults and for teens. When you go to Al-Anon meetings or Alcoholics Anonymous (AA) meetings, you realize you aren't alone. I attended a meeting with my mom just to experience what it was like. A girl stood up to speak. This is her story:

> Holly is twelve years old. She decided to start drinking because her father was an alcoholic. She wanted to screw up her life so her dad would realize he had to stop drinking, but she went to an Al-Anon meeting first. The speaker that day was eighteen. When he was sixteen, he had done exactly what Holly was about to do. He started drinking, thinking that would make his dad stop drinking. But instead, he and his dad became drinking buddies. When the boy finally realized his plan wasn't working, he had already become an alcoholic. He began showing up at Alcoholics Anonymous meetings and eventually he was able to get himself straightened out. By listening to this story, and realizing that there were other ways she could deal with her problem, Holly was able to keep herself from messing up her life.

Another story I heard that night was about a twenty-three-year-old man named Nathan who began drinking when he was four years old. He said:

> My dad was an alcoholic. When I was thirsty, my dad would let me drink from his beer can. When I passed out, my dad would pick me up and carry me to the bathroom so we could throw up together. Then, he would throw me in bed and we passed out. By the time I was thirteen, I was an alcoholic. When I was sixteen, I tried to commit suicide because I felt like my life had hit rock bottom. Fortunately,

251

I was able to turn my life around. To this day,
I still hate my dad for screwing up my life.


If you are treated in a way that is inappropriate, mean,
or abusive, the most important thing you can do for yourself is to choose to deal with it in a positive way. Nathan
was able to turn his life around. He chose to go to AA
meetings instead of continuing to be an alcoholic. Holly
was able to stop herself from making a terrible mess of
her life. She realized there were other ways to deal with
her father without screwing up her own life at the same
time. You are the one who has to decide to make choices
that build your character. Everything you do in life is
about the choices that you make.

The deputy sheriff from Northern California I had interviewed said, "We have laws for a reason, and people
choose whether or not they are going to obey them. You
just have to decide what you want to do." We have to
learn to respect the laws so we can reduce the number
of teenagers who are killed by drug abuse, smoking-
related diseases, and drunk driving.

---

Teenagers are becoming an endangered species.

—*H. Samm Coombs*

---

If you are in a situation where your friends have been
drinking, don't get in the car even if the driver only had
one beer. His driving skills could be screwed up without
his even knowing it. You're risking your own life by getting in the car. To avoid getting stuck in this situation,
you can:

- take the keys away from the drunk driver.
- always have a designated driver. You don't have to drink if you are the one driving, because everyone depends on you to get them home safely.
- always have some extra cash with you so you can call a taxi if you need one to drive you home.
- make a preagreement with your parents: If you need a ride home, you can call them at any time of the day or night, and they'll come get you without starting a fight. (Be sure you really thank them for this one.)

## Make Smart Choices

By making smart choices, you let yourself create change and improvement in your life. But there is a difference between smart, safe choices and stupid, dangerous ones.

Many people think pot is a safe, nonaddictive drug; but according to the National Institute on Drug Abuse, marijuana can lead to psychological dependence and withdrawal symptoms. Taking drugs is a choice, but not a safe one. Not having safe sex would also be a stupid thing to do, because you risk losing your life to AIDS. We all think, "Oh, it isn't going to happen to me." In a way, we have to think like that for our own sanity, but we still have to play it safe.

If you get caught doing something that is against the law, you will end up having a lot less freedom. Besides the fact that you will make your parents really mad, which always causes kids to lose privileges, you could end up in Juvenile Hall or on probation. That will really limit your freedom! If you take drugs, it is possible for them to permanently damage you or actually kill you. I think it's much wiser to take safe, exciting risks like rock climbing, scuba diving, or riding on roller coasters, which can be thrilling and can't get you into trouble. For an altered state of mind, you can try meditation.

---

Learn to live life to the fullest without crossing the lines of danger.

---

## Deal with Your Feelings

Life is always filled with ups and downs. Growing up has its many stages: some good and some not so good. Preteens and teenagers can easily get stressed out or feel depressed. If you feel like you're going through a hard time right now, it may be just another passing stage. The only way to get through a really tough stage is to acknowledge your feelings, and then either talk about them with someone you can trust, or just stay with your thoughts and think about what's going on in your life.

If you're depressed because you aren't doing well in school, or you have a fight with your boyfriend or girlfriend, or you're really upset with your parents, try not to sink into a deeper depression. Think about why you're upset. Go deep inside and take a close look at the feelings you have. We all have intense feelings at some time in our lives. It's possible for these feelings to be softened by letting them out. Your feelings may not completely go away, but here are some things you can do so they are not as bad:

- Talk to a friend, family member, therapist, or a hot line about your problem and your feelings. If you call the right hot line, you can find the exact advice you need. They will listen to everything you have to say, and they will help you only if you want help. It's completely confidential. You don't have to give them your name, and you can hang up whenever you want. Plus, the number doesn't show up on the phone bill as long as it's an 800 number. These numbers are usually listed in the Yellow Pages of your local telephone book, or you may be able to get them at your school.

• If you're mad at your parents, write a letter about how you're feeling. You can use the Feeling Letter Format which I explain in chapter 8. After you write the letter, there are several things you can do with it. You can give it to your parents, rip it up, burn it, throw it away, or keep it.

• Talk to your parents. This may be the hardest option, but sometimes it's the most successful. The best way to handle this is to use "I" messages, which I explain in chapter 5. You can say something like "It really upsets me when I'm grounded and I'm not told why." Remember to stop and take a break if your conversation turns into a screaming match.

By choosing one of the options listed above, using the ideas I gave you at the beginning of this chapter for releasing stress, or using some of your own ideas, you will be able to express your feelings in a non-violent way instead of turning to drugs, alcohol, or smoking.

Unfortunately, the majority of people in today's society aren't used to dealing with feelings. You're supposed to "forget about it," or, "be cool." But the truth is, everyone needs to let out their feelings, otherwise that energy can get transformed into anger. Before you know it, the anger turns into rage and the rage turns into violence. Maybe we have to stop thinking about ourselves as much and spend more time listening to each other.

When you have too many unhappy feelings cooped up inside, you aren't able to think clearly or make your own decisions. You may find yourself caught up in a bad situation you don't know how to get out of. Life is all about the choices we make. If you choose to take drugs and smoke as a kid and you become addicted, your life as an adult may not turn out to be as wonderful as you had expected. If you screw up your life, you may not even make it to being an adult.

Don't let other people pressure you into doing things you don't want to do. And realize that smoking, drinking, and taking drugs do not really relax you. By doing these things, you may be severely damaging your body. There are safer ways to deal with stress like the examples I gave in this chapter. Try not to do things that damage your life or anyone else's. You can make safe choices and still have a great life.

## *Personal Goals*

1. Be different and unique by just being yourself.

2. Don't let people pressure you into doing things you don't want to do.

3. Find healthy, positive, safe ways to express your anger and release stress.

4. If your parents smoke, drink, or get high, don't do it with them. Be strong.

5. Don't forget: Drugs and alcohol are not the answers to anything.

6. Never get in a car with someone who has been drinking or doing drugs.

7. Make smart choices. Don't get back at your parents by ruining *your* life.

8. Be sure you have safe sex. (But don't start having sex too soon. Wait until you are old enough and mature enough to be sexually and emotionally responsible.)

9. If you feel depressed, find someone to talk to who you can trust.

10. Deal with your feelings instead of trying to numb them.

## What Matters
(author unknown)

One hundred years from now,

it will not matter what kind of car I drove,

what kind of house I lived in,

how much I had in my bank account,

or what my clothes looked like.

But the world may be a little better

because I was important

in the life of a child.

# CHAPTER 8

# The Gift of Self-Esteem

## *PARENTS:*

*Teach Your Children to Love Themselves*
*Unconditionally*

Positive self-esteem is a powerful force. It lays the groundwork for a healthy personality that lasts a lifetime. On the other hand, people with no self-worth show many more serious problems including substance abuse, eating disorders, learning problems, destructive behavior, suicide, and violence. A child who grows up liking herself will function well in school, will be capable of relying on herself, will trust her intuition, will accept responsibility, and can develop into a responsible adult who feels physically, intellectually, spiritually, and emotionally strong.

Children of all ages need guidance to help them grow and develop properly. This can be done using praise and encouragement. This is not to say that a parent must never say no or correct his or her child's behavior. Reinforce the positive behavior instead of dwelling on the negative. Kids need to know that if they fall down, they are capable of getting themselves back up again. By reinforcing the positive nature of the whole child, you strengthen his or her self-esteem.

From the time your children are young, begin instilling in them a sense of pride.

- Show them they are loved by being kind, supportive, and respectful.
- Acknowledge their feelings.
- Forgive them when they make mistakes.
- Show them you care so they can learn to care about themselves and others.
- Love them unconditionally with no expectations in return.

## Love Them

Self-esteem depends on unconditional love: love with no strings attached. Loving someone unconditionally means you love them for better or for worse. You stand by them and support them, even when it may seem hard to do. Seeing the beauty and the imperfection in another human being and loving her the way she is without changing anything about her is unconditional love.

When you can love people regardless of their fear, rage, anger, or confusion, then you can love them unconditionally. Loving them even when they challenge you to the limit, or push your buttons, or make you want to scream is the true test of this kind of love which all beings so desperately crave. Unconditional love and compassion are the foundation for successful relationships.

Conditional love manipulates behavior. "I love when you act like that" implies "I don't love you when you act the other way." Adrian's mother always told her, "I love you because you are my child, but I don't like you." As a fifty-year-old woman, Adrian now says,

I have a lot of friends, and I know many people love me, but I've always had this little voice inside me saying "you're not good enough, and if you aren't really careful, no one is going to like you anymore." I now know this feeling comes from the conditional love I received as a kid. I guess I just wasn't perfect enough to please my parents all the time.

Parents must learn to address the behavior that is wrong, not the personality of the child. A better way to express this feeling would be to say "I'm really upset because of what happened." Kids who grow up being loved "conditionally" may never really trust the love they receive as adults. Adults and children who never felt unconditional love often try to earn love by becoming people-pleasers, trusting others more than they trust themselves, and repeatedly forsaking themselves in the process. Saying "That kind of behavior makes me angry" gives children the opportunity to change their behavior and not feel like they are bad people.

---

There is no difficulty that enough love will not conquer.

—*Emmet Fox*

---

## Acccpt Them

It may be easier to feel love and acceptance for your children when they dress and act the way you want them to, or when they make choices you feel are smart. But what happens to your feelings as a parent when your kid comes home after school with a friend you do not approve of, a note from the principal, or a pierced navel? What happens to your feelings of acceptance and unconditional love then?

Just loving your child when he "behaves properly" (according to whose standards one might ask?) is not unconditional love. You may be furious with his behavior, outraged at his attitude, or embarrassed by the way he dresses. You do not have to approve of or like the situation, the behavior, or the attitude, but loving your child even when he acts unlovable is the true test of unconditional love.

---

No one ever said parenting was easy.

---

Guide your children toward more appropriate behavior by opening the lines of communication. It is important to express the feelings you have in your heart, which include:

- your thoughts
- your fears
- your desires
- and your hopes

Instead of screaming, yelling, and threatening, approach your child the way you would want someone to talk to you if the tables were turned. Express your feelings in a positive manner, without put-downs, shame, or guilt. Remember to use "I" messages, which allow you to own the problem by expressing your own feelings and concerns; and ask open-ended questions that encourage conversation by allowing for several possible responses.

You can give them feedback about unacceptable behavior, but do not withdraw your love. Children flourish in an environment where unconditional love is constant and always present.

Here are some examples of what you might say if your child does something that makes you angry:

- I feel frustrated and disappointed when you don't take responsibility for your actions.
—This allows you to express your feelings without creating major power struggles.
- I get really angry when you leave your dishes in the sink, because it makes more work for me.
—This gives your kids an opportunity to change their behavior on their own.
- How can we solve this problem so I don't worry and you get to make some of your own decisions?
—Asking open-ended questions allows your adolescent to explore alternatives and make wise choices.

Suggesting options rather than dictating the behavior you prefer empowers your kids and helps them to determine their own ways of coping with any given situation.

## Inspire Them

Children and teenagers can be inspired to feel capable and valued through the continual use of positive encouragement and praise. Genuinely praising the behavior or action of your child, not the personality, allows them to grow to their full potential.

Monique was in a parenting seminar I gave in northern California. She said, "When my ten-year-old son kicks our dog out of his way, I say, 'stop doing that, it's mean. You're a bad boy.'"

Her son is not a "bad" boy. It has nothing to do with being good or bad. It has everything to do with unacceptable behavior. Monique said, "I get really mad when this keeps happening. It's hard not to yell at him, because he doesn't listen to me."

When a child of any age is testing his or her limits or goes out of control, parents must keep cool. You can redirect the child's focus so he stops the negative behavior or distract the child so he does something else instead. Perhaps just stating how the behavior makes you feel will stop the unappreciated behavior. Use words that are age appropriate for clear understanding. Teach your child that certain behaviors are not acceptable, while keeping his or her self-esteem intact.

Such statements include:

- I need you to be kind to the dog.
- How would you feel if you were a dog and someone didn't want you around?
- Please walk around the dog if he's in your way.
- I know you can find a respectful way to deal with the dog.
- Hey, why don't you put the dog in the yard so he doesn't bother you anymore?

Be understanding as you teach your child to cooperate. Cooperation requires focus and consideration. Start with little tiny baby steps if necessary. Have faith in your child and in your ability as a parent.

## Show Them

If your teen says, "I forgot my homework at school," you could get angry at her forgetfulness, or acknowledge that she actually remembered it! Janine, mother of two, turned the situation around to make it positive instead of negative. She said, "Hey, I'm glad you remembered where your homework is!" Her son still had to deal with the consequences of not being able to finish his homework assignment, but his mom did not belittle or berate her son.

When you speak to a teen who has already shut you out of his or her life, you must use "baby steps" to get your foot back in the door. Instead of nagging, criticizing and blaming, parents must continually acknowledge, praise, and encourage their teenagers whenever possible.

Think about the times you have forgotten your keys, or left your checkbook at home, or forgotten to return an important phone call. People of all ages get caught up in the fast pace of life and are prone to forgetting even the smallest things. Who wants to be lectured for forgetting his or her work or yelled at for being late?

Help them find what was lost, go back to school to pick up forgotten homework if you have the time, or let the experience be one they can learn from. With little children or taller-than-you teenagers, offer your help whenever you can. This does not mean you have to solve their problems or always fix their mistakes; you can simply acknowledge their actions. For example, you might say:

- You forgot your math book at school? That's terrible!
- Sounds like you're really angry with yourself for missing soccer practice.
- You tore your favorite shirt? I'd be glad to show you how to fix it.

Be sensitive, compassionate, and understanding when you can. If the situation warrants your input or advice, offer it and wait for your teenager to accept. By doing this, you delicately demonstrate how your own child might help you or someone else in the future. Children learn from your examples. It is up to you to set good ones.

## Encourage Them

Parents have incredible power to encourage or discourage their children. Some parents want their children to be high achievers, more successful, more productive. Overly ambitious parents seem to push their kids to do more or be more. Pushing kids can often backfire and foster rebellion. They cannot always live up to your expectations. A father told me, "My son is very smart and I want him to get ahead, so I push him to be the best he can be." His thirteen-year-old son said, "My dad always tells me I'm the best, but I still have to do better. If I don't do that well in school, I feel really guilty, like I've let him down. He gets really disappointed and the stress makes me nuts. I can't wait till I'm outta here."

---

By the time a man realizes that maybe his father was right, he usually has a son who thinks he's wrong.

—*Charles Wadsworth*

---

Here are two additional stories in which the kids were pushed by their parents:

- Melissa's mom gets angry if her fourteen-year-old daughter does not score in the "top three" runners at the track meet. Melissa always runs her fastest, pushing herself beyond her limits. When she finishes the race, she often throws up or passes out in her unconscious quest to please her mother.

• Courtney is in fifth grade. Her dad is a math teacher. Courtney told me, "If I don't do well in math, I feel like I have failed my dad and myself. I just can't do what he does. I hate math."

Parents who are overbearing in their involvement with their children, along with those parents who show no interest or involvement whatsoever, often end up with kids who feel guilty, inadequate, or rebellious. Their children's self-confidence becomes fractured. Parents must find a comfortable balance between running their kids' lives and being uninvolved or uncaring. Being the mentor or guide allows you to step back from overmanaging or overparenting your child and to move into a role that promotes trust in your adolescents' growing judgment.

Give your children a healthy dose of love and support. Try not to focus on your teens' weakness or mistakes; encourage their positive traits instead. This helps them to focus on their own strengths and abilities, allowing them to feel more confident and self-assured.

## Praise Them

Your words and attitude let your children know you love them even though they may have done something you do not like. Use encouraging statements that acknowledge feelings, capabilities, acceptance, contributions, and accomplishments, while avoiding criticism or value judgments. We all have room for improvement somewhere in our lives, but teens especially need to feel that what they are doing is accepted and appreciated. When they do not receive the positive input they so desperately crave, they will seek it elsewhere. In gangs they can find acceptance, with drugs they can escape their inadequacies, with you they can find love. The approach you use is up to you.

When children are very young, parents offer their love and praise freely. They joyfully applaud any new change in growth, and the young child feels acknowledged, appreciated, and proud. When toddlers take their first step, or preschoolers learn the alphabet, everyone celebrates and applauds. As young children develop into adolescents, parents forget to continue the acknowledgments, appreciation, and praise. Everyone needs to feel valued and appreciated; it is crucial for the development of self-esteem. When you praise, encourage or acknowledge your child of any age, use specific words to keep your messages clear. You can say something like, "Thanks for helping your sister with her homework. I really appreciate that." Patronizing, overly elaborate, or manipulative praise or statements can backfire and your child will see right through you. When you say "I need the trash taken out before ten P.M. tonight," you still hold the master plan. Your children look to you for strength and boundaries.

Teach your kids to accept compliments with grace by modeling graceful behavior. Do not shrug off compliments you receive by responding with "What, this old thing?" or "You look great, too." Just say thank you and accept the compliment you have received. As you breathe in compliments and praise, your children may learn to accept and give praise to others through your example.

Here are a few do's and don'ts when talking to kids:

**Do say**
I really like the way you folded the laundry. Thanks for your help.
**Don't say**
I could use your help more often.

**Do say**

I know you worked really hard.

**Don't say**

Just think how much better you could have done if you'd worked even harder.

**Do say**

You must be really hurt by what happened today.

**Don't say**

It's no big deal, forget about it. You'll feel better tomorrow.

**Do say**

I understand you feel overwhelmed.

**Don't say**

If you had started everything sooner, you wouldn't be bogged down today.

**Do say**

Your music sounds really loud to me. Will you please turn it down?

**Don't say**

Turn down that damn music!

**Do say**

I like the way your room looks today. It looks like you worked really hard.

**Don't say**

So, you *finally* cleaned your room. Too much of a pig sty even for you?!

**Do Say**

*I love you.*
*You're a shining star.*
*I'm glad you're my son/daughter.*
*I love you just the way you are.*
*Thanks for being in my life.*

Be clear with your statements so that they are focused, direct, and to the point. Remember to avoid statements that are manipulative, critical, or judgmental. Offer advice only when your child asks for it. If your adolescent says, "My homework keeps piling up and I have too much to do," do not start lecturing him. If you imply superiority by lecturing, you deprive your child of the esteem-building experience of solving his own problem, and you may encourage dependency. If your child does ask for your advice, have fun brainstorming together. You both can come up with numerous ideas to make his workload more manageable. Ask questions that will help him clarify his thoughts and feelings, and explore ways to manage time or prioritize. Help your kids believe in themselves.

## Write Little Love Notes

When my children were small, my mornings were always hectic at best: making breakfasts and lunches, finding socks that matched, and locating misplaced homework and sweatshirts. But I always managed to scribble a quick little note to put in their lunches every few days. The kids never knew when to expect these little love notes, but they always came home telling me how much they loved their lunches.

- If we squabbled in the morning, the note might say, "Sorry we had a fight today, but I love you anyway!"
- Other notes read, "Good luck on your test, I'll be thinking about you."
- "Hope you feel better today."
- "It's Friday! Here's to a great weekend."
- Some days the message was a simple, yet powerful, "I love you."

When they were really too young to read the written word, I used drawings and stickers to portray messages of love and affection. My kids told me the notes made them feel special.

As they got bigger, they did not want messages in their lunches anymore because it embarrassed them. Honoring their requests, I began sticking little notes on their bathroom mirror, or on their pillows at night. Once in a while, I placed a little note of love or encouragement on their dinner plates.

Over the years, my children began leaving notes for me. Journey still leaves love notes on the washing machine or on my bedside table. She also leaves me a note whenever she is going somewhere, or to tell me of her plans. "Leave me a note so I know where you will be," she asks of me and her dad in return. I feel confident that my kids will always let me know where they are or where they will be. The groundwork for mutual trust and respect has been laid.

---

People have a way of becoming what you encourage them to be, not what you nag them to be.

—*Scudder N. Parker*

---

## When It's Hard to Give Love

Helping someone else feel good about himself is a wonderful and fulfilling task, especially if it is for your own child. But what happens when you have a child who is shutting you out? In our stressed-out, trying-to-get-ahead lifestyle, it is so easy for parents to lose themselves in the process of child rearing.

Some parents have told me they honestly do not like their children. The atmosphere at home becomes one of abandonment, loneliness, and sadness. Children who are viewed as tyrants or an "inconvenience" will demand negative attention at home, wreack havoc in the classroom, and find ways to disrupt the public at large in an attempt to find any kind of attention.

I asked a sixteen-year-old girl at a local high school why she dyed her hair bright blue and what prompted her to get so many nose rings. She replied, "People look at me, ya know? It's cool to be different and I stand out in the crowd." According to many kids, negative attention is better than no attention at all.

You can help your teenager deal with negative emotions by listening to them, acknowledging the positive things they do, encouraging their strengths and capabilities, and giving them fair choices within appropriate limits from the time they are young. Many discipline problems can be prevented by involving your kids in constructive family decision-making. This gives them positive power.

## When You Are Running on Empty

After you have had a long day at work, or are just trying to make ends meet, your children come home from school needing your support, understanding, and unconditional love. When you have nothing more to give, it can be exasperating even to try.

Suffering from Chronic Fatigue Syndrome, Sue, the mother of four, was always exhausted. She would wake up feeling tired and go through her day like a zombie.

> I'm not operating at my full capacity. Everything in my day is stressful. Just waking up and getting my kids off to school is such a big deal for me these days. It's hard for everyone around me, too, because I don't have flu symptoms or a broken leg that they can see. My

> handicap is silent and runs very deep. At the
> end of the day, it's virtually impossible for me
> to give my kids the encouragement they need.

When your own tank is running on empty, it may be difficult to find the energy to fill someone else up with encouragement and love. I have felt it myself. I can remember a time when Journey was feeling sad. "I need a hug, Mom." I put my arms around her for a moment and was ready to send her off to bed so I could finish the laundry and my work, and get to bed myself. Journey held me tighter and said, "A real hug. I need a real hug, please."

For a fleeting moment I felt pressured and trapped. Within a split second, I looked into my own heart and told myself that my daughter needed me. I hugged her tightly with the intention of holding her for as long as she needed. She sank into my loving embrace and began to cry. I silently stroked her hair. "If you want to talk, I'm willing to just listen," I said softly. Her crying intensified. "I just need to cry and have you hold me, okay?"

In that magical moment, I held my little girl. Mysteriously, my exhaustion disappeared! I was able to move outside of myself and be there for the child who trusts me, needs me, still knows that her mom will always be there for her, no matter what.

When she fell asleep content and relaxed, I wondered if I had just played the martyr. Was I a doormat, always putting my own needs aside for others? As I went into my heart, I realized I was not a martyr or a doormat, but a mother who has the ability to step out of my own pain and sorrow momentarily to give love and empathy to a child in need. The unconditional love I gave my daughter at that moment healed a wounded piece of the little child within my own soul.

## Remember What Life Was Like

Think for a moment about the kind of family you grew up in. Were your parents strict? Were they overbearing? Were they permissive? Were they ever home? If each one of us could go back home to our family of origin knowing that is the place where we received pure, unconditional love, we would always have a safety net where we could turn for support. Unfortunately, not that many people can go back home or would even want to.

I have found that the majority of parents I have worked with have had unhappy childhoods. So many parents have vowed never to use their parents' style of raising a family, while others say, "If it worked for me, it will work for my kids." Perhaps you were lucky enough to have been raised in a family where trust, flexibility, understanding, and caring were balanced with love, allowing you to grow up to be a strong, powerful, considerate, loving, successful adult. In today's world, very few families are able to grow in love. Yet, it does happen. When parents and their children are able to respect and accept their differences, and work toward mutual understanding utilizing the tools and techniques for good communication, then love has a chance to blossom.

We must not forget that we relate to life differently than our children do. Yet, in our everyday interactions with our children, we often have difficulty remembering these differences. Often with the most loving intentions in mind, parents become demanding, judgmental, intolerant, and unsupportive. In response, children become defensive, secretive, develop "attitude problems," and rebel. Communication within the family breaks down as the child strives for independence and control. By the time the child becomes a teenager, all hell has broken loose. By remembering the concerns and struggles you had as a child growing up, and thinking about how you would have liked to have been treated by your ideal parent, you can bring more understanding, compassion, and empathy into your relationship with your kids.

Think back for a moment: What was your life like when you were an adolescent? What thoughts did you have? What feelings did you experience? Were you wild or a wallflower? What issues did you have about growing up and becoming a teenager? Whatever they were, please remember that your child may not have the same issues as you did. This child is not you. The way your adolescent deals with problems may be completely different from the way you did. Kids have minds of their own that should be respected and reasoned with. Remember your own confusion while growing up as you put yourself in your child's place. Think about how it might feel to be loved and accepted just the way you are, then give him or her the gift you would have loved to have experienced all your life: unconditional love.

---

Love is the answer, whatever the question.
*—A Course in Miracles*

---

## Love Yourself

Verbalizing love to your children is not enough; actions can speak louder than words. It is up to parents to teach their children to feel good about themselves. Teach through example.

- Learn to accept yourself.
- Respect your body.
- Take care of your health.
- Appreciate your capabilities.

- Believe that you are here for a special reason.
- Trust your instincts.
- Be compassionate.
- Tell the truth.
- Radiate love.

Acknowledge yourself for all the things you do.

- Find the place inside yourself where you may feel weak, confused, unheard, hurt, or unloved, and work on healing those fragmented parts of your soul.
- Tame your own fear and find healthy, sane ways to heal your personal pain.
- Be accountable for your own life so your kids can be proud of you.
- Apply the steps in this book to yourself.
- Express your love through loving actions.
- Treat yourself well as often as possible.
- Thank yourself for taking such good care of yourself and your kids.
- Be a good example by healing your relationships.
- Show love, respect, and faithfulness in all your relationships.
- Demonstrate through action how to be an honest, responsible, caring human being in our world.

Remember that on the road of life you will have only one constant companion, so make sure that you are good company for yourself. Give your children the same message.

---

The deepest desire in human nature is the craving to be appreciated.                                    —*William James*

---

If you feel overwhelmed, do not panic. Take time for yourself: go for a walk, go to a movie by yourself or with a friend, or have an unscheduled coffee break. Do whatever you can to be good to yourself. If you grew up in a family where unconditional love was nonexistent, take a parenting class so you can gain an understanding of the family dynamic and learn new parenting skills. Create a protective environment for yourself and your family that is supportive, loving, and safe. Practice what you preach. The more you practice appreciating, praising, and encouraging yourself, the easier it will be to instill self-esteem in those around you.

## *160 Ways to Show You Care*

1. Tell them you are glad they are alive!

2. Show them how to speak kindly and encourage each other.

3. Acknowledge your child's competency, no matter how big or small.

4. Thank them for doing little things no matter how insignificant it may seem to you.

5. Honestly express your appreciation as often as possible.

6. Help them trust their own intuition.

7. Trust their instincts, as well as your own.

8. Honor the Divine in each child.

9. Love each child for who he or she is.

10. Help them see their own goodness.

11. Teach them to honor and respect their own bodies.

12. Give them space.

13. Work problems out as soon as possible.

14. Listen from your heart.

15. Guide them toward making informed decisions.

16. Celebrate their accomplishments both big and small.

17. Leave fun, silly, or loving notes for them to find.

18. Encourage them to speak positively about themselves.

19. Reinforce positive behavior with praise, applause, congratulations, smiles, and hugs.

20. Compliment them on their talents.

21. Respect their ideas.

22. Praise them in public (but don't embarrass them).

23. Reprimand them in private so they can focus on the issue, not on feeling embarrassed.

24. Acknowledge good behavior immediately.

25. Use eye contact when talking to them, but don't force them to look at you.

26. Have fun with them; they will feel great about themselves afterward.

27. Keep directions simple and to the point.

28. Play noncompetitive games with them so everyone wins.

29. When they come home dirty, tell them it looks like they had a great time.

30. Tell silly jokes and laugh together.

31. Praise them unconditionally for being lovable, wonderful, miracles of life.

32. Praise their little accomplishments as well as the medium and big ones.

33. Reinforce behavior you want to see repeated.

34. Tell them you like how they are growing up.

35. Tell them they did a good job.

36. Acknowledge the way they pay attention to what they are doing.

37. When they tell the truth about something they have done, thank them for being honest.

38. Acknowledge the choices they make.

39. Believe in them so they can believe in themselves.

40. Rejoice in your children.

41. Give trust, not unsolicited advice.

42. Validate their feelings.

43. Let them express feelings without your judgment or comments.

44. Be supportive.

45. Give them a pat on the back.

46. Go places they like and have fun.

47. Frame their work and display it on the refrigerator.

48. Show them that their opinion matters to you.

49. Tell them they are wonderful.

50. Give positive feedback without negative emotion attached to it.

51. Use an attitude of respect.

52. Take your kids seriously when they speak.

53. Appreciate their efforts.

54. Feed their spirits with compliments.

55. Bestow special nicknames on them that you only use in private.

56. Cherish their innocence.

57. Describe what you appreciate about them so they know for sure.

58. Talk to them as if the angels could hear you.

59. Give them permission to be individuals.

60. Tell them their ideas are intelligent.

61. Let them know how much you learn from them.

62. See the best in your child each day.

63. Appreciate their creativity.

64. Set reasonable limits and let them know you care.

65. Do not shame or embarrass a child when he or she makes mistakes.

66. Praise them at least ten times every single day!

67. Let them experience and acknowledge their feelings.

68. If you cannot be interrupted, tell them how soon you will be available.

69. Sing and dance with them.

70. Surprise them by doing one of their favorite things, without any notice.

71. Get down on the ground and play with them, even if they are big!

72. Have a family water fight with the hose in the rain.

73. Help them to see that a mistake is merely a "miss take" and, gently, try it again.

74. Thank them for being gentle with animals.

75. Thank them for being kind to younger children.

76. Thank them for showing respect to the elderly.

77. Thank them when they do not interrupt you on the telephone.

78. Stand up for your child in a wrongdoing, especially if your child is with you.

79. Gently touch your child's face as she lies sleeping.

80. Tell them how much you love them.

81. Give your child one beautiful rose tied with a ribbon.

82. Secretly wink at one another when you are in a serious environment.

83. When you are out to dinner or at home, have a family toast. Let your kids come up with the toast.

84. Give them your undivided attention.

85. Treat them the way you want them to treat you and others.

86. If you are having a rough time—stop; everyone take a three minute break in silence—draw a flower for one another and start anew.

87. Help them to learn from their mistakes.

88. Share stories of something positive you both accomplish every day.

89. Identify something your child did today that made you thankful.

90. Get to know your children's friends.

91. Validate their feelings when they are upset.

92. Make a special "date" with your child and go somewhere fun for the day.

93. Schedule extra time when going out together so they do not always have to rush.

94. When you take time out to cool off, talk about what was bothering you in a nonblaming way when you come back.

95. When your child talks to you, turn off the TV or

put down the newspaper and give her your full attention.

96. If your child is home alone after school, call from work just to say "I love you."

97. Give your kid a foot massage. It will relax him and give you some special time together.

98. Be patient when your child is talking. Don't keep saying "Hurry up and get to the point."

99. Do not grab the channel changer away and start watching a different show when your child is watching TV. Be respectful and give her advance notice before you change the channel on the TV.

100. Buy their favorite foods.

101. Bake cookies together and decorate them with wild designs.

102. Be understanding if your teen decides to change outfits often.

103. Buy them little presents from time to time.

104. Put little encouraging notes in their lunch boxes.

105. Take a class together and learn something new.

106. Communicate instead of arguing.

107. Fix toys that are broken as soon as you are able to.

108. Mend broken hearts with love, understanding, and affection.

109. Encourage them to think for themselves.

110. Let them know you missed them when you went away.

111. Go for a walk in nature.

112. Go on a family bike ride.

113. Let the phone go unanswered when they are talking. It makes them feel important.

114. Say "please" and "thank you" when asking them to do something for you.

115. Appreciate their sense of humor.

116. Cuddle in bed together and read stories or poetry.

117. If your child is sick, give him extra love and attention.

118. Always say good-bye when you are leaving. Don't sneak away.

119. Take time to talk together each day.

120. Honor their separateness from you.

121. Respect their courage.

122. Use eye contact when listening to them talk.

123. Set reasonable and healthy limits.

124. Encourage them to go after their goals.

125. Acknowledge their inner wisdom.

126. Plant a garden together and teach them to nurture Mother Nature.

127. Send them notes in the mail.

128. Teach them to believe that little things do make a difference in life.

129. Create clear agreements and rules that everyone feels good about.

130. Tell them what you appreciate about their friends.

131. Learn how to say "I love you" in sign language, and send "secret" messages to one another.

132. Make up your own secret handshake.

133. Demonstrate how your kids can take pride in the environment: don't litter.

134. Take pictures of your kids and keep an ongoing photo album.

135. Teach them that giving is as important as receiving.

136. Let them know that we live in a world of infinite possibilities.

137. Celebrate rites of passage such as: special birthdays, graduation, menstruation, and personal achievements in a cherished and meaningful way.

138. Participate in your kids' school gatherings, events, fund-raisers and celebrations.

139. Turn off the television, computer, and telephone, then spend luxurious family evenings together.

140. Make up a special family song and sing it on special occasions.

141. Pray together.

142. When they are fearful, remind them that their guardian angels are watching over them.

143. Congratulate instead of criticizing.

144. Do not dictate, control, or give your opinion too often.

145. Provide a safety net for your kids to fall back on.

146. Give them rules they can count on. It helps them establish rules of their own.

147. Tell them they are your dream-come-true.

148. Help them identify and name their feelings.

149. Light a candle for a special talk with them.

150. Establish rituals for special days of remembrance.

151. Tell them they will be good parents someday.

152. Light candles in the bathroom and draw a bubble bath for them.

153. Tell each of your children that he or she is an unrepeatable miracle.

154. Teach them to be brave enough to cry.

155. Let your kids express themselves.

156. Share your values with them.

157. Have patience.

158. When they need you, let them find sweet acceptance in your eyes.

159. Make home a haven.

160. Treat them as if this day were their last.

# *KIDS:*

## *Self-Esteem Isn't Anywhere But Inside Yourself*

Sometimes kids get really depressed when they don't feel good about themselves. It's important to know that you are the only one who can make yourself feel better about who you are. If you have low self-esteem, people will most likely avoid you and not want to hang out with you. If you have high self-esteem, people will feel drawn to you and more people will want to become your friend. You have to learn to be yourself and love yourself before anyone else can like you.

If you feel good about yourself for a few days, you can't expect that all of a sudden you will be bombarded with friends. Things take time. When the time is right, new people will start heading your way. Your present friends will probably want to spend more time with you, too. This will all happen because you feel better about yourself; therefore, everyone else feels more comfortable being around you.

## Believe in Yourself

If your family or the people around you are always putting you down, you can still create your own self-esteem. The first thing you have to do is believe in yourself: know your own capabilities, and be proud of yourself. Don't put yourself down when you make a mistake. Just learn from your mistakes and move on.

Believing that you are a good and talented person doesn't mean that you're conceited. To be conceited means you think you're better than everyone else. If you act better than everyone else, no one will want to be around you because it makes them feel like they can't match up to you. When people are conceited, they aren't fun to be with because they are so caught up in themselves. They usually spend a lot of time bragging. But there is a huge difference between being conceited and believing in yourself. It's okay to love yourself and believe in the things you do; just be careful not to tell people you are better than they are.

We all have at least one thing about ourselves we can feel proud of, and probably a few others we feel uncomfortable about. You may be confident in your ability to play basketball, but when it comes to singing you would much rather bury your head in the sand like an ostrich. Even though no one has one hundred percent self-esteem all the time, you have to keep focusing on your good qualities, and the things you are proud of about yourself. Once you believe in all the things you're good at and realize you're a good person, you will feel more confident, and it will be easier to deal with the negative stuff in your life.

## Make a Praise List

One way to feel good about yourself is to make a list of all the things you're good at, or even slightly good at. By focusing on what you're good at and writing each thing down, you can look at what's good about yourself every single day. Write down even the little things that you know make you a good person. Anything you can come up with that is positive is worth writing down. You will probably discover a few good traits you never knew you had. For example, write it down if you:

- are good at sports.
- enjoy playing an instrument.

- are a good friend to others.
- take good care of your dog.
- are nice to your little brother or sister . . . sometimes.
- are good at riding your bike or Rollerblading.

Find a special place to keep the list. Look at it every morning and every night. Whenever you think of something new to add, jot it down on the paper. Keep looking at this list until you believe it and know that it is YOU who is special and who can do all those things. If you keep focusing on the good things about yourself, you should eventually start to notice a big difference in your self-esteem.

---

When we look for the best in the world, we find it in ourselves.     —*Irish proverb*

---

## Feel Better About Yourself

I asked a group of eleven- to thirteen-year-old boys and girls, "What do you do when you want to feel better about yourself?" Here are some of the responses I received:

- I write in my diary.
- I scribble on paper really hard to get my feelings out.
- I use a stress ball and squeeze it hard to let my anger out.
- I punch my pillow. That way I won't hurt anyone.

- I play my drums and pound really hard. That gets my anger out.
- I think things over in my room.
- I talk to my parents. When they listen and understand me, I feel better.

If you're wondering why you should do anything to make yourself feel better, the answer is simple: to liven up your life a little bit! Who wants to have a depressing, miserable life? People who are always depressed, or have low self-esteem, are shut down to life. When you feel good about yourself, you are automatically more open to everything around you. Sooner or later, good things are bound to come your way.

## Use Positive Affirmations

Affirmations are another tool you can use to feel better about who you are. You can create any affirmation you want to believe about yourself as long as it's realistic. If you write affirmations stating that you can fly, obviously that won't happen. Affirmations are things that are possible. Don't put yourself down by saying "It isn't possible for me to be smart," because it is possible if you believe in yourself.

Here are a few affirmations you can choose from, or you can try to come up with your own:

- I am a good person.
- I am smart.
- I love my family.
- I am thoughtful.
- I am a good friend.
- I am strong.
- I am a caring person.
- I am proud of myself.

- I take care of my body.
- I am courageous.
- My family loves me.
- There are many people who care about me.
- I like myself.

What you have to do is:

1. Pick one or two affirmations from the list I created above, or make up your own.
2. Write each affirmation down on a piece of paper at least ten to twenty times every single day until you start to believe it.
3. If negative thoughts start to come up as you're writing, then write the negative stuff down on the next line. Eventually, the positive thought will take over the negative one and you will start to believe in yourself. Don't worry about spelling or your handwriting.
4. Keep writing the positive thought every day until you finally start to believe it and it becomes a part of who you are.

Here is an example of what an affirmation with a few negative thoughts might look like:

-I am smart.
-I am smart.
-I am smart. No I'm not; I get bad grades.
-I am smart. No I'm not; my dad says I'm stupid.
-I am smart. No I'm not; I'm really dumb.
-I am smart. No I'm not; I'm stupid.
-I am smart, maybe.
-I am smart, sometimes.
-I am smart.
-I am smart.
-I am smart.

Writing affirmations may not make you feel better right away. But if you keep practicing, you'll be amazed at what you can learn about yourself in the process.

---

You have brains in your head.
You have feet in your shoes.
You can steer yourself
Any direction you choose.
—*Dr. Seuss*

---

## Write a Feeling Letter

A Feeling Letter can help you if you are really upset with someone and you don't know what to do with your anger. Writing a Feeling Letter allows you to express your feelings without hurting others or getting yourself in trouble. I have written Feeling Letters to my parents when I was really angry, and it helped me a lot.

Copy the first part of each sentence shown below, and finish it with your own situation. Just use the sentences that sound right to you. Some people don't even pass the first level, which is anger. If you write a really angry or "monster" letter, it is not a good idea to give it to the person you wrote about. You can safely burn the letter, bury it, rip it up, or throw it away. Here is how a Feeling Letter is structured. Start your letter by saying:

I am writing this letter to share my feelings with you.

**Begin with Level 1: Anger**
I do not like ...
I resent ...
I feel frustrated ...
I feel angry ...

I feel furious . . .
I want . . .

**Go to Level 2: Sadness**
It hurts when . . .
I feel disappointed when . . .
I feel sad . . .
I feel unhappy . . .
I wish . . .

**Continue with Level 3: Fear**
It is painful when . . .
I feel worried when . . .
I feel afraid . . .
I feel scared . . .
I need . . .

**Follow with Level 4: Regret and Apology**
I apologize for . . .
I feel embarrassed . . .
I am sorry . . .
I feel ashamed . . .
I am willing . . .

**End with Level 5: Love, Understanding, Gratitude, and Forgiveness**
I love it when . . .
I appreciate it when . . .
I realize . . .
I forgive . . .
Thank you . . .
I would like . . .
I trust . . .
Sign your name and write the date at the end.

You could also do this process in your mind. Find a

comfortable and quiet place to relax and think through your feelings. Just say to yourself what you feel, what you think, and what you want. What happens when you go through all the negative feelings is, you eventually get to the positive feelings and you can start to feel better about yourself and the people you are angry with.

## Write a Response Letter

If you don't want to give the letter to the person you are upset with, you can create your own response. After you're finished writing the Feeling Letter, read it over carefully as if you were the other person. Then take out another piece of paper and write your own response, pretending you are the other person. It just takes a few more minutes to write your ideal response as if the person was writing back to you.

Here is how it works: Imagine that your parents have just read your feeling letter and completely understand how you feel. Write a short letter to yourself pretending they are writing back to you. Write all the things you would like to hear them say. Start your letter by writing:

- Thank you for . . .
- I understand . . .
- I am sorry . . .
- You deserve . . .
- I want . . .
- I love . . .

If you can't do the love part in the Feeling Letter or you can't write a Response Letter, that's okay. Just keep noticing your feelings and find ways to let them out safely so no one gets hurt, and you take control of your feelings.

## What Goes Around, Comes Around

Everyone has feelings, and we all know what it's like to get our feelings hurt. If you don't want to be embarrassed or made fun of, then don't do it to others. There is a very popular expression that says "What goes around, comes around." What you do to others will eventually be done back to you, even if it isn't exactly done in the same way. What benefits do you get by putting someone down? Do you really have to put someone else down to build yourself up? What will it take to get people to leave each other alone? Here are what three teenagers who have experienced the thrill of embarrassing others and the not-so-big thrill of being embarrassed by others have said.

> Leah is in eighth grade. She said, "I used to make fun of people at my school all the time. But one day, some girl came up to me, right up in my face in front of all my friends, and told me off. I was so embarrassed and I felt really stupid. Everyone kept teasing me about what happened. It made me really mad. For a while, I didn't change. I kept making fun of other people. But I saw the reactions on their faces and I knew how they felt. After a while I made myself stop teasing them because I could relate to what they were going through."

> Cameron is a sophomore in high school. He said, "I used to get a major kick out of tripping people. I loved watching them fall flat on their faces. People would try to get me back all the time, but I was always expecting it, so they missed me. Of course, one day right before an assembly was going to start, I was walking along the front row of bleachers looking for a seat, when some jerk tripped me. That was the first time I had ever been tripped. The whole school saw it and everyone was cracking up. I

was mad, but I was also really embarrassed. I promised myself never to trip another person for the rest of my life."

Kirsten is a junior in high school. She said, "I guess I've been kind of mean to people for a while now. I never really cared about hurting people's feelings before. I always made fun of this girl who I used to be friends with. I don't know why, but I just hated her, so I made up a bunch of stories about her and told everyone at school. Then I got raped and went through some really horrible feelings about myself. I went through counseling and realized that I need to be nice to myself because the rape wasn't my fault. I also learned that I don't have the right to make other people feel bad by putting them down or making fun of them."

---

To the questions of your life, you are the only answer.
To the problems of your life, you are the only solution.
—*Jo Coudert*

---

Don't forget: what goes around, comes around.

## Make New Friends

You slam your locker and walk through the halls and out the door. You see rows and rows of benches in front of you. There is a large grassy area to your right and the cafeteria to the left. If you sit in any of these places, everyone will see you sitting by yourself and that would be very embarrassing. So you walk around a little bit. It is your first day at a new school, half way through the first semester. Everyone has already made their groups of friends. You have walked around the whole lunch area and no one asked you to come eat with them. You don't have a car so you can't drive away, and you don't know if there is anywhere to go within walking distance. The only thing you can think of is to forget about lunch and go to the library. You can pretend you are doing homework or something.

Wouldn't this be a horrible situation to be in? I'm sure no one would want that to happen to them, yet it has happened to so many people. There are many ways to make new friends. Here are some ideas:

- Go up to a group of people you think you would like to be friends with and ask them if you could eat lunch with them.
- Join clubs, sports, or do other extracurricular activities so you can meet new people who have your same interests.
- Ask people you would like to become friends with if they would like to do something with you. You could ask them over to your house, go to a movie, go swimming, or hang out.

If you have lost touch with your old friends, it may be time to make new ones. People change and move on. As things in life change, you have to learn to adapt to them. Even though you may have been best friends with some kids in elementary school, you might not have the same interests as they do now.

An important thing to remember when making friends is to be a good friend:

- Keep their secrets.
- Listen when they have problems.

- Don't talk about them behind their backs.
- Don't spread rumors about them.
- Treat them the way you want them to treat you.

Making new friends can be challenging. It makes you vulnerable and sets you up for acceptance or rejection. If you have a problem finding friends you can talk to, try these techniques and see how things work out. The teenage years are the most confusing years, because everyone is trying to figure out what they believe in and where they belong.

## Create Your Own Self-Esteem

Don't get yourself worked up about what other people think and do. If you need to, remember the saying you probably repeated when you were younger: "I'm rubber, you're glue. Whatever you say, bounces off me, and sticks to you." If someone says something mean to you, as hard as it may be, try not to let it bother you or make you upset. Just blow it off. Whatever comes your way during your life, try not to let it get you down too much. Learn from your experiences and then move on.

Even if your family or friends are treating you bad, never lose respect for yourself. If you're feeling down, use some of the techniques from this chapter to raise your self-esteem. People who are depressed and don't like themselves usually end up without a lot of friends or in a bad crowd. Once you have increased your own self-esteem, you will feel proud of yourself and more people will want to be your friend. Hopefully your family will appreciate you more often too.

No one can make you feel better about yourself except YOU. You are the only one. No one is responsible for your moods or your actions except you-know-who. Don't blame other people for getting you mad, because you're responsible for your own feelings. Self-esteem comes from creating peace within yourself.

Self-esteem is something that everyone needs in order to be happy in life. It also helps you to be confident enough to make new friends. Don't get discouraged with yourself; no one is perfect and everyone makes mistakes. That's why there are erasers on the ends of pencils. Find good things about yourself that will make you feel more confident about who you are. Whatever you do, don't try to be someone you're not; just be yourself and relax.

---

### *Personal Goals*

1. Be yourself.
2. Focus on the good things in your life.
3. Make a list of all the great things you do.
4. Keep writing down your affirmations until you begin to believe them.
5. Believe in yourself.
6. Write a Feeling Letter when you get angry at someone.
7. Try exercise or meditation to manage stress.
8. Take good care of yourself.
9. Find friends who will encourage you to be the best that you can be.
10. Be grateful for the things or people you have in your life.

---

CHAPTER 9

# For Parents and Kids

## *COMMUNICATING TOGETHER*

Parenting, letting go, learning to trust, and growing up all take an incredible amount of courage. Creating good communication skills and healthy, strong, loving relationships takes time and effort. Consciously creating an environment of respect and reverence can be challenging for both parents and kids, especially when your instincts kick in and you both become emotional. You do not need the patience of Job or the wisdom of Solomon to be able to use the tools and techniques we provide in this book. Simple respect, an understanding of the differences between adults and kids, a willingness to communicate better, and a lot of trust go a long way toward bridging the gap between parents and their children.

After giving one of our parenting talks, we were stopped by a woman named Renée, who is the mother of six-year-old Tayler. She was concerned about the effort and time involved in creating a good relationship with her daughter.

**Renée:** When my six-year-old is a teenager, I want to be able to have the kind of relationship you two have. What do I have to do?

**Journey:** It takes a lot of effort.

**Andrea:** It takes constant effort and devotion to raise an incredible human being.

**Renée:** I want what you two have, but I work every day. I have the desire, but I don't have the time. I think there is too much work involved, and I'm not sure I can find that kind of time.

**Andrea:** You have nothing but time. When you decided to raise a child, you made a commitment to life itself. This is your job. Of course, you need to work to make money so you can put food on your table and a roof over your head. But your job as a parent is the highest position you will ever hold. The time you do spend with your child is the moments that ensure the future of your relationship together, and the future relationship your child may have with her own children and others around her. Then you can stand back and be proud of the job you have accomplished as your child walks into the future with an ability to communicate well, independence in her stride, and love and compassion in her heart.

As other parents gathered around, Santiago and Cecilia, the parents of four children between the ages of four and eleven, began asking us more questions about raising children. We want to share our conversation with you.

**Cecilia:** I know my relationship with my daughter is going to be the same as the one you

301

two have. See, when I was a kid, my mother didn't trust me. So now I'm trying to trust my daughter as much as I can. And I see it's working already. If I say "Don't touch that," she doesn't touch it. Or if I say, "Stay out of that room," she doesn't go in. She's four years old, and she's already proving that she will listen to everything I say, and that I can trust her.

*Journey:* If you tell kids what to do throughout their lives, when they grow up, they won't be able to make their own decisions as easily. Kids need to be able to have choices in their lives. When they are little, you can say, "Do you want to wear your blue sweater or your green sweater?" That way they are able to make their own decisions, but at the same time the parent is making sure his or her child is wearing something to stay warm. To older children you can say, "Do you want pizza for dinner or do you want pasta?" This gives them a chance to make their own choices, but you make sure they are eating dinner. Just because your daughter does everything you tell her to do now doesn't guarantee that she will continue to listen as she gets older.

*Santiago:* That is so true. When I was growing up, my mother always told me what to do without allowing me to have any choices about anything. Now, at thirty-seven, I'm so indecisive when it comes to making my own decisions.

*Journey:* So you understand what I'm saying, then. See, if a kid never has a chance to make her own decisions while she's growing up, when she becomes a teenager and is offered drugs, she won't be able to decide what's right. This person would be so used to being told what to do all her life that if someone says "Here, take this. Go on, take it," the kid wouldn't feel strong enough inside to make a good decision.

**Santiago:** Wow! It's really true. And that's pretty much how I am now, I can never make up my mind. I guess we have to find a way to talk to our daughter so she understands why she shouldn't be doing something. Then she'll be able to figure things out for herself.

**Cecilia:** We're moving, so our daughter will be going to a different school. I'm really afraid of what goes on in schools today. For example, something I just don't understand: Why do kids join gangs? Sometimes I just want to shake these kids and say "Wake up!"

**Andrea:** A lot of that has to do with the love they get in their families, or lack of it. Gangs are an extension of the family unit: a place where kids think they can feel accepted and protected. For some, it takes an incredible amount of self-knowing and strength to stay out of the gang, but for others who are seeking approval and love, the gang is a welcoming place. The thing I find most ironic is that kids often leave home because of "too many rules and restrictions," yet gangs are known to have an incredible amount of restrictions, rules, and harsh discipline for rules that are broken.

**Journey:** Another reason why kids turn to gangs and drugs is because they aren't sure of themselves. I know who I am completely. And I know what I want out of life. No one can make me do something I don't want to do. Peer pressure doesn't affect me in any way whatsoever.

**Santiago:** But how were you able to become like that?

**Journey:** I owe it all to my parents. All my life, my mom and dad told me how wonderful I was. I was praised for everything I did, even if what I did was no big deal. When I was younger, my parents would say how wonderful I was (they would only say that when I behaved myself) and how much everyone loved me. Even if only a few people said that, it was important to exaggerate a little bit. Or if I made a picture at school, my parents would act as if it should be in a famous art gallery, and they would hang it up on the wall somewhere and show everyone who came in the house. They were so proud of me for everything. Because of all this, I grew up feeling good about myself. I remember when I was in fourth grade, some kids would make fun of my name. They would say things like "Hey, Journey, you wanna go on a journey?" And I would say something like "Okay, where are we gonna go?" At that age, kids can be really mean and they make fun of everyone. The point is that I was able to stand up for myself, even when I was little. When I couldn't stand up for myself, my mom and dad were always there to listen to my feelings.

They never made me feel ashamed of how I felt.

**Cecilia:** So you have a relationship built on love and trust. Tell us more about that.

**Journey:** I'm really lucky to have such a great relationship with my parents. We fight sometimes because we're all human—we're not perfect, but we're able to work really well together. They trust me so much and I would never do anything to mess that up. It isn't like they let me do everything. But if they say I can't do something with friends one night, I know they'll let me do something another night. One time, I wanted to go out with my friends, but my mom said no. She wasn't being mean or trying to control my life, but she needed me to help around the house that day. Instead, she said I could go out the next day. Being offered another chance to do something with my friends helped me accept the fact that I couldn't go out that afternoon. I wasn't happy, but she was being fair. Relationships are about give and take.

**Cecilia:** Don't you ever try to sneak out or do something you aren't supposed to do?

**Journey:** I would never want to do anything to break the freedom, respect, and trust that my parents have given me. They don't let me do everything, but they let me do a lot because they trust me and I love the feeling of being trusted so completely. If my parents say I can't do something that is really important to me, there is no way on Earth that I would try to sneak out. If I did sneak out, my parents wouldn't hate me, they just wouldn't trust me nearly as much. And then I would end up with a lot less freedom. If my parents say I can't do something, we talk about our feelings and try to compromise. Sometimes when my parents say no, I get upset. But my parents are parents, and sometimes they have to say no. That isn't always easy for me to understand, but I love them anyway.

**Santiago:** How are you able to understand the adult point of view?

**Journey:** First of all, I realize that adults and kids think very differently. Our whole book is based on this theory. So, I try to remember that we are different and that my parents will respond to things in a way that I might not. It really helps when my mom expresses her honest feelings about something; then it's easier for me to realize how she's feeling. When I have compassion for others, I can look at what I'm doing and try to think about how it feels for them. Because of our close relationship, my mom has a hard time letting me go.

She doesn't stop me from doing things, in fact, she gives me a lot of freedom to grow, but she has her own feelings about it. I understand because she shares her feelings with me, and she doesn't make me feel guilty. She tells me how much our relationship means to her, and how it feels for her to be a mom. She has been honest about her fears, which, by the way, are not my fears. My mom always says, "I trust you completely, but I don't always trust everyone else out there!"

***Andrea:*** Journey, what do you trust about me and your dad?

***Journey:*** I trust that you will always be there for me, and that you will always love me. I trust that when I screw up, you'll still love me. I know you and Dad won't just forget about it and let it go, we'll have to talk about what happened. I trust you will always forgive me, even when you're disappointed in me. I trust you guys will always be my friends. I love the relationship we have, and I think it would be really stupid if I did something to destroy the trust you have in me. I know I'll make mistakes in life, and even though you might not approve of what I do in the future, I know you and Dad will always love me.

***Santiago:*** When I was a kid, I asked my mom if she could be more like a friend to me, and she went crazy. Is it good or bad to be friends with your child?

***Journey:*** The type of friendship is important. My parents are my friends, and I can count on them to be supportive of me. A lot of parents drink or get high with their kids. These parents think they are being their child's friend, but they are actually abandoning them. Kids need parents who are emotionally strong to support them and make sure they are safe.

***Andrea:*** I would like to say that I think it is important to establish a relationship with your children that includes both parent-in-charge, and forever-friends. What I mean by parent-in-charge is: The parent is the person to whom the child looks for guidance, shelter, support, food, and boundaries, to name a few of the many things a parent must do. Parents must set limits and guidelines, establish and uphold healthy values for the family, and demonstrate love, compassion, appreciation, and respect. The forever-friend maintains a relationship of trust, honesty, support, and unconditional love, no matter what. Parents should strive to be parent and friend to their children to maintain a harmonious relationship that will last. I have met some parents who take drugs, go on double dates, or drink with their teenagers. This kind of behavior or "friendship" sends mixed messages to the kids, causes confusion, creates blurry boundaries, and ultimately leads to disrespect and a breakdown in the relationship between parents and kids.

*Cecilia:* Don't you two ever fight?

*Andrea:* We had a fight just the other day. My husband came home and asked us if we were writing, and I said no—we were fighting instead! I didn't need to discuss the fight with him because I knew it would be over soon. I knew that Journey and I were right in some ways, and we were both wrong too. Things happen in relationships. Journey and I don't fight that often but when we do, we seem to move through it fairly quickly. We don't hold grudges, and I find I am much more forgiving than I used to be.

*Journey:* I think it's the way that I talk to my mom

that makes a difference. I don't like fighting with her, but it happens. We are two
different people with two different viewpoints, so fighting is really normal. We
move through it so quickly because we use
our own techniques. Sometimes we start
laughing because we use our own advice
straight from the book. We love each
other, and we aren't going to stay mad
forever.

**Santiago:** My wife and I don't always agree on the
way we are raising our daughter. What do
you think parents can do about that?

**Andrea:** Often parents disagree about child rearing. When you have two different people
who come from two different families, you
are bound to have some conflicting viewpoints. For the sake of the children, I feel
it is important for parents to find a middle ground. The best way to do this is to
discuss your differences when the children
are not around. If you can work things out
together and then present your ideas to
your kids, they will experience less conflict and you will experience more harmony. It is perfectly okay to say to your
child "I don't have an answer right now,
and I need some time to think about it."
Or you can say, "I need your mother's
opinion on this. Let's wait until she gets
home and then she and I can talk it over.
I'll let you know what we decide." If the
communication between parents is shut
down, family counseling may help. Sometimes one parent can get help or advice
to work on his or her own issues, before
trying to deal with the uninvolvement or

closed-down attitude of the other parent. Reading books, taking parenting seminars, talking to other parents or school counselors can all be helpful ways to bridge the gap between parents and their children. The bottom line is to find some common ground where the two of you can lovingly and respectfully guide your child into being the best person she can be.

*Santiago:* You two have certainly bridged the gap between parents and kids. What was it like writing a book together?

*Journey:* Writing this book was the hardest project I have ever had to do. After we got the fun stuff out of the way, like finding an agent, a publishing house, and signing the contract, I began to understand that we had a serious deadline that would be coming up soon. This wasn't some project that I could get a decent grade on and just let it slide. This project had to be the best it could be. I had made a serious commitment to write this book with my mom, and I didn't realize what I had gotten myself into.

I hardly ever fought with my parents, until I began writing this book. After a while, I couldn't take it anymore. I felt drained and confused. I felt as if I didn't have any more answers. I didn't want to be writing this book anymore. It was a drag and nothing more. I hated everyone and everything. I went through a few weeks feeling like this, until I came to the realization that the deadline was only weeks away and I was months behind in my writing. I knew I had to finish what I had started. With a lot of personal dedication and support from my family, I was able to get myself back on track.

I felt like I had to give up everything. I couldn't go to friends' houses on the weekends or stay out late because I had to get up early in the morning to work. My life felt like it was always about work, work, work! It was work all morning at school, and then homework in the afternoons, and then if I had time, I worked on the book in the evenings. Once in a while, I would manage to spend some time with my friends. It was crazy and I can't believe I lived through it. But, I proved to myself that I am capable of following through with my commitments. I'm really proud of myself.

I finally realized what I was accomplishing. I don't know many kids who want to do anything with their parents, and I certainly don't know anyone who is writing a book with her mom! I started to see this as an exciting project. It felt incredible, and I loved it. But I would never do it again, at least not until I'm out of school. I already have a few ideas for another book I may write someday, but for now, I just want to be a teenager.

**Cecilia:** What about you, Andrea? What is it like to raise a teenage daughter who you are also writing a book with?

**Andrea:** We have embarked on a new beginning. All the hours spent writing have taken up most of our time. As any writer knows, writing a book becomes all consuming; it becomes your life. Because of this, my daughter felt she had no life. As any writer also knows, writing with a partner can be challenging at best; as any adult knows, writing with a teenager must be an interesting endeavor; but as any parent might guess, writing with a partner who is a teenager who also happens to be my daughter brought its own set of challenges. It also brought us closer together.

Journey and I work well together. We find we are a single mind with one thought, and we also find we are a mother and daughter struggling for comprehension and independence, respectively. As I try to understand what she needs as she continues to grow up and spread her wings, she keeps spreading those wings and trying to fly farther and farther from home. The feelings that come up for both of us are constant and confusing. But we continue to share our feelings with each other, which keeps us close. I work very hard to stay in the present and deal with each situation on an individual basis as it arises.

*Santiago:* Are you worried about the boys she goes out with?

*Andrea:* My very first reaction when she began dating was intense, dramatic, and humorous all at the same time. Journey introduced me to three of her friends and asked if they could go to the movies together. After I shook hands with the boys and talked to them for a while, they went off with my daughter. As I watched them leave, my dramatic feelings overtook me. I decided the boys looked as if they did not have any spines. They walked around like big apes, hunching over in their over-sized clothes. They said "Hey" instead of "Hello." They shook hands like wimps with sweaty palms. I searched them for beady eyes or sour breath, any telltale sign I could come up with to make them bad, to make them wrong, to keep them away from my daughter. The wound of separation in my heart is so deep. The pain of separation is searing. This is my baby, this is my child, MINE, MINE, MINE. I own her. I brought her up. I gave her life. She belongs to me. Now I am told I have to play second fiddle to these hunkering creatures masquerading as teen-age boys.

But then I remember that boys are not so bad. In fact, I have a son of my own. He is a good-natured, respectful, gentle person. Both of my kids have some really great male friends. And after all, I do not really own my daughter's body and soul. All these feeings are so confusing.

The potential danger that lurks around every corner is now in my own backyard. It used to be if my daughter went outside, she could catch a cold. Now if she leaves the house she could contract AIDS. Some of her peers smoke, some drink, some smoke pot. So what if some of my friends did those things when they were young. WE were different. Somehow it wasn't so dangerous then, or was it?

It's absolutely terrifying to let go. I am told I must feel safe enough and secure enough to trust not only my daughter and her ability to make good judgments, but I have to put my trust in the universe, for those times when her judgment may not be so good. But how do I let go? How do I let her make decisions that I don't agree with? How do I let her have experiences I don't want her to have? These feelings can be frightening and confusing to parents.

So many parents operate from this place of fear and don't even realize it. It is from this fear for the very safety of our children's lives that we hold on, dictate, mandate, and control them. And it is from this same place of control that children rebel. They fight with their lives to make their own decisions. If we don't let them have reasonable control over their lives, they do everything within their limited power to do something, anything, to exert control. When they have not been given the chance to exert reasonable control over their lives as they are growing up, then they will seize their freedom and run in directions we can only imagine.

Letting go is not easy. It can be deeply painful and heart wrenching, but they have to go, like the little bird who tries to fly. It is true, some little birds never make it past that first attempt. But nature miraculously provides a successful way for almost all the little birds to fly away from home. As parents, it is up to us to create a safe path for our little birds to take flight. Without us, they will be led astray. With us trying to hold on too tight, they will still fly away, perhaps never to return.

**Renée:** Most parents don't think that deeply about their kids growing up.

**Andrea:** If all parents could be aware of how they feel on such a deep level, and be able to convey their feelings to their kids on a regular basis, without overwhelming or frightening them, there would be such a deeper level of communication, respect, love, compassion, and bonding. You are correct when you say that it can be difficult to get so deep into your own feelings and be able to convey them. I think most parents just don't do that.

**Journey:** Growing up is really hard for kids, too. Everything changes before our eyes: our friends, our family, our limits, and ourselves. Some parents try to control their kids so strongly that they do things that harm their kids physically and emotionally. For some reason, they think that's the only way they can teach their children to be strong and successful in life. I want to tell the kids that you're not alone. Everyone goes through thousands of ups and downs in life. And growing up can be tough. We rely on our parents for support and encouragement. Unfortunately, so many parents don't know how to help their kids along the path to adulthood.

**Andrea:** Journey, if you had one last message to give to the kids, what would you say?

**Journey:** I want to say that I hope this book will help you and your parents learn how important it is to communicate successfully with your family. Hopefully you will be able to use the techniques my mom and I have given you so you can create a better relationship and gain the trust, freedom, and respect you deserve. It will be hard work, but stay committed.

No matter how many skills and techniques you have learned and used, once in a while you can expect a major fight or two where everything goes back to the unfair, parent-in-control situation where you think your parents don't understand, and don't care. At the same time, you might forget everything you learned, as you blow up and start screaming. It happens. No one is perfect and every family has fights. Once you read this book and you feel that you know enough of the skills to be able to make a difference in your family, don't expect your family relationship to change overnight. Things take time. This is a lifetime process.

I hope with all my heart that the information we have given you will help you and your family. The experiences and the feelings you encounter as a child influence your life growing up. It's important to try to make those experiences as wonderful as possible. Now that the information is here, I hope you will be able to work with it to find the techniques that work best for you. Don't get discouraged or upset if your family still breaks out in one of those crazy fights once in a while. It still happens in my family. Just try to use the techniques and the skills in this book as often as you can so you can get used to them, and make them part of your everyday routine.

In order to work through this process,

we have to love ourselves and trust ourselves. The only person you will ever be with every second of your whole life is you. If you don't love and respect yourself, you won't be able to love anyone or anything else around you. Believe in yourself and your ability to make a difference in your life. Remember to keep cool and communicate!

## From an Address by Mother Teresa

We must bring the child back to the center of
our care and concern.
This is the only way that our world can
survive because our children are the only
hope for the future.
As older people are called to God, only their
children can take their places.

(Excerpted from the address by the late Mother
Teresa—Nobel Peace Prize laureate, founder of
the Missionaries of Charity, and champion of the
poor—to the National Prayer Breakfast on
February 3, 1994, in the United States of
America.)

# Recommended Reading

## FOR PARENTS:

Anderson, E., Redman, G., and Rogers, C., Ph.D. *Self-Esteem for Tots to Teens.* Wayzata, Minn.: Parenting & Teaching Publications, Inc., 1991.

Bean, R. *How to Be a Slightly Better Parent.* Los Angeles: Price Stern Sloan, 1991.

Berends, P. *Whole Child/Whole Parent.* New York: Harper & Row, 1987.

Briggs, D. *Your Child's Self-Esteem.* New York: Doubleday, 1970.

Cecil, N. L. *Raising Peaceful Children in a Violent World.* San Diego: Lura Media, Inc., 1995.

Chopra, D., M.D. *The Seven Spiritual Laws for Parents.* New York: Harmony Books, 1997.

Clinton, H. R. *It Takes a Village.* New York: Simon & Schuster, 1996.

Coloroso, B. *Kids Are Worth It!* New York: Avon, 1994.

Dinkmeyer, D., and McKay, G. *Systematic Training for Effective Parenting of Teens: Parenting Teenagers.* Circle Pines, Minn.: American Guidance Service, Inc., 1990.

Eyre, L., and Eyre, R. *Teaching Your Children Values.* New York: Simon & Schuster, 1993.

Faber, A., and Mazlish, E. *How to Talk So Kids Will Listen and Listen So Kids Will Talk.* New York: Avon Books, 1980.

Faber, A., and Mazlish, E. *Siblings Without Rivalry*. New York: Avon, 1987.

Ford, J. *Wonderful Ways to Love a Teen . . . even when it seems impossible*. Berkeley, Calif.: Conari Press, 1995.

Gordon, T. *Parent Effectiveness Training (P.E.T.)*. New York: Plume, 1975.

Gray, John, Ph.D. *Mars and Venus Together Forever*. New York: HarperCollins, 1996.

Gray, John, Ph.D. *Men Are from Mars, Women Are from Venus*. New York: HarperCollins, 1992.

Gray, John, Ph.D. *What You Feel, You Can Heal*. Mill Valley, Calif.: Heart Publishing, 1984.

Hart, L., Ph.D. *The Winning Family*. Berkeley, Calif.: Celestial Arts, 1993.

Jackson, Deborah. *Three in a Bed*. New York: Avon, 1989.

Kamin, B. *Raising a Thoughtful Teenager*. New York: Dutton, 1996.

Kelly, K. *The Complete Idiot's Guide to Parenting a Teenager*. New York: Alpha Books, 1996.

Kitzinger, Sheila. *The Crying Baby*. New York: Penguin Books, 1990.

Kurcinka, M. *Raising Your Spirited Child*. New York: Harper Perennial, 1991.

Leidloff, Jean. *The Continuum Concept*. Reading, Mass.: Addison-Wesley, 1985.

LeShan, Eda. *When Your Child Drives You Crazy*. New York: St. Martin's, 1992.

Loomans, D. *Full Esteem Ahead*. Tiburon, Calif.: H. J. Kramer, Inc., 1994.

Loomans, D. Kolberg, K., and Loomans, J. *Positively Mother Goose*. Tiburon, Calif.: H. J. Kramer, Inc., 1994.

Markova, D., Ph.D. *Kids' Random Acts of Kindness*. Berkeley, Calif.: Conari Press, 1994.

Mendelsohn, R., M.D. *How to Raise a Healthy Child . . . in Spite of Your Doctor*. New York: Ballantine, 1984.

*Mothering* magazine. P.O. Box 1690. Santa Fe, NM 87504-9780.

Nelson, J. *Positive Discipline*. New York: Ballantine, 1987.

Nelson, J., and Lott, L. *Positive Discipline for Teenagers: Resolving Conflict with Your Teenage Son or Daughter*. Rocklin, CA: Prima Publishing, 1994.

Packer, A., Ph.D. *The Nurturing Parent: How to Raise Creative, Loving, Responsible Children*. New York: Fireside/Simon & Schuster, 1992.

Packer, A., Ph.D. *365 Ways to Love Your Child*. New York: Dell, 1995.

Pearce, J. C. *Magical Child*. New York: Plume, 1991.

Pipher, M., Ph.D. *Reviving Ophelia: Saving the Selves of Adolescent Girls.* New York: Ballantine, 1994.

Popenoe, D. *Life Without Father.* New York: Simon & Schuster, 1996.

Riera, M. *Surviving High School.* Berkeley, Calif.: Celestial Arts, 1997.

Riera, M. *Uncommon Sense for Parents with Teenagers.* Berkeley, Calif.: Celestial Arts, 1995.

Riggs, M. *Natural Child Care.* New York: Harmony Books, 1989.

Rutter, V. *Celebrating Girls.* Berkeley, Calif.: Conari Press, 1996.

Saavedra, B. *Meditations for Mothers of Toddlers.* New York: Workman, 1995.

Sears, W., M.D., and Sears, M., R.N. *The Discipline Book.* Boston: Little, Brown, 1995.

Shure, M. B., Ph.D. *Raising a Thinking Child.* New York: Pocket, 1994.

Sifford, D. *The Only Child.* New York: Harper & Row, 1989.

Strasburger, V., M.D. *Getting Your Kids to Say No in the 90's, When You Said Yes in the 60's.* New York: Simon & Schuster, 1993.

Stoppard, M., M.D. *Complete Baby and Child Care.* London: Dorling Kindersley, 1995.

Terdal, L., Ph.D., and Kennedy, P. *Raising Sons Without Fathers.* Secaucus, N.J.: Carol Publishing Group, 1996.

Thevenin, T. *The Family Bed: An Age Old Concept in Childrearing.* New York: Avery Publishing Group, 1987.

Vissell, B., and J. *Models of Love: The Parent-Child Journey.* Aptos, Calif.: Ramira Publishing, 1986.

Wyckoff, J., Ph.D., and Unell, B. *Discipline Without Shouting or Spanking.* New York: Meadowbrook Press, 1991.

## *FOR TEENS:*

Childre, L., Ph.D. *Heart Smarts: Teenage Guide for the Puzzle of Life.* Boulder Creek, Calif.: Planetary Publications, 1991.

Coombs, H.S. *Teenage Survival Manual.* San Francisco: Halo Books, 1995.

Packer, A., Ph.D. *Bringing Up Parents: The Teenager's Handbook.* Minneapolis: Free Spirit Publishing, 1992.

Palmer, P., Ed.D., and Froehner, M. *Teen Esteem: A Self-Direction Manual for Young Adults.* San Luis Obispo, Calif.: Impact Publishers, 1989.

# Index

# Index

Independence of child (*continued*)
 and parental rules, 199–201
 and rules, 199–201
 and sense of time, 198
 separating from child, 176–177
 sexuality, 181–184
 and trust, 201–203
 and unconditional love, 174–175
 and uniqueness, 205–210
Individuality
 of child, 3–4
 finding personal uniqueness, 205–210

Kids' Rules, 12, 34–35
Kindness, teaching of, 60–62
*Kissing-up*, 72–76

Letter writing
 Feeling Letter, 102–103, 255, 291–294
 love notes, 270–271
Letting go by parents, 153, 154–155
 meaning of, 173
 *See also* Independence of child
Listening, 103–106, 114–118
 active listening, 103–104, 114–118
 and communication, 86–87
 listing of good listening skills, 104–105
 poem about, 81
Logical consequences, 88–91
 examples of use, 89–90
 guidelines for use, 88–89, 90–91
Love
 parental self-love, 275–277
 physical displays of, 223–224
 saying "I love you," 37–38, 223
 and self-esteem, 260–261

tips for showing care/love, 277–286
 unconditional, 21, 174–175, 260–261
 verbal displays of, 224–226
Love notes, 270–271
Lying
 alternatives to, 39–40
 reasons for, 120
 to self, 121
 versus softening truth, 120–121

Marijuana, 245, 247–248
 negative effects of, 248–249
Meditation, stress reduction, 241
Mistakes
 and apologizing, 167–169
 learning from, 135–137
Mood, and timing of talk, 157–158
Mornings, getting ready in, 131–132

Negotiation, teaching about, 57–58

Parental control, negative control, 8
Parenting, 4–6
 authoritarian, 5
 guidelines, 31
 learning from kids, 30
 negative parental behavior, 4, 5
 and parental upbringing, 14–15, 21, 274–275
 permissive, 6
Parents
 common ideas of, 38
 compared to kids (survey results), 32–33
 unreasonable behavior of, 36–37
Permissive parenting, 5–6

# About the Authors

**Andrea Frank Henkart, M.A.,** has a bachelor's degree in sociology and two teaching credentials from UCLA. She holds a master's degree in psychology from Sonoma State University.

Andrea took a break from teaching children to teach yoga for Club Med. As a G.O., she had the opportunity to interact with thousands of families in Hawaii, the Bahamas, France, Spain, Switzerland, and the two coasts of Mexico.

After leaving Club Med, Andrea continued her studies, receiving additional degrees as a Holistic Health Educator, Certified Massage Practitioner, Certified Childbirth Educator, and Certified Professional Childbirth Assistant. She was the cofounder and former president of the International Cesarean Awareness Network in Marin County, California, and assisted over two hundred women in having healthier, happier babies in her private practice as a childbirth assistant. Author of *The Cesarean Challenge*

(Henkart & Cie, Publishers, 1991) and *Trust Your Body! Trust Your Baby!* (Greenwood Publishing Group, 1995), she has over twenty-five years of experience in the fields of health, parenting, childbirth, and personal growth.

As an international public speaker and seminar leader, Andrea has worked with over 3,000 preteens and teenagers. With a focus on building self-esteem and strong communication skills between parents and kids, Andrea and her teenage daughter, Journey, coteach "Cool Communication for Parents & Kids." Together they also lead mother-daughter workshops, speak to Mother's Groups and local PTAs, and are a regular feature at the San Francisco Whole Life Expo.

She developed her wildly popular workshop, "Super Sitters: A Positive Approach to Baby-Sitting," which teaches ten- to sixteen-year-olds to be active, responsible, fun sitters. The main focus is on professionalism, communication skills, positive discipline, basic safety concerns, and building self-esteem.

Andrea also leads her popular "Positive Parenting" workshops in which she blends her famous communication skills with profound common sense, to help parents of infants through teens create strong, nurturing families.

She is also the mother of a preteen son, and is regarded as the "Cool Mom" by her children's friends. In her spare(!) time, Andrea enjoys the peaceful joy and quietude of gardening.

**Journey Henkart** is sixteen years old. She is a student, actress, model, and writer. When she graduated from middle school, she was president of the Honor Society and a Peer Advisor. Journey is currently a sophomore in high school.

For three years, Journey wrote an advice column for teens in the *FastForward* newspaper in northern California, called "Journey for Answers." In addition, she was

West Coast correspondent to *Blue Jean* magazine, an East Coast magazine for teen girls.

Together with her mom, Journey gives talks on self-esteem and communication skills, facilitates mother-daughter workshops, and teaches personal-empowerment seminars. She has also helped teach her mom's workshop, "Super Sitters: A Positive Approach to Baby-Sitting."

Journey has acted in numerous national commercials and school plays, and holds a purple belt in Karate. Every summer, she works as a camp counselor, and in her spare time, she enjoys traveling, hiking, kayaking, windsurfing, and wake-boarding.